The paranoia was starting to get to him

But he didn't have time to dwell on it. First Bolan had to keep both eyes wide open for his upcoming contest with the Russians—and, perhaps, with agents from the Company. At the same time, he had to narrow his focus, try to penetrate the wall of secrecy Brognola had raised between them, without losing track of those he knew to be his mortal enemies.

And if Brognola stood in their ranks, what then?

Bolan was pledged to never kill a lawman, even if the cop in question was a criminal. His long friendship with Hal Brognola made that promise to himself doubly imperative. And yet this time it was not simply Bolan's life at stake. His brother's was riding on the line.

If Brognola had turned, would either of them survive?

MACK BOLAN ®
The Executioner

#193 Hostile Action
#194 Deadly Contest
#195 Select Fire
#196 Triburst
#197 Armed Force
#198 Shoot Down
#199 Rogue Agent
#200 Crisis Point
#201 Prime Target
#202 Combat Zone
#203 Hard Contact
#204 Rescue Run
#205 Hell Road
#206 Hunting Cry
#207 Freedom Strike
#208 Death Whisper
#209 Asian Crucible
#210 Fire Lash
#211 Steel Claws
#212 Ride the Beast
#213 Blood Harvest
#214 Fission Fury
#215 Fire Hammer
#216 Death Force
#217 Fight or Die
#218 End Game
#219 Terror Intent
#220 Tiger Stalk
#221 Blood and Fire
#222 Patriot Gambit
#223 Hour of Conflict
#224 Call to Arms
#225 Body Armor
#226 Red Horse
#227 Blood Circle
#228 Terminal Option
#229 Zero Tolerance
#230 Deep Attack

#231 Slaughter Squad
#232 Jackal Hunt
#233 Tough Justice
#234 Target Command
#235 Plague Wind
#236 Vengeance Rising
#237 Hellfire Trigger
#238 Crimson Tide
#239 Hostile Proximity
#240 Devil's Guard
#241 Evil Reborn
#242 Doomsday Conspiracy
#243 Assault Reflex
#244 Judas Kill
#245 Virtual Destruction
#246 Blood of the Earth
#247 Black Dawn Rising
#248 Rolling Death
#249 Shadow Target
#250 Warning Shot
#251 Kill Radius
#252 Death Line
#253 Risk Factor
#254 Chill Effect
#255 War Bird
#256 Point of Impact
#257 Precision Play
#258 Target Lock
#259 Nightfire
#260 Dayhunt
#261 Dawnkill
#262 Trigger Point
#263 Skysniper
#264 Iron Fist
#265 Freedom Force
#266 Ultimate Price
#267 Invisible Invader
#268 Shattered Trust

DON PENDLETON'S
THE EXECUTIONER®
SHATTERED TRUST

The
Conspiracy
Trilogy

BOOK I

A GOLD EAGLE BOOK FROM
WORLDWIDE®

TORONTO • NEW YORK • LONDON
AMSTERDAM • PARIS • SYDNEY • HAMBURG
STOCKHOLM • ATHENS • TOKYO • MILAN
MADRID • WARSAW • BUDAPEST • AUCKLAND

If you purchased this book without a cover you should be aware that this book is stolen property. It was reported as "unsold and destroyed" to the publisher, and neither the author nor the publisher has received any payment for this "stripped book."

To Eamon Collins, executed by the IRA
at Newry, Northern Ireland, on 27 January 1999

First edition March 2001
ISBN 0-373-64268-7

Special thanks and acknowledgment to
Michael Newton for his contribution to this work.

SHATTERED TRUST

Copyright © 2001 by Worldwide Library.

All rights reserved. Except for use in any review, the reproduction or utilization of this work in whole or in part in any form by any electronic, mechanical or other means, now known or hereafter invented, including xerography, photocopying and recording, or in any information storage or retrieval system, is forbidden without the written permission of the publisher, Worldwide Library, 225 Duncan Mill Road, Don Mills, Ontario, Canada M3B 3K9.

All characters in this book have no existence outside the imagination of the author and have no relation whatsoever to anyone bearing the same name or names. They are not even distantly inspired by any individual known or unknown to the author, and all incidents are pure invention.

® and TM are trademarks of the publisher. Trademarks indicated with ® are registered in the United States Patent and Trademark Office, the Canadian Trade Marks Office and in other countries.

Printed in U.S.A.

Anarchy is the stepping stone to absolute power.
—Napoleon Bonaparte

Various are the uses of friends, beyond all else in difficulty, but joy also looks for trust that is clear in the eyes.
—Pindar, *Odes*

Trust is in short supply these days—and so are friends. Deciding which friends can be trusted may turn out to be the ultimate final exam.
—Mack Bolan

THE
MACK BOLAN®
LEGEND

Nothing less than a war could have fashioned the destiny of the man called Mack Bolan. Bolan earned the Executioner title in the jungle hell of Vietnam.

But this soldier also wore another name—Sergeant Mercy. He was so tagged because of the compassion he showed to wounded comrades-in-arms and Vietnamese civilians.

Mack Bolan's second tour of duty ended prematurely when he was given emergency leave to return home and bury his family, victims of the Mob. Then he declared a one-man war against the Mafia.

He confronted the Families head-on from coast to coast, and soon a hope of victory began to appear. But Bolan had broken society's every rule. That same society started gunning for this elusive warrior—to no avail.

So Bolan was offered amnesty to work within the system against terrorism. This time, as an employee of Uncle Sam, Bolan became Colonel John Phoenix. With a command center at Stony Man Farm in Virginia, he and his new allies—Able Team and Phoenix Force—waged relentless war on a new adversary: the KGB.

But when his one true love, April Rose, died at the hands of the Soviet terror machine, Bolan severed all ties with Establishment authority.

Now, after a lengthy lone-wolf struggle and much soul-searching, the Executioner has agreed to enter an "arm's-length" alliance with his government once more, reserving the right to pursue personal missions in his Everlasting War.

PROLOGUE

Johnny Bolan Gray wasn't sure what woke him up at 4:09 a.m. that Tuesday. It had been after midnight when he went to bed, and while he understood that everyone dreamed each night, he could recall no mental images that might have shocked him back to grudging consciousness.

A sound, perhaps?

He didn't wake as most men do, by fits and starts. There was a certain grogginess, of course, but he didn't roll over, seeking comfort in the crisp new sheets that swaddled him. He had no sense of dislocation or forgetfulness. He knew exactly where he was, and why.

The Desert Rose Motel, outside of Aztec, Arizona.

With business slow enough, renting two adjacent rooms hadn't been a problem. In the morning, U.S. Highway 8 could take them east or west, depending on their mood. They'd made that choice at breakfast, in the coffee shop next door.

But it was morning now, albeit well ahead of the alarm that Johnny had set to wake him at sunrise. Why the hell was he awake?

He checked out the room, thankful now for the reflected glow of neon from the motel sign outside. The room was small, a ten-by-fifteen stucco box, with nowhere to hide. The door was still chained from inside, meaning no one had entered while he was asleep. He had checked out the bathroom window earlier, determining that anyone attempting to escape or enter by that route would have to smash the frosted glass.

Then *what?*

He sat up, facing east, toward the connecting door between his bedroom and the woman's. He didn't know if it was locked on her side, hadn't tried it earlier, resisting the temptation. They were traveling on business, of the life-and-death variety, and he wasn't prepared to let his guard down for a one-night stand. Beyond that, he couldn't forget about the lady's situation and wasn't prepared to take advantage of her weakness at the moment, when she needed him for more important things.

He sat and listened, head cocked, alert to any sounds that might have emanated from the room next door. Nothing. He wasn't aware of frowning, but the short reach for the pistol on his nightstand was a conscious move. He found the Glock by touch and brought it back to rest against his thigh. There was a live round in the spout, no safety catch to fumble with. He was prepared.

And yet, he still had no idea what had awakened him.

It took another moment for his mind to focus on the sound, and even then he only recognized it after it had stopped, the silence offering a contrast to the missing background noise. A car, the engine idling. Not outside his room, exactly, but it had been close enough. The driver had decided he would stay a while.

So what?

Johnny told himself that he was being foolish, paranoid. By definition, motels catered to a populace on wheels. Unless the person had two heads, the only motel customer who earned a second glance was one who came in off the interstate *without* a set of wheels.

Okay. A car pulled into a motel. Big freaking deal. He could forget about it. Time to sleep.

Not yet.

Who started looking for a motel room at 4:09 a.m.? If a

person was driving through the night toward Casa Grande, to the east, or Yuma, westbound, why stop now? Why here? Fatigue could do it, he supposed, perhaps anxiety about the predators who trolled in search of targets parked along the interstate. But it was timing that compelled him to reject the thought. Who drove all night and suddenly conked out at 4:09 a.m.?

A person couldn't travel fifty miles along I-8 without discovering another tiny desert town, where low-rent lodgings were available. Most of the pit stops wouldn't rate two stars in any decent travel guide, but they were cheap and reasonably clean.

Maybe someone was checking out? An early bird.

No good. If they were checking out, why switch off the engine? They should be pulling out, hitting the road.

He stood, naked in the darkness, feeling goose bumps crawl across his chest and shoulders. It was weird about the desert: bake all day and shiver all night long, as if the climate were incapable of moderation, bound to pitch and yaw between extremes.

Unfortunately, it wasn't the temperature that made his skin crawl or set his teeth on edge.

His clothes were folded on a nearby chair, but he ignored them. Check first, then decide. Three steps and he was at the window, shifting toward the corner farthest from the door. No sudden moves. Be cool.

He hesitated as he reached for the curtain, fingers grazing cloth. How many fright flicks had he watched, with scenes like this? The curtain opened to reveal a monstrous, leering face pressed up against the glass, and a living nightmare smashes through to claim its prey.

He held the pistol ready as he nudged the curtain back an inch, no more. It would be difficult for anyone to catch the subtle movement there, unless his face *was* pressed against the glass. In which case, he would get an eyeful, but not the sort he was expecting.

The motel was laid out in a V-shape, I-8 making it a triangle. Johnny's room was near the inner angle of the V, the woman's room to his left, as he stood facing toward the wedge-shaped parking lot. He had a clear view of the rental office, last room on his right, the east arm of the V, adjacent to the highway.

He could see the Lincoln Town Car parked outside the office, though he couldn't read its license plate or verify its color in the garish light. Maroon, perhaps, but it could just as easily have been light gray, reflecting color from the neon sign that towered overhead. He counted three heads in the car, no driver, and decided that the wheelman had been sent inside to rouse the motel's manager.

Four groggy travelers decide to stop and give the Desert Rose a try? No damn way.

He double-checked the parking lot from force of habit, picking out the shiny grille and bumper of a Cadillac, not quite concealed behind the west end of the motel. It wasn't where a guest would park for easy access to the nearest room, and there had been no vehicle in that position when he checked the lot before he went to sleep.

Two cars, at least. Four men in one of them. He could assume four in the other.

Eight men, eight guns. At least.

He scrambled for his clothes, stepped into Jockey shorts and blue jeans, grappled for a precious moment with his sweatshirt, slipped the Galco shoulder holster over that and topped it with a leather jacket. Socks and boots came last, hopping on one foot, then the other.

He hadn't unpacked his suitcase. It was standing by the door, with nothing inside that he couldn't afford to lose, but he was thinking of it more as body armor now, instead of luggage. With his clothes inside, the Samsonite should slow most pistol bullets enough to spare his life, but it wouldn't survive repeated hits. If they had something heavier—assault rifles, perhaps—then he would be shit out of luck.

When he was dressed, Johnny went to wake the woman. He was surprised to find the door between their rooms unlocked and couldn't help wondering if it had been a simple oversight, or whether she had lain awake after they parted, hoping he would come to her.

No time now, dammit!

Moving through the neon backwash, four strides brought him to her bed. He cupped one hand across her mouth, prepared to fend her off in case she came up swinging. There was panic in her eyes when they snapped open, instantly alert.

"It's me," he whispered in the semidarkness. "We've got company. We have to leave right now."

THE MOTEL MANAGER was well past middle age, a scrawny man whose skin resembled ancient leather, tanned and cracked by long exposure to the desert sun. His hair was thin and streaked with gray, receding from a freckled forehead. At the moment, it was flattened on one side, from contact with his pillow, while the rest of it stood up in swirls and spikes.

"Help you?" he challenged, scowling from behind a pair of steel-rimmed spectacles.

Ilya Zarudniy had been forced to ring the little bell five times before the manager appeared, scratching himself through sweatpants that had obviously missed their last appointment with the laundry. It was tempting to reach out and grab the old man by his spiky hair, dribble his face across the counter like a basketball, but Zarudniy forced a smile instead, remembering his English when he spoke.

"I'm looking for a friend," he said.

The old man closed one eye, then opened it again, a lazy wink. "That be a special friend, or you just window shopping?"

Careful not to lose the plastic smile, Zarudniy reached inside his jacket for the photograph. His fingers grazed the

Taurus Model PT 92, reminding him that he could simply kill this peasant where he stood. Instead, he palmed the snapshot, placed it on the counter, sliding it across. Two faces smiling in the sun.

"The girl," he said.

"You know what time it is?" the old man asked.

There was a large clock on the wall behind him, but Zarudniy checked his Rolex watch, making sure. "Eleven minutes past the hour of four o'clock," he said.

"Uh-huh." The old man winked his other eye this time. "People in this motel are all asleep right now. I oughta be asleep, myself."

"It's an emergency," Zarudniy said.

That much was true. They had already missed the woman twice, and he didn't look forward to reporting yet another failure. It wasn't good to appear incompetent in his line of work.

"Emergency, you say." The old man made a snuffling sound, as if about to spit, but swallowed something instead.

They had been checking motels since shortly after sundown, working westward from the town of Red Rock, forty miles northwest of Tucson. Zarudniy had stopped counting after twenty, but they kept on, because they had no other choice, no better plan. They took turns going in to show the photograph, the two cars splitting up if there were motels close enough together that a man could see one from the other. Even so, the time had dragged, and they were turned away each time with frowns, a head shake.

No. Not here.

"Emergency," the old man said again. He had no pockets, so he tucked both bony hands inside the waistband of his sweatpants, leaning forward for a closer look at the snapshot. When he blinked this time, it was both eyes at once, a nervous flick of eyelashes.

"Ain't seen her," he said, as he straightened again.

The man was lying, and Zarudniy had a choice to make.

He consciously ignored the little thrill of triumph, almost sexual in its intensity, and focused on the old man's eyes. He could try money, or produce the phony badge he carried in a leather wallet, as a prop to fool the peasants. Either way might loosen the old man's tongue, but what would be the point?

The man had lied, which meant the woman had to be here. The last near-miss had been in San Diego. That was yesterday, and now she was somewhere in the state of Arizona. One night's passage meant that she wouldn't have stopped at multiple motels. If the old man had seen her, she was here.

And now that he had seen Zarudniy, the old man would have to die.

But not before he talked.

Instead of reaching for his bankroll or the badge, Zarudniy drew the Taurus semiautomatic pistol, thumbed its hammer back and aimed it at the old man's chest.

"Shit fire!" the old man blurted. "You want money, there's the register. Go on and help yourself."

"The woman," the Russian told him. "I require the number of her room."

The old man hesitated. Chivalry was strongest in the old ones, Zarudniy found, where it survived at all. Younger Americans had grown up in an age when women were proclaimed as equals, sometimes hated for it, rarely coddled or protected. With the older ones, he recognized, there was at least a fleeting tendency to guard the "weaker" sex.

Zarudniy dropped the pistol's sights in the direction of his target's groin and watched the old man jitter. "That would be room 19," he said. And added helpfully, "They took two rooms, in case it matters. Maybe she ain't cheating on you after all."

Ilya Zarudniy reached across the counter, raised his gun and shot the old man in the face at contact range. No mess on his end; everything went out the back and spattered on the wall, streaking the round face of the clock.

He walked to the back to check the bedroom, just in case the old man had a wife, and found it empty. Spartan quarters with a musty, sour smell. It would smell worse before the day was out.

He walked back to the Lincoln, slid behind the steering wheel. The others watched and waited for him, saying nothing, even though he thought they had to have heard the muffled gunshot. "Two rooms," he said. "The woman's in nineteen. Vanya, go tell the others."

One of the Lincoln's rear doors opened, then closed quickly. Zarudniy watched as Vanya moved across the parking lot, in the direction of the Caddy.

"Guns," he said.

Sergei opened a duffel bag and handed up an MP-5 K submachine gun, double magazines secured by friction tape. Zarudniy accepted it and cocked the stubby weapon, waited while Ivan, beside him in the shotgun seat, received its twin. Sergei was rummaging around inside the bag, choosing a weapon for himself. A backward glance revealed the others, stepping from the Cadillac, neon reflecting from the well-oiled hardware in their hands.

"Let's go," Zarudniy said.

SUZANNE KING HAD nearly lost it when she awakened to find a hand clamped tight across her lips. She saw the gun first, then the profile limned in neon, and it registered before she heard him speak.

He stepped back from the bed and turned his back as Suzanne scrambled clear. She didn't mind if Johnny saw her in her underwear—in fact, she had been hoping he would come through that connecting door before she fell asleep—but any budding thoughts of fun and games were driven from her mind by sudden fear.

"Who's 'company'?" she asked him, as she tugged on jeans, a T-shirt and reached for a windbreaker.

Getting no answer, she turned to find him just returning

from his room, toting a suitcase and a leather gym bag. When he dropped the gym bag on her rumpled bed, it made a clanking sound.

"I said, 'Who's company'?"

"Don't know," he told her, "but I counted eight of them. They're armed and headed this way, as we speak."

Suzanne was reaching for a bedside lamp when Johnny snapped, "No lights!" He couldn't see her blushing in the dark, which was a blessing, but she still felt like an idiot.

Of course, no lights.

"Are they police?" she asked and knew it was a stupid question. Wishful thinking.

"Cops don't drive around in Cadillacs and Lincolns," he replied. "Most of the cops in Arizona don't have ponytails or wear custom-tailored suits."

"Well, who, then?"

"If I knew that," Johnny said, "we'd have the answer to your other questions, too." He unzipped the gym bag and removed a pistol that resembled his. "Can you use one of these?"

"Don't know," she told him honestly. "I never tried."

He racked the slide, reversed the weapon in his grip and gave it to Suzanne butt first. "It's cocked," he said. "No safety. All you have to do is pull the trigger, so be careful."

"Right." She kept her index finger flush against the outside of the pistol's trigger guard.

"The sights are rimmed in white to help you aim," he told her. "You've got seventeen shots. When it's empty, the slide will lock open."

"And then what?" she asked him, wide-eyed.

"If we're not in the Blazer and rolling by then," Johnny answered, "it won't make much difference."

"Oh." So much for wishful thinking.

Johnny withdrew a larger weapon from the bag—some kind of sawed-off shotgun, Suzanne thought, although she wasn't sure—then slung the bag across his shoulder.

He checked the curtain without touching it, just peering through a narrow slit, and said, "They're halfway here. What are you taking with you?"

"Well..." She waved the pistol toward her scattered things. A blouse and skirt, more underwear, hair dryer and cosmetics in the tiny bathroom.

"Never mind," he said, handing her his own suitcase. "Hold this in front of you the best you can when we're outside. It's not Kevlar, but it may stop a pistol round."

Kevlar? Outside?

"We'll go through my room," Johnny said. "It's closer to the car, and with any luck they'll be focused on your room."

"Some luck. Who are these guys?"

"You want to hang around and ask them?"

"No."

"Then follow me."

She picked the suitcase up and hugged it to her chest. Though it was awkward, Suzanne found herself wishing the bag had been larger, heavier. If she turned it on end, it would cover most of her torso, while leaving face and legs exposed. Her most secure grip was to wrap an arm around it, clutch it like a lover, but that left her arm exposed, as well. If she used both hands, though, the pistol would be useless.

By the time they stood in Johnny's room, his fingers wrapped around the doorknob, clutching it, Suzanne had found a compromise. The suitcase had a towing handle on one end, wheels on the other. If she gripped the handle, she could hold the bag in front of her, shielding herself from chin to groin. The muscles in her arm were trembling, burning, but she managed to ignore it.

How did she get here? she thought, and almost laughed aloud.

That was easy. She had needed help and picked a total stranger from the phone book to assist her. She had hired him by the day, her trust fund money good for something more than kicks, this time. Four days, and they were still no closer to answering her mystery.

Or, were they?

If someone was hunting them, they had to be closer. Too close for comfort, in someone's opinion. What had Billy blundered into this time? Was her brother dead and buried somewhere? Or were these men friends of his, mistaking Suzanne's interest for a threat?

Another thought occurred to her almost immediately. There were men with guns outside, and Johnny reckoned they were after her, but what if he was wrong? Private investigators made no end of enemies, from what she understood. They were mercenary muckrakers, going to the highest bidder in messy divorce cases, corporate fraud, skip-tracing fugitives from justice, missing persons cases like her own. They weren't police, of course, but all that meant was they lacked protection from the system. Some of their investigations ruined—maybe even ended—other people's lives.

For all she knew, these gunmen might be hunting Johnny Gray to settle some old score. The problem being that, when Suzanne thought about it in those terms, it didn't help her case a bit. If they were bent on killing or abducting Johnny, they wouldn't leave witnesses behind. If she wasn't the target, that meant she was simply in the way. Expendable.

Goddammit!

She was in the middle of it now, no matter who or what the gunmen wanted. Truth be told, Suzanne was happier believing they *were* after her, instead of Johnny. That way, at least, the whole damn thing wasn't some stupid accident she had stumbled into. That way, if she survived the night, Suzanne would have a reason to believe they were making progress.

All she had to do was make it from the doorway to the Blazer parked outside, climb in and hope Johnny survived to slide behind the wheel. If she was lucky, Johnny's suitcase would protect her when a gang of total strangers started shooting at her, with intent to kill. Then, all they had to do—assuming no one killed them in the parking lot—was drive away and hope they weren't followed.

Bullshit!

"Ready?" he asked her.

"As I'll ever be," Suzanne replied.

"On one," he whispered. "Three...two...go!"

Johnny was already moving, out the door and hustling toward the Blazer in a crouch. She followed him, the suitcase held in front of her, as the night exploded into chaos.

THE SHOTGUN WAS an Ithaca Mag-10 Roadblocker, with a pistol grip in place of the usual walnut stock. The barrel was sawed off at twenty inches, while the magazine had been extended to hold five 10-gauge Magnum rounds, instead of the standard three. The piece was semiautomatic, and it kicked like hell. Tailored for law-enforcement use, it had been tagged the Roadblocker because it was designed for stopping cars—and drivers—after all else failed.

Johnny had calculated they should have two seconds, maybe three, after emerging from the motel room, before all hell broke loose. He didn't think the gunmen wanted prisoners, but if they did, their hesitance to fire could buy another second. That would put him at the Blazer, maybe even in the driver's seat.

He had the pinky on his left hand looped inside his key ring, thumb poised on the button of his keyless-entry tag. Two clicks unlocked the Blazer all around. He figured he could manage two clicks, even in the middle of a firefight.

Sure, unless someone shot him first. Another down-and-out scenario: suppose he got the doors unlocked, but never made it to the car himself? That left Suzanne a sitting target, dead in microseconds flat.

So many things to think about. He had seen eight shooters, but what if there were others—maybe snipers on the roof, or lining up a long shot from the Cadillac? What if the goons were armored up?

It wouldn't matter, Johnny thought. The 10-gauge might not penetrate a Kevlar vest, but it would damned sure knock his targets down if Johnny scored a solid hit. Likewise, the spray of buckshot would also puncture faces and extremities, unless he let the shooters get too close.

In which case, he was dead.

He whipped the motel door back, lunged outside, the gym bag slapping heavily against his hip. Johnny ignored it, concentrating on his enemies. The Blazer screened three of them from his view, but that was satisfactory for now. It meant they couldn't shoot him, either, and he concentrated on the gunners he could see.

They were spread out, professional, not bunching up to let him take down two or three at once. He took the gunman nearest to the Blazer first, firing from the hip, strong arms absorbing the Ithaca's recoil. It sounded like a cannon in the predawn stillness of the motel parking lot, and its impact was commensurate with the report. His target vaulted backward as if yanked by cables, rolling through a clumsy backward somersault as he hit the pavement.

One down, and the rest of them were reacting on instinct, weapons swinging into target acquisition. Johnny willed Suzanne to use the Glock and was rewarded with gunfire from the far side of the Chevy Blazer. He hoped it was Suzanne and wished her luck. There was no way for him to cover her just now.

His second shotgun blast slammed out before the echoes of the first had finished rattling windows in the Desert Rose. The target had some kind of stubby automatic weapon in his hands, already spitting muzzle-flame, but Johnny's buckshot took him down before he found his mark, a life-sized rag doll flopping on the asphalt as he fell.

And everyone was firing now, the bullets whining past Johnny like mosquitoes on steroids, hungry for blood. Ducking lower as he ran, he punched the door-lock button twice and saw the Blazer's dome light come alive, a signal that the locks were disengaged. It was supposed to let you check and see if anyone was hiding in the car, but he wasn't concerned with lurkers at the moment.

He had all the action he could handle from the guys who had already shown themselves.

The Blazer was already taking hits, but nothing critical. A window, a fender, the tailgate. It would run.

"We're open," Johnny shouted at Suzanne, in case she'd missed the light or didn't grasp its significance. Just then, a shooter stepped around the left-rear fender of the vehicle, some kind of automatic rifle swinging into line with Johnny's face.

The guy was only eight or nine feet out when Johnny fired the 10-gauge, and the buckshot never had a chance to spread. It hit the gunner squarely in the face and vaporized his skull, a crimson mist wind-whipped and gone before his body hit the deck.

Johnny grabbed for the driver's door handle and found it, yanked it open, silently cursing the dome light that would now remain illuminated for at least another thirty seconds. Never mind. The shooters didn't need a light to find him in the driver's seat; they simply had to spray the vehicle with automatic fire, and they—

Suzanne! Where was she?

Johnny flinched and raised his shotgun as the other door whipped open, easing off the trigger as he recognized Suzanne. She fired two shots at someone in the parking lot before she slammed the door.

"Let's go, for Christ's sake!" she demanded, wild-eyed.

"Right."

He twisted the ignition key, his head ducking lower as the Blazer started taking concentrated fire. How many shooters were left? A bullet clipped his side view mirror off its post before he had a chance to check it out, but Johnny had the engine running by that time. He put the Blazer in reverse, released the brake and stood on the accelerator, cranking hard right on the steering wheel. Tires yelped and lurched across some unseen obstacle, as they whipped through a tight U-turn and wound up pointed toward the open highway.

Suzanne had her window down, exchanging fire with someone on what had been Johnny's side a heartbeat earlier. The windshield blew into their laps, an avalanche of pebbled safety glass, as Johnny shifted into forward drive and stomped on the pedal. Another squeal of rubber, and the Blazer leaped ahead, passing the shooters who were still alive and firing.

Steering with his left hand, Johnny braced his 10-gauge on the dashboard, muzzle aimed across the broad black hood. He glimpsed one shooter leaping clear and let him go. A second stood his ground, hoping to nail the driver, but the Blazer nailed him, rolled him up across the hood and into Johnny's line of fire. The shotgun finished it, a point-blank blast that punched the body off the hood and send it tumbling into darkness.

Johnny took a chance and slowed as they drew even with the Lincoln. "Shoot the tires!" he told Suzanne and heard her weapon barking as he swung around to bring the Caddy under fire. One round remained in the 10-gauge, and he chose the car's radiator, watching coolant spew and splash.

There was more gunfire from behind them, but he shook it off, a hard right turn onto the highway, running dark until the Desert Rose was well behind them, when he switched on the headlights.

"Are you all right?" he asked Suzanne.

"I think so." She was breathless. "Oh, shit!"

"What is it?"

"I lost your bag."

The laughter came from out of nowhere, Suzanne watching him as if she thought he were insane, then joining in, as the absurdity of her remark hit home. It carried them another three or four miles down the road before he caught his breath.

"I'll get another bag," he said. "And, come to think of it, we'll need another car. But first there's someone I need to call."

1

A sun-bleached, bullet-punctured highway sign identified the town as Many Farms, population 250, but Mack Bolan saw neither people nor farms as he made his approach, driving south from Round Rock and the Navajo Indian Reservation on U.S. Highway 191. His Audi Cabriolet ate up the miles, running cool despite the full-blast air-conditioning that spared him from the broiling desert heat.

Two hours down from Moab, Utah, on a drive that should have taken three or more, if Bolan gave a damn about the posted speed limit. He had been cautious to a point, slowing through little dried-up towns that eked their meager living out of speeding fines, letting the Audi rip when he was on the open road.

The man known as the Executioner didn't like the ghost town vibe that emanated from the shops on Main Street. Half of them were vacant, windows painted over from the inside or festooned with faded signs that read For Sale or Lease. The first pedestrian he saw was such a shock that Bolan almost started rubbernecking. An old man in overalls, his face shaded by a straw sombrero, looked every bit as dried-up as the town. As Bolan watched, he disappeared inside an ancient hardware store that featured socket wrenches and a set of dusty cookware in its window.

Bolan didn't like the feel of Many Farms because it felt like death, and that played into Johnny's tone from their brief conversation on the telephone. No details yet, but Johnny never mentioned trouble on the phone, unless the cause was life or death.

And this time, he had mentioned trouble twice.

The coffee shop was called Marv's, across the street from the Sleepy Pines Motel. Bolan assumed the pines in question had been felled to clear the way for all those farms he couldn't see. The one car in the motel parking lot was a Jeep Cherokee, black underneath a layer of khaki dust. A sign out front assured him there were vacancies.

He drove past, checking out the coffee shop. Two customers positioned in a window booth appeared to have the place all to themselves. He checked for lurking traffic cops and made a U-turn, doubling back to park outside the coffee shop. He killed the air-conditioning, switched off the Audi's engine and stepped out into blinding sunlight and baking heat.

The coffee shop had air-conditioning, but it was listless, tired, in keeping with the restaurant's decor. Pea-green linoleum had faded out to something like chartreuse, and Bolan guessed the walls hadn't been painted in a decade, maybe more. A waitress who had tagged her left breast "Maybelle" watched him from behind the counter.

"Anywhere you wanna sit, hon," she announced.

He nodded toward the couple in the window booth. "Just catching up," he told her, putting on a weary smile. "Got separated on the road."

"It happens, hon."

"I'll have a Coke and check out the menu," he said.

"Sure thing. Right with ya."

Johnny and the woman faced each other in the booth, both of them watching Bolan as he closed the gap. It still surprised him sometimes when he saw his brother all grown up, remembering the youth Johnny had been when Bolan launched his lonely war against the predators. The boy had grown into a fine, strong man—a fighting man, at that, a sometime fellow warrior in the struggle that would never end.

Bolan resented that, to some extent. Not Johnny's choice,

so much, but circumstance. He thought one member of his family at least should have been spared. Of course, that would have meant that life was fair.

So much for fairy tales.

His brother scooted over, making room, and Bolan sat beside him in the booth, vinyl and duct tape squelching as he settled in. Maybelle was at his elbow with the cola and a plastic-coated menu that was long on deep-fried foods.

"You order yet?" he asked of no one in particular.

"The trucker's combo," Johnny said. "Cheeseburger, fries and slaw."

"I'll have the same."

"Three mother truckers," Maybelle said, and laughed her way back to the kitchen with his order.

"So, Suzanne," Johnny began, "this is my good friend, Mike Belasko. Mike, meet Suzanne King."

They smiled in lieu of handshakes, Bolan pegging her at twenty-six or twenty-seven, maybe five foot six, perhaps 120 well-proportioned pounds. Her auburn hair was shoulder length and framed a face that would be worth a second look in any circumstance. She went easy on the makeup, and the shadows underneath blue eyes suggested that she had been going easy on the sleep of late, as well.

Since neither one of them was sporting any bandages that he could see, Bolan dispensed with any questions on their health and cut directly to the chase. "What's going on?"

His brother shared a glance with Suzanne King and said, "I'll start. Suzanne's been looking for her brother, Billy, for a month or so."

"Six weeks next Thursday," she corrected him.

"She talked to the PD in San Diego, where Billy lives, but they just blew her off."

"No foul play evident," she mimicked some anonymous detective. "They'll make some attempt to look for missing children, but adults can disappear without a trace and no one gives a damn, unless they find a body in the gutter."

She was right, of course. Adults were free to pull up stakes and vanish on a whim unless they were parolees or indicted felons pending trial. According to the last statistics he had seen, more than a hundred thousand did exactly that in the United States each year. Most of them surfaced somewhere else, in time, alive or dead, but roughly ten percent were simply gone. They changed names, picked up new ID, skipped out on debts and built new lives.

Or maybe not.

"What does your brother do?" Bolan asked Suzanne.

She frowned and broke connection with his gaze. "Odd jobs," she said. "He's not…oh, hell, why lie about it, right? He's been in trouble all his life, with one thing or another. Joy-riding when he was still in junior high school. Later on, receiving stolen property, shoplifting, bunco scams, that kind of thing. He's done some time—a year in Chino, plus a couple shorter terms in county jail. My brother's not an angel, okay? I don't know why I still have trouble saying it."

"He's not locked up right now, by any chance?"

"I checked that out first thing," Johnny replied.

"He always called me when he took a fall," Suzanne put in. "He didn't have a lawyer or a bondsman he was tight with. I'd take care of things."

"Billy is your younger brother?" Bolan asked.

"I'm younger, by a year and change," she said, "but I was always more…I don't know…levelheaded or mature, I guess. Our mother died when he was twelve and I was eleven. I sort of started taking care of him and Dad. I got promoted to the lady of the house, you know? And when our father went away, four years later…"

"Went away?"

"He started drinking after Mama died," Suzanne explained. "Sometimes, he got a little rowdy in the bars. One night, there was some kind of argument. This guy went for a knife, and Daddy hit him with a bar stool. Anyway, the man died. They called it manslaughter and sent him to prison.''

''How long was he gone?''

''Forever,'' Suzanne said. She stroked one forearm with an index finger, saying, ''Daddy had this rebel flag tattoo, right here. I'm not sure why. He wasn't even from the South. He was barely in the joint two weeks before another prisoner—a black man—stabbed him in the yard. Some lawyer from Corrections said they thought it was a racial thing. The black guy noticed his tattoo and thought he was associated with a bunch of Aryans. I told them he was wrong, for all the difference that it made.''

The burgers arrived, and Bolan caught a lazy wink from Maybelle as she turned away. The possibilities of small-town life.

''I won't pretend to know your brother,'' Bolan said, as Johnny and Suzanne got started on their burgers, ''but from what you've told me, two scenarios suggest themselves. The first would be that Billy got in trouble and decided it was time to split, lie low and let the heat blow over.''

''I thought of that myself,'' Suzanne replied. ''He's skipped before, a time or three, I grant you. But he always called me, so I wouldn't worry. Even when he wouldn't tell me what was wrong or how long he'd be gone, he always called. We're close. Please understand that.''

Bolan glanced at Johnny, saw concern for this young woman in his brother's eyes.

''In that case,'' Bolan said, ''you should prepare yourself for the eventuality that Billy hasn't called because he can't. The kind of lifestyle you're describing, there's a chance that something may have happened to him, either accidentally or otherwise.''

''We've checked the hospitals and morgues from San Diego, up as far as Bakersfield,'' said Johnny, ''but they haven't seen him. It's a washout.''

"You know—" Bolan thought about it, frowned and took a bite of cheeseburger instead of finishing the thought.

"Go on, please," Suzanne urged him. "If there's something on your mind I haven't thought of, I want to hear it. Nothing's worse than wandering around, not knowing."

"Fine. I was about to say that lots of bodies never make it to the morgue. Some people make a point of covering their tracks and leaving the police department short on evidence."

"That's possible, of course." Her eyes were brimming, but her voice was strong. There was a core of steel inside this one. "But if he's dead—murdered—I know it wasn't done by any of the two-bit punks he hung around with normally. Whatever happened to him, I want to know. I want to find out who's responsible and make them pay."

The burger wasn't bad, but Bolan's second bite went down like wet cement. The woman had more in mind than simply tracking down her missing brother. She was talking vengeance, if he turned up dead.

He turned to Johnny with a frown. "This isn't the kind of case you normally take on."

His brother's face was deadpan. "Like I said, it started out a basic missing person job. I ran the standard checks—jails, hospitals, obituaries. Three days into it, I figured out I wasn't working on the case alone."

"Explain."

"The first thing was a phone tap," Johnny said. "You know I sweep the lines three times a week. Last Thursday morning, when I checked, it came up positive. Somebody had installed a tap outside my office, at the junction box. Nothing sophisticated, but effective."

"Traceable?" Bolan asked.

Johnny shook his head. "Basic equipment. Anybody with the right patch on his overalls could have installed it. Up and down the pole, ten minutes, max."

"What makes you think the tap's related to this case?"

"Slow trade, for one thing," Johnny said. "The only other

case I had on-line was a divorce job, and I'd already submitted my report."

Alarm bells started going off in Bolan's mind. He thought about the times his brother had collaborated with him in the past, on missions that were definitely life-or-death, and said, "You never know. It could be something else. Old business, maybe."

Johnny shook his head. "I thought about that, too," he said. "There's nothing that connects. Besides, you haven't heard the rest."

"I'm listening."

"Someone broke into my apartment Friday night," Suzanne informed him. "They went through the place trashing everything. They left a message on the bedroom wall. Spray paint, two words—'Butt out.'"

Bolan didn't attempt to rationalize the vandalism. He saw where this was going, and he sensed there was more. "Go on," he said.

"Same night," his brother said, "there was a break-in at my office. I suppose it pissed them off to lose the tap, or maybe they were flexing, sending me a message. Anyway, you know my filing system. They got nada."

Johnny's filing system was a masterpiece of orchestrated chaos on computer that allowed him to retrieve a given file at will, employing codes and cutouts that would baffle any outsider.

"There's more?"

"Two nights ago, somebody firebombed Sue's apartment." Bolan picked up on the nickname but ignored it. "We were meeting on the case that night, as luck would have it. When we saw the fire trucks hosing down the ashes, I picked up some gear and we split."

"And now, they're after you."

"They found us," Johnny said, "last night. Pick up a local paper, and you're bound to read about the shooting. Right now, the police are playing it as drug related."

"Oh?"

"Turns out our uninvited drop-ins were a bunch of Russians with 'suspected criminal connections.' What's that tell you?"

It told Bolan that his brother and Suzanne had somehow run afoul of what was often called the Russian Mafia. The term was a generic tag, of course, and not restricted to the States. Even in Mother Russia, where the very mention of a syndicated criminal conspiracy had been forbidden ten years earlier, the newspapers were filled with *mafiya* reports. A special unit from the FBI had been dispatched to Moscow, as a gesture of goodwill, to help the locals cope with home-grown gangsters.

Not that it was doing any good.

There was no single, monolithic Russian Mafia, of course. As in America and every other land where crime was semiorganized, the network was composed of different gangs and "Families," some allies, other fierce competitors, who worked together when they could, and sometimes fought among themselves. Their first concern, above all else, would always be the dollar—or the ruble.

Bolan had dealt with the Russian mobsters in the past and found them cunning, ruthless, savage. None of that set them apart from any other predators he had encountered, though the Russians showed a certain careless disregard for human life more often seen in the Jamaican posses or Colombian cartels than in the Cosa Nostra. When they sought revenge against any given individual, it was assumed his parents, siblings, wife and children would be killed, as well. The extra victims were a message to the world at large: Don't fuck with us.

Bolan addressed himself to Suzanne King. "Was your brother hanging out with any Russians?"

"None," she said. "You have to understand, he didn't fill me in on everything that he was doing. Scams and such, I mean. He knew I disapproved of how he made his living, so he kept it mostly to himself.''

"But you were close."

"That's right!" she answered, leaning forward, lowering her voice but speaking with a new intensity. "He called me when he needed me, all right? The rest of it, he left me out because he was protecting me. He didn't want me thinking badly of him. If you had a brother, maybe you would understand."

He kept his eyes away from Johnny, holding Suzanne's gaze. "I understand this much," he said. "Your brother's into various unspecified activities outside the law. He's disappeared, and now it looks like someone in the Russian Mafia's determined not to let you find him. They've already tried to kill you, maybe twice. You're eating burgers in a ghost town, and you're clueless as to what comes next."

"Well, not exactly," Johnny told him.

"What?"

"We have one lead," Johnny replied. "That's why we're here. I mean, in Arizona."

"Billy had this friend in Tucson," Suzanne said. "His name's Ted Williams. Like the old-time baseball player?"

"It's familiar," Bolan said. "You have some reason to believe this person is connected to your brother's disappearance."

"Not exactly," she admitted. "But he talked about Ted all the time, more so the last few months. It's always, 'Ted says this,' or 'Ted thinks that,' you know?"

He didn't know. "Nothing specific, then?"

"About two weeks before he disappeared, he told me Ted had turned him onto something hot. That's how he phrased it. I asked him what that meant, but he just said I wouldn't want to know. That pissed me off. I told him he was stupid, risking any trouble with the record he already had. We've got that three-strike law in California now. There was an ex-con who got thirty years for shoplifting some candy bars, a little while ago.''

"So, you advised him not to follow through on this arrangement, whatever it was.''

"That's right," Suzanne replied. "He blew up on me, telling me I didn't understand where he was coming from, because I had it made. Yeah, right. I have—well, had—a two-bit secretary's job in a real-estate office, studying nights to get my license. Billy calls that big success.''

"You had an argument.''

"He pissed me off so bad, I said some things I shouldn't have, and he walked out.'' Her eyes spilled over now, and she dabbed them with her paper napkin. "That's the last I saw or heard of him. I gave him two weeks to cool off, then started calling him, but he was never home. I went around to check on him—I've got a key to his apartment—and I saw that he'd been gone a while. He's no great housekeeper, you understand, but there was all this dust on things he'd handle every day, if he was home.''

"No signs of struggle or intruders?'' Bolan asked.

"I checked it out,'' his brother interjected. "There was nothing I could spot to indicate a snatch from home. It's like he left the place, expecting to come back, but never did.''

"You have a number or an address for this Williams character?'' Bolan asked.

"Both,'' Suzanne replied. "I found it in Billy's address book.''

"We didn't want to call ahead and spook him, maybe put him in the wind,'' Johnny said. "If it hadn't been for last night's fireworks show, we were supposed to visit him today. A drop-in, to surprise him.''

"See what's up?'' Bolan asked.

"Right.'' His brother hesitated, then remarked, "There's something else.''

"And that would be…?''

"Suzanne?''

"Well, Billy said this friend of his was hooked up with intelligence, somehow. I asked him, one time, if he meant the CIA, but he just gave me Groucho eyebrows, making fun. It could be nothing."

Right. So far, he had a missing small-time criminal, the Russian Mafia, and now a shady stranger "hooked up" with intelligence. The name of Billy King's good friend in Tucson suddenly assumed a new significance. At one time, in the CIA, it had been fairly common for field agents to adopt the names of American icons as pseudonyms, when they went under cover. "Jack Armstrong," the proverbial "all-American boy," had been lifted from a comic strip and recycled dozens of times by contract agents working for the Company. Why not Ted Williams? Hell, why not Babe Ruth or Mickey Mantle?

Bolan was silent for a moment, felt the others watching him before he spoke again. "Why don't I check this out?" he said to Johnny. "You can take the lady somewhere safe, and I'll get back to you."

"No way," Suzanne objected, before Johnny had a chance to speak. "This is my brother, and I'm not about to run and hide while someone else does all the work."

Unspoken in her protest, but implicit in her tone, was Suzanne's natural mistrust of Mike Belasko. They had never met before that afternoon, and Bolan understood why she would be reluctant to accept reports from total strangers.

"What I'm saying," he informed her, "is that this could be a dicey situation. Someone could get hurt."

"Someone already has," she answered back. "A dozen people lost their homes and nearly died when my apartment house burned down. I shot a man last night. He may be dead for all I know. And Johnny...well...I'm just not backing off. That's it. End of discussion."

Bolan studied her more closely. It would be no challenge to immobilize her, lock her up somewhere with Johnny standing guard, but that had never been his style. Besides, he knew the draw of family, especially when there was danger to a member of the clan. It had been something very similar that launched his own long war against the savages. In that case, Bolan's parents and his teenaged sister had been killed, Johnny near death, before he even realized the family was threatened. Bolan's vengeance had been swift and terrible, apocalyptic, but he quickly learned there was no such thing as getting even.

Once you lost your loved ones, they were gone for good, and no amount of blood spilled in the streets would ever bring them back.

"Know this," he told Suzanne. "From here on out, it's an entirely different game. Last night was nothing. You have zero expertise in this domain. We do." His nod included Johnny. "If you're set on doing this your way, ignoring our advice, the best that you can hope for is a quick, clean death. I have no great desire to die for you, or sacrifice my oldest friend." Another nod toward Johnny, and the faint suggestion of a lump in Bolan's throat.

"You think I'll just be in the way," Suzanne responded, not quite pouting.

"That depends on how you play it," Bolan said. "I can't do anything to help your brother if I have to spend all day reminding you to watch your back and keep your head down."

"I'm not an idiot," she said. "I won't pretend I wasn't scared last night, but I came through. I'm still alive."

"Beginner's luck."

"We're all beginners, once," she said. "Besides, why would you want to?"

"What?"

"Help me," she said. "Help Billy."

"Johnny called and asked me to."

"That's it?"

"You've had it rough," Bolan replied. "I understand that.

And frankly, I suspect the worst is yet to come. That doesn't mean you have to face it by yourself.''

She thought about that for a moment, staring out the window at the street, where heat waves shimmered off the pale, cracked sidewalks. He could almost see the cog wheels turning in her mind. To trust, or not to trust?

"All right," she said at last. "If Johnny wants you in, that's cool. You need to understand, I don't have cash to burn."

The smile on Bolan's face was pure reflex. "I won't be billing you," he said.

"Why not?" she asked.

"I do pro bono work from time to time," Bolan replied.

"So, now I'm charity?"

"You're paying Johnny, right?" He waited for her grudging nod. "Okay, then. Say I owe him one and let it go at that. Don't look a gift horse in the mouth."

"In my experience, gift horses have a tendency to come up lame," she said.

He turned to Johnny, caught his brother smiling, too. "You've got a live one here," he said.

"I'd like to keep it that way," Johnny replied.

"Don't worry," Suzanne said. "If I get killed, I promise not to ask you for a refund."

"Great. I feel much better now."

"So what's the program?" Suzanne asked. "Where do we go from here?"

"Tucson," the Executioner replied. "I need to see a man about a baseball game. With any luck, he just might know the score."

2

Ted Williams lit his forty-third unfiltered cigarette of the day and took a long drag, waiting for the small, familiar rush. Damned things were killing him, he knew, but that was life. He had to die of something, and experience had taught him there were much worse ways to go than coughing out his lungs in some low-rent retirement home.

Not that he figured it would come to that. There were too many other hazards in his life for the Big C to rank as anything more than a small, distant blip on the radar screen.

His suitcase was packed and sitting in the middle of the living room, all scuffed and scarred from years of traveling the world on other people's errands. He had lugged that bag along with him from West Berlin to Bangkok, from Angola to Algiers. If it could talk...

Ted Williams.

It wasn't the name typed on his birth certificate, but he had used that other name—his first—so rarely in the past three decades that he sometimes had to think a while before he could recall exactly what it was. John Something, he remembered now. Who gave a shit?

Ted Williams was the one they counted on to get things done, and when he let them down—or, rather, when they *thought* he'd let them down—Ted Williams was the one who could expect a midnight visit, with an all-expense-paid one-way trip into the desert.

He took another long look at the suitcase. Williams had

spent the best part of a month debating what he should take with him when he finally left Tucson. He had packed, unpacked and repacked twenty-five or thirty times, until he realized that he was turning into a compulsive basket case. The last time, fifteen days ago, Williams had packed some socks and underwear, a couple of his nicer shirts and a half million bucks in crisp, new hundred-dollar bills.

He didn't pack the Smith & Wesson Model 4026 or its spare magazines, preferring to have firepower available at need. The pistol was a .40-caliber, the old 10 mm round renamed in order to secure a contract with the mighty FBI. He also kept a Mossberg "Special Purpose" shotgun in the bedroom, its 9-shot magazine loaded with alternating deer slugs and double-aught buckshot rounds.

Just in case.

Williams was paranoid and didn't care who knew it. The folks who mattered were as paranoid as he was, maybe more so.

It was how they all stayed alive.

Once he had finished packing, Williams had to think about the two real problems: when to leave and where to go. Two weeks and counting on those questions, and he didn't have a goddamned clue.

The timing, he supposed, was less important than his choice of destination, though each day he spent procrastinating whittled down his chances of survival. Christ, for all he knew, he might have waited too long, as it was. He had to smile around his cigarette at that, the notion that he could have stumbled on a new technique of suicide. Simple inaction. Not starvation, mind you. Hell, no. You just sat around, ate what you pleased, watched Jerry Springer on the tube and waited for some grunt to show up on the doorstep and put a bullet in your head.

The problem with deciding when to leave was, simply, that he wasn't absolutely sure the trip was necessary in the first place. Williams wasn't positive he needed to escape at all—

and if he didn't, if the men he feared were really satisfied with his performance, then a sudden break would change their minds, become a self-fulfilling prophecy of death.

It was enough to drive a man to drink. Of course, with Williams, that didn't take much. He had polished off a six-pack of Coronas in the past two hours, and he still had ten or fifteen long-necked bottles waiting for him in the fridge. When he got up that morning, he had planned to make the beer last two whole days, but it was looking like he'd have to make another run tomorrow morning, early, for a fresh supply.

Assuming that he hadn't left by then.

It was already well past ten o'clock, and even thinking that it would be best to leave at night, still meant he had wasted two full hours of travel time. On top of that, he had a fairly decent buzz on, and he didn't really feel like driving. Not until he had a sure-fire destination, anyway.

The obvious selection would be Mexico. A forty-something gringo with a suitcase full of hundred-dollar bills could finish off his life down there. Pick out some little village where the tourists didn't congregate and no one gave a damn about his name, connect with some sweet señorita who would keep an old man happy for a reasonable price, and he was set.

Until the bastards tracked him down.

So, maybe Mexico wasn't quite far enough away from home. He thought about Costa Rica, maybe Venezuela, but the street scenes ran together in his mind, and then, before he knew it, he was back in Guatemala, Nicaragua, Chile, pulling shit that made him wonder what the hell he had been thinking at the time.

Too late.

What was done was done, and there was nothing he could do about it now, except keep trying to survive.

From out of nowhere, Williams thought about something he'd heard on the radio a couple days ago. One of the morning jocks was rambling, waxing philosophical—or trying to—when he proclaimed, "The past is gone, the future's unknown, but today is a gift. That's why they call it 'the present.'"

He had laughed at the time, a cynical hoot, but the more he thought about it now, the more Williams was starting to suspect the jock was onto something. There were ways to turn a life around, no matter how fucked-up it was. Junkies got clean and sober. Thieves went straight. They even had a regimen of drugs and therapy these days that was supposed to make your basic psycho-rapist safe to walk the streets. Why not an aging cloak-and-dagger type who lost his way while he was working in the dark?

Why not, indeed?

The problem was that if he ran, the very men he wanted to avoid were rich enough to find him anywhere on Earth, and they were known for holding grudges. Nothing drove them crazy like unsettled scores, the thought of enemies enjoying life and living to a ripe old age. The Russians were a lot like the Colombians, that way.

Of course, it wasn't only Russians he would have to think about if he took off. Had it been only Russians, Williams could have asked his longtime friends back east for help, a little cover, maybe even some financial aid. These days, with everything mixed up the way it was, he would be running from his so-called friends, as well as from his lifelong adversaries. And his friends would have an even greater reason to make sure his lips were permanently sealed.

Ted Williams almost missed the noise. It was soft and subtle, nearly covered by the rasping of his lighter as he fired up cigarette number forty-four. Still, there was something, like a scuffling in the kitchen, that immediately made the short hairs bristle on his nape.

A last glance toward the suitcase, as he drew the Smith & Wesson from the waistband of his faded jeans. He always kept it cocked and locked, only the safety stopping him from cranking off a hot round down the crack of his ass. He thumbed off the safety now, held the piece against his thigh as he began a slow walk toward the kitchen. It was probably another lizard, snuck in through that hole he never got around to patching in the window screen.

Two steps inside the kitchen, he was reaching backward for the light switch with his free hand when the cold steel of a weapon kissed the naked patch of skin behind his ear.

"Let's take it nice and easy," the voice said.

THEY HAD CONVOYED down to Tucson, Bolan trailing Johnny's Jeep and watching out for any shadows on the way. They took Highway 191 as far as Sanders, where they picked up U.S. Highway 666—a tag that had to have given certain drivers pause, as they drove south through desert country that was hot as hell.

Ted Williams occupied a small-frame house on Escalante Road, southeast of Tucson. The incessant noise of training flights from nearby Davis Montham Air Force Base hadn't depopulated Escalante Road, but it insured that those who bought or rented houses there wouldn't be members of the local upper crust. It was a neighborhood of faded, peeling paint, and small, untended yards that went to seed before the grass baked brown and died. If all the junk cars parked in yards and driveways had been up and running, their respective owners could have mounted an impressive demolition derby.

It was nearly sundown by the time they finished scouting out the neighborhood. Retreating into Tucson proper, Bolan found a parking lot where he was guaranteed the Audi would be safe. He walked two blocks from there to meet his brother and Suzanne King in a café, where they drank coffee, working out the details of the probe.

"You're staying with the car," he told Suzanne, first thing.

"That isn't fair," she said.

"It's nonnegotiable."

"May I ask why?"

"You've never done this kind of work before," he told her. "You're a liability. You'd slow us down, get in the way, present a possible distraction. If it falls apart, you might get someone killed."

"Don't sugarcoat it," she replied sarcastically. "Go on and tell me what you really think."

"We also need someone to watch the car," Johnny said.

"I'm your driver now?"

"Think you can handle it?"

"This is my brother, dammit!"

"Do you have some reason to believe he's in the house with Williams?"

"No, I meant—"

"You're in the car," Bolan repeated. "Or we scrub the deal right here, right now. Your choice."

"Looks like I'm in the car."

"You'll have a weapon, but it's strictly as a last resort. Can you remember that?"

"I'm not Ma Barker," Suzanne told him, "and I'm not an idiot."

"Then you should be all right. We may need to extract him, but I'm hoping we can get the information that we need on-site. Whatever happens, keep a lookout and be ready for a hasty getaway."

"Do I keep the engine running?"

"Not unless the Jeep has trouble starting."

"It's brand-new," Johnny reminded him.

"Then never mind. You'd only draw attention to yourself."

"In that neighborhood?" she said. "It didn't look like anyone would call the cops."

"You're right," Bolan replied. "More likely, they'd come out to check on you themselves. We don't need any witnesses."

"You're only *talking* to this guy about my brother, right?"

"That's what I had in mind. Of course, he may not want to share."

"It just keeps getting better. Christ, I don't believe this."

"If you'd rather just forget about it, we can all go home."

"Now that a bunch of crazy people want me dead?" Suzanne retorted. "I don't think so."

"I'd be very much surprised if they were crazy," Bolan said.

"They looked professional to me," Johnny put in.

"That makes it better?" she asked.

"That makes it worse."

"How did I know you were about to say that?" Suzanne raised her coffee cup, considered it, then set it down again. "I need to use the ladies' room. Have we got time?"

"Go ahead."

"I don't like this," Bolan informed his brother after she had left the table. "Russian shooters, now this Williams character. It reeks."

"What are you thinking?" Johnny asked him.

"Nothing, yet. There are too many wild cards in the game, and Suzanne's one of them."

"I checked her out," Johnny replied. "She's clean."

"What kind of check?"

"The usual. She's got no record, other than some parking tickets. Nothing in the way of wants or warrants. Her employment history is stable. Squeaky clean."

"Which means she's either never been in trouble, or she's good at covering her tracks. Unlike her brother," Bolan added.

"So, the brother was a waste. She wants him back, or to find out what happened to him, anyway. You can't hold that against her."

"If that's all it is."

"If I didn't know you better," Johnny said, "I might suggest that you've got a suspicious mind."

"It's caution," Bolan told his brother. "Maybe you could use an extra helping for yourself."

"What's that supposed to mean?"

"Don't let a pretty face confuse you. Make damned sure you know which head you're thinking with before you act."

"That's cute," Johnny said. "You don't trust her."

"I don't know her," Bolan said. "Neither do you."

"The Russians tried to take her out last night. She dropped one, maybe canceled him."

"I heard that. Are you positive she was the target?"

Johnny nodded without hesitation. "Absolutely. There's no reason for them to be after me, except through my association with Suzanne."

"That stock thing, late last year," Bolan reminded him.

Johnny had been retained to ID an embezzler in a San Diego brokerage firm after close to a million dollars in stock had fallen through the cracks. The senior partners were avoiding contact with police to save their public face, and Johnny had been able to identify the man responsible: an aging associate whose sluggish progress with the company had prompted him to think in terms of mixing profit with revenge. He had been fencing the securities to a small-time Russian operator in L.A., and both of them had gone to prison after Johnny testified.

"It's been too long," Johnny replied with perfect confidence. "Besides, I'm still not sure the guy in that case was connected."

Bolan frowned. "Assume the worst. That way—"

"—'you'll always be prepared, and seldom disappointed,'" Johnny finished for him, grinning. "I remember. This is something else."

"I hope you're right," Bolan said. "Otherwise, we're both out on a limb."

They saw Suzanne returning from the ladies' room, and Bolan slipped his poker face back on. He had no reason to distrust the woman, but he had survived this long by covering the angles, making sure that none were overlooked, nothing was left to chance.

"When do we go?" she asked.

"Right now."

They drove back to the seedy stretch of Escalante Road in Johnny's Cherokee, with Suzanne at the wheel. It wouldn't hurt to let her try the route one time, in case she had to do it in a hurry later on. If Bolan was supposed to trust her, there was no time like the present to begin.

Most of his hardware had remained locked in the Audi's trunk. The only weapons Bolan carried were his usual Beretta 93-R pistol in a Galco shoulder harness, as well as a double-edged dagger disguised as the buckle of his black leather belt. The Beretta held twenty 9 mm Parabellum rounds, with two clips in reserve, and it was fitted with a custom-tailored sound suppressor. Johnny was packing a Glock, and if they needed more than that to question one man in a run-down bungalow, they would be out of luck.

A Honda Civic parked in front had led them to believe someone was home during their first pass, and lights inside the house confirmed it when they made another drive-by, looking for a place to park the Cherokee. Bolan directed Suzanne to continue past the house and had her pull into a littered alleyway that ran behind the homes on Escalante Road. They parked two houses short of their intended destination, and she killed the lights and switched off the engine.

"What's the drill again?" he asked her.

"Me? I'm staying with the car."

"That is exactly right. Do not step out for any reason, even for a second."

"What if I get rousted by the cops?"

"Unlikely," Bolan said. "But if they do show up, you keep it casual and tell them that you're waiting for some friends."

"Out here?"

"They're moving, you're the driver. If—and only if—an

officer should order you to step out of the car, you give the
horn a tap. A little accident, okay?''

"I hear you."

"Right."

To Johnny, he said, "Let's go."

They tugged on lightweight ski masks as they moved along
the alley, passing battered garbage cans. The fence around
the small backyard was chain link, nothing to suggest a
watchdog on the premises. The yard was dark, same story
for the windows facing it. There was no challenge as they
crossed the crunchy, dried-up grass and crouched beside a
door that seemed to open on a smallish kitchen.

Two locks on the door, a dead bolt and a simple push-
button. The latter popped when Bolan used a strip of plastic,
probing briefly in between the door and jamb. He had to pick
the other, Johnny standing watch, and he was sweating by
the time he got it done.

The kitchen smelled of grease. The house was quiet, no
TV or stereo in play, lights burning toward the front. Bolan
moved silently to the connecting door and risked a glance
around the corner, picking out a man of average height and
build. He stood with his back to the kitchen, smoking and
staring out the broad front window, toward the street outside.

Bolan turned to Johnny, glancing at the small, square dining table in the middle of the kitchen, ringed by mismatched
chairs. He pointed, Johnny picking up on it and stretching
his leg to gently nudge one of the chairs. It made a muffled
scraping sound on the linoleum, nothing too obvious, but
loud enough.

They heard Ted Williams coming, even though he tried to
keep it casual. Bolan was waiting on the blind side of the
kitchen door as Williams entered, reaching out with the
Beretta to make contact with the stranger's skull.

"Let's take it nice and easy," he suggested.

"Sure thing," Williams replied. "You're the man."

"The gun," Bolan instructed, sensing that he wouldn't have to spell it out.

Williams raised the automatic, shifted it so that the weapon balanced on his open palm. Bolan retrieved it with his free hand, flicked on the safety and tucked it inside his belt.

"Just make it quick, okay?" Williams said. "That's not asking much."

Bolan reached back and found the light switch, near the door, and brought the kitchen into clear relief. He could feel Williams checking out Johnny, though he made no attempt to turn his head. The guy was cool, so far. Bolan could almost hear him wondering if Johnny's mask was any cause for optimism. Why hide faces, if he was about to die?

"Sit down." A nudge from the Beretta got him moving toward the table.

"Where?" Williams asked.

"Take your pick."

He sat, and Bolan took a seat across the table from him, Johnny staying on his feet, prepared to head off any sudden bolt toward either exit.

"Listen," Williams said, "I'd just as soon not drag this out, if you don't mind. We both know why you're here, and—"

"Why is that, again?"

"Tie up loose ends," Williams replied, but for the first time, he was sounding less than certain.

"And who is it that you think we are?" Bolan asked.

Williams blinked at that. His mind was working, but he couldn't seem to get beyond the expectation that had sent him to the kitchen with a pistol in his hand.

"I guess you'd better tell me that," he said at last.

"You were a friend of Billy King's."

Another blink, impossible to say if it was prompted by surprise or fear. Williams was stalling, trying to decide how he should answer. Bolan took it that the men he was expecting would have known the answer for themselves, and probably wouldn't have mentioned it.

"If you say so," the man replied.

"I'm asking what *you* say."

"I know him," Williams answered. Present tense. Did that mean King was still alive? "We do some business, now and then."

"When was the last time that you heard from him?" Bolan asked.

Williams sat back in his chair, hands in his lap. He turned to look at Johnny, then swung back toward Bolan, answering the question with a query of his own. "Who are you guys?"

"Let's say we've got an interest in his welfare," Bolan said, "and let it go at that. I'm waiting for an answer to my question."

"And the question was...?"

Bolan was raising the Beretta when Williams jerked a hand up, open palm positioned to accept the bullet. "Wait! I haven't heard from Billy in six weeks, maybe more."

That coincided with Suzanne's date for her brother's disappearance. "Did he call you here?"

"He called, but not here. I've got another place I use for business." Williams shrugged, as if the rest were understood between them.

"When you spoke to him, how did he sound?"

"The same as always." Lying. It was there, behind his eyes.

"Try that again." A twitch of the Beretta, angling toward his face.

"Okay, he sounded nervous. Told me he was having problems with some business in L.A."

"Same business that he did with you?" Bolan asked.

"I didn't say that."

"It's the question on the table," Johnny told him, moving closer, but remaining clear of Bolan's line of fire.

"You guys should know this shit already," Williams said.

"We should?"

The message sinking in at last. "Say, what the hell is this? You guys aren't Russian, and you sure as hell aren't from the Company."

The words were barely past his lips, when Williams realized that he had said too much. Some of the starch went out of him, his shoulders slouching as he leaned back in his chair.

"You're right on both counts," Bolan said, "and I can't wait to hear how Langley figures into this."

"Who's Langley?" Williams asked, hands fidgeting just out of sight, as if the guy were twiddling his thumbs.

"I'd like to sit and talk to you all night," Bolan said, "but the fact is that we're on a schedule. If you want to dick around, the options for a civilized discussion will be limited."

"I see your point." The man's right hand came up, as if to scratch behind his ear, then made a hasty detour toward his mouth. Not yawning, though his mouth was open now. Something—

His gut told Bolan it was too late, even as he lunged across the kitchen table, striking Williams on the wrist with his Beretta, knocking down the arm. He heard a crunch like someone biting on a Chiclet, something mashed between the molars there.

Williams's eyelids drooped as he slithered from his chair. Johnny was there to catch him underneath the armpits, halfway to the floor, but he was limp already, his pale face lolling over on one shoulder like a hanged man's.

Leaning in, Bolan could smell the bitter almonds on his breath. A glance down at his lap revealed the open belt buckle, a simple but effective place to stash the cyanide capsule.

Death before dishonor, more or less.

"That's it. He's gone."

"I don't believe this shit," Johnny said. "This guy's CIA?"

"Not necessarily. It could have been a blind." But even as he made the comment, Bolan's gut was saying otherwise.

Johnny released the flaccid body, Williams oozing from his chair to wind up underneath the table. Bolan's mind was racing as he stepped into the living room, remembering the suitcase he had glimpsed when he first saw the man now lying dead behind him on the kitchen floor.

"Looks like he was about to leave," Johnny said. "Want to see what's in the bag?"

When Bolan opened it, the first thing that he saw was folded shirts, some underwear beneath. He twitched the fabric back with the Beretta's muzzle, saw the cash and made a hasty estimate.

"He wasn't leaving empty-handed, anyway."

"You want to leave it?" Johnny asked him.

Bolan shook his head, already pulling out the clothes. No fingerprints on cotton fabric. "Langley and the Russians have enough cash, as it is. We may need this before we're done."

"You're buying this? About the Company, I mean?"

"I don't know what to think right now," Bolan replied. "But I know where to check it out."

3

Hal Brognola had been swearing off cigars the past ten years or so, but every once in a while he'd just have to smoke. It was an ongoing battle—quit for six months, smoke for two months. It was a weakness he confessed to, but he stopped short of regarding it as an addiction. Nowadays, he decided he'd have a cigar but not light it. A nice compromise.

This Thursday morning, the man from Justice was wishing that cigars were all he had to think about. Unfortunately, he had operations up and running in four different jurisdictions that demanded his attention, none of them revealing any hints that they would be resolved within the next few days. The biker syndicate that operated out of Florida was hanging in there with their methamphetamine production and had recently completed treaty talks with a Colombian cartel to handle cocaine shipments coming through the Keys. In Utah, a mixed bag of "patriots" and flat-out Nazis had been robbing banks and armored cars for seven months, bagging an estimated thirteen million dollars toward their goal of financing a "racial holy war." The Yakuza was buying up a series of hotel-casinos in Nevada, while the state commissioners insisted that their "Black Book" was sufficient to protect the gaming industry, with its list of thirty-odd aging Italians and Jews who were banned from casino operations in the Silver State. A doomsday cult in San Francisco was about to pull up stakes and move to Yucatán, provoking cries of panic that another Jonestown was about to break.

The last thing Hal Brognola needed at the moment was to hear the red phone on his desk ring, announcing he had an urgent call. No other kind had ever been received on that line, and there were only seventeen or eighteen people in the world who had the number. One of them lived in the White House, while the rest were scattered far and wide, from the ultracovert Stony Man Farm in Virginia, to the shifting battlefronts where the director of the Sensitive Operations Group deployed his meager troops.

He lifted the receiver on the second ring and told the caller, "Speak to me."

"We scrambled?"

The big Fed recognized the voice, experienced an instant of relief, then lost it as he realized that Bolan wouldn't call between assignments unless he had a problem on his hands.

"We will be," Brognola responded. "Just a sec." He pressed a button to engage the built-in scrambler, and a green light blinked alive to tell him it was operative. "Okay, it's cool."

"I've stumbled into something here," Bolan said, "and I'm hoping you can help me with some gaps in the intelligence."

"Where's 'here'?"

"Out west."

He noted the evasiveness and wondered what was up with that. It wasn't vintage Bolan, and it put the big Fed on guard. "It's warm out there, this time of year," the man from Justice said.

"And getting warmer," Bolan said. "Do you know anything about the Company cooperating with the Russians recently?"

It wasn't quite the sound of an alarm bell going off, Brognola told himself. More like tinnitus, really, that insistent, pesky ringing in the ears that seemed to have no cause or cure.

"That's pretty vague," Brognola said. "There've been all

kinds of overtures since '91. It goes both ways. I'd need more details.''

''Right. Let's start with an illegal operation in the States,'' Bolan suggested. ''Something that would put the Company in bed with members of the Russian Mafia. Make it a deal they'd kill for, to prevent it going down the tubes.''

Brognola felt his stomach tighten. Perspiration made the telephone receiver difficult to handle. ''Any operation by the CIA on U.S. soil is automatically illegal,'' he reminded Bolan. ''As we know from personal experience, that hasn't stopped them in the past. There's been one kind of covert action or another going on behind the scenes since Langley set up shop way back when.''

''I need to find out if there is an operation running at the moment,'' Bolan told him. ''If there is, I'll need to know if it's a sanctioned program, or if Langley's got another rogue.''

A well-placed traitor in the Company had mounted operations against Bolan and Stony Man Farm, some time back. Lives had been lost, including one that Bolan held most near and dear. The aftermath of that betrayal amply verified the biker motto that explained that payback was a bitch. In spades.

''I told you—''

''Any operation in the States is banned, I know,'' Bolan said, interrupting him. ''And we both know that certain programs get the green light out of Langley anyway. They've never had much interest in the law, except when it protects their secrets. I've got one I need to crack, and soon.''

''It's still not much to go on,'' Brognola said, shifting in his swivel chair. ''You say the Russian Mafia. Which Family? They're everywhere these days. I don't—''

''Start looking in the Southwest,'' Bolan said, interrupting again. ''So far, I've got contacts in Tucson and in San Diego.''

''San Diego?'' Now, the ringing in his ears was definitely more pronounced. ''Is Johnny—''

"Two names," Bolan cut him off. "The first is Billy King, white male, an ex-con who's done time in California. Different kinds of theft, from what I understand. He disappeared about six weeks ago."

"An ex-con's missing? Stop the presses! Look, I—"

"His connection out of Tucson was a guy who called himself Ted Williams. Forty-something, white, with salt-and-pepper hair cut in a military buzz. I talked to him last night."

"What did he have to say?" Brognola asked.

"Not much. When he worked out that Langley hadn't sent me, he decided it was time to swallow cyanide."

"He mentioned Langley?"

"I believe his words were, 'You aren't Russian, and you sure as hell aren't from the Company.'"

"Well, that could mean anything."

"It *could* mean Sears and Roebuck, but I'd bet against it," Bolan said. "The guy was packed to leave, with something like three-quarters of a mill in C-notes. When we dropped in on him, he assumed it was a hit at first, then took himself out when we started asking questions about King."

"What do you mean, '*we* dropped in'?"

"It's Johnny's case," the Executioner stated, confirming the Fed's apprehension. "Simple missing person, when it started. Now, we've got some kind of hit team trailing Johnny, who knows how, and the one guy who could have shed some light on it has decided he'd rather die, spook-style, than talk."

"The Russians have a lot of people scared these days," Brognola said. "They're working with the old-line Mafia, the Yakuza and Triads, the Colombians, you name it."

"Lots of people don't mention the Company ten seconds before they swallow a cyanide capsule hidden in a belt buckle, Hal. When was the last time you even heard of that happening? Bay of Pigs? Some cold war operation out of East Berlin?"

"You're right, Striker," Brognola said, using Bolan's code

name. There was no point denying it. The ugly mess had CIA written all over it. "I'm still not sure how I can help you, though. If they've got shooters out, my money's on the Russians. Either way, it doesn't sound like something Langley would admit to me, sanctioned or otherwise."

"You've still got ways," Bolan reminded him.

"Two names, and one of them most likely false." Brognola didn't have to feign a tone of hopelessness. "That's not a lot to start with, Striker."

"See if this helps," Bolan replied. "On Tuesday night or early Wednesday morning, several shooters got their tickets punched in Arizona. Little town called Aztec, down on U.S. 8. They bought it at a motel called the Desert Rose. They had two cars, and neither one of them were fit to drive away. You may get something from the local sheriff's office on ID or license plates. For all I know, the Bureau may be looking into it by now."

"How is Aztec this time of year?" Brognola asked.

"I've never had the pleasure," Bolan said. "They came for Johnny and his client."

"Shit, I'm sorry, man. Is he all right?"

"So far, so good," the Executioner replied.

"About this client…"

"No apparent link, except an interest in the welfare of the missing person."

"Billy King," Brognola said, as he began to jot notes on a pad.

"The very same."

"You figure he's alive?"

"My gut says no, but it's been wrong before. If he was into something with the Russians and the Company, he may have gotten scared and decided it was time for a vacation. Still, from what the client says of their relationship, he would have called to say goodbye, at least."

"I'm guessing the authorities in California weren't so hot to put an APB out on an ex-con who's dropped out of sight."

"You win the big cigar," Bolan replied.

"Johnny's done the usual routine with morgues and hospitals, I take it?" Brognola queried.

"For the southern quarter of the state, at least. Beyond that, it becomes unmanageable for a single operator," Bolan said. "And if it was some kind of contract, there's at least a fifty-fifty chance they took him somewhere, made him disappear."

"Your brother's client needs to come to terms with that."

"It's understood. Hope's hard to kill, though."

"So," Brognola asked, doodling along the left side of his pad, "what's next?"

"We can't sit still and wait," Bolan replied. "I'll check back later in the day to see if you've come up with anything. Meanwhile, I'm thinking that it couldn't hurt to shake the Russians up a little, see what happens there."

"If you don't mind my asking—"

"It apparently began in San Diego," Bolan said, "at least for King. But San Diego's really just a big, extended suburb of Los Angeles, these days. The last I heard, the Russian Mafia still had its West Coast headquarters in Los Angeles."

"Those guys play rough," Brognola told his second-oldest living friend. "You need to watch your back."

"Sounds like a plan," the soldier said. "I'll catch you later."

Cradling the red receiver, Brognola was driven by a sudden urge to pick it up again and smash it down with force enough to crack the plastic. "Dammit! Dammit all to hell!"

He stared at the disordered jottings on his notepad, scowling as he underlined the final word.

L.A.

"I HATE the fucking desert," Christian Keane announced to no one in particular. He stared out through the tinted window of the Lexus LS 400, watching the wasteland roll past, and made a sour face at his own ghostly reflection in the glass.

None of the Russians answered him, which was par for the course. Four of them stuck together in the car for hours, driving down from Phoenix, and he seemed to be the only one who wasn't mute. God only knew why they hadn't flown into Tucson straightaway; some kind of great diversionary plan, no doubt, devised by geniuses who didn't give a shit if Christian Keane was absolutely bored out of his fucking mind.

He understood the job was necessary, even recognized its urgency, and hadn't complained when Noble Pruett tagged him for the ride-along. The sole redeeming virtue of the trip would be if they found Ted Williams sitting home and waiting for them. That way, Keane would get to watch the Russians work him over, maybe getting in a few licks of his own.

That sounded like fun, he thought, but realized it was unlikely to play out that way. They had called his house, Keane plugged in with a special telephone that altered voices on command, tuned in to make himself sound like a woman. It was just a simple check, to see if Williams was at home. They couldn't afford to spook him. Keane had written out a little script, pretending he had time shares in a Vegas condominium to sell. Williams would blow him off, of course, but all they needed was some kind of confirmation that the target was in place.

The bad news was that Williams hadn't blown him off. The asshole didn't answer, period, though Keane had let the phone ring thirty-seven times. He'd actually counted, shooting for an even forty, but it started getting on his nerves, and so he gave up in disgust.

Now, they had no idea if Williams was at home or not, but they were still obliged to check it out. Keane didn't like to think what it would mean if Williams slithered through their grasp, but it was unavoidable. Another damned loose end that needed tying up at any cost, and it would be *his* problem all the way, until he settled it.

The California segment of the operation had been bleeding dollars for a while now, but it wasn't easy keeping tabs on leakage in black operations. For a start, the cash was dirty in the first place, either skimmed from government appropriations where it wouldn't show, or generated by the kind of businesses that Langley didn't want to hear about. Black operations also meant that much of what went on was never written down on paper, logged on a computer disk, or otherwise recorded for posterity. Suppose one of the operators paid twelve thousand dollars for a vehicle and then reported back thirteen. Who had the time or cared enough to run around behind the pack and check on every little thing?

Of course, the biggest problem, right up front, was working with the Russians in the first place. Keane would have advised against it, but no one had asked for his opinion when the plan was being organized. He simply followed orders and expected his subordinates to do the same. The Russians, though, were snakes, and that would always be the bottom line. Shake hands with one of them, and you had to count your fingers afterward to make sure they were still intact and fully functional.

It had surprised Keane, therefore, when the leak was finally traced back to Williams and his San Diego flunky. It didn't amaze him that an ex-con on parole would steal, if given half a chance, but Williams had been working for the CIA since he got out of the Marine Corps, sixteen years and counting. He had never made a false step prior to this one.

Keane had confirmed that Williams was involved by talking to his junior partner. Billy King had cracked in something close to record time, admitting his part in the skimming operation, holding out a brutal quarter of an hour more, before he finally identified the brains behind the theft. Now, Williams wasn't answering his telephone, and that was bad.

The Russians had been all for taking Williams out as soon as King had spilled his guts, but Noble Pruett wanted more. It troubled Keane to think the old man might be getting sentimental, bogged down in weird notions of fair play, but Pruett had insisted that they give the guy some extra rope and let him tie the noose himself. When King dropped out of sight, they reasoned, Williams might react in any one of several ways.

If he was truly guilty, he might panic and take off for parts unknown. If he was innocent—fat chance—he should begin to look for King, try to discover what had happened. As it was, he had done neither. After logging King as MIA, Williams had simply gone about his business, just like any other member of the team. Six weeks, and he had yet to make a move. Pruett refused to take him out as long as they had nothing but King's unsupported word. No safe deposit box, no secret bank account, no living friends or relatives who might have helped Williams hide the cash.

To Keane, that simply meant he had the money in his house, but Pruett wouldn't authorize a search, assuming—probably correctly—that a veteran like Williams would be quick to spot the signs. As far as sweating him, the word had been: hands off.

Until last week.

The news had filtered through that King's sole living relative, the nosy sister, wasn't satisfied with the brush-off she got from San Diego's finest. She had hired a private investigator, which was no great source of consternation in itself— they wouldn't find the stupid bastard checking hospitals and such, no matter how far out they cast the net—but someone in the Russian camp had started stewing over it, deciding on his own that they should take the woman out, and maybe the PI as well, just for insurance.

It was extravagant, a stupid waste of energy, but that was how the Russians handled things. Scorched earth. Unfortunately, what the Russian's *didn't* do was clear their plans through Pruett. That arrogance had been a stumbling block on more than one occasion, and it was the Russians' fuck-up that had placed Keane in the Lexus, cruising through a desert wasteland with three stone-faced mutes, en route to kill a man who probably wasn't home.

One thing he had to give the Russians: when they broke the rules and killed without express permission, they were normally efficient to a fault. This time, for no apparent reason, they had dropped the ball—not once, but twice. The first time, they had sent a team of cleaners to the sister's place in San Diego, but she wasn't home. An address book one of them found, while they were tearing up the place, had given up a listing for "T.W." in Tucson, with an address and unlisted phone number that matched Ted Williams's.

The second try, just one day later, had occurred in some pathetic pissant town in southern Arizona where the sister and her private investigator had stopped off for the night. Eight guns had been dispatched to bag the pair, and only three had walked away—literally, since both of their cars had been trashed in the firefight. It had been a cluster fuck par excellence, and there was nothing Keane or Pruett could have done to help the Russians clean it up, even assuming they had wanted to.

He shot a quick glance toward Kropotkin, sitting ramrod straight behind the steering wheel. It seemed to Keane that members of the Russian Mafia fell into two distinct categories. There were former military men, who brought a certain discipline to crime, albeit with the same damned Russian attitude the Kremlin had espoused in 1917 until the great collapse in 1991; and, then, there were the sleazoids who resembled greasy street thugs, magically transplanted into thousand-dollar suits, most of them sporting hair down past their shoulders like some kind of strung-out heavy metal band.

The three who shared the Lexus with him were a mix from Column A and Column B. The skinhead Kropotkin at the wheel, so military in his look he may as well have had his tailor stitch the three-piece suit in olive-drab. The two goons in the back seat, names dismissed as rapidly as they were introduced, were from the heavy metal school, both smoking cigarettes that smelled like shit and whispering between themselves, their speech so weighted down with slang that even with his fluency in Russian, Keane could only make out roughly half of what they said.

Screw it. All three of them were killers and exactly what Keane needed for the job at hand, whether Ted Williams was at home, not answering his phone, or they were ultimately forced to track down the bastard.

A highway sign told Keane they were within ten miles of Tucson, and he started thinking through the hit. They had already wasted too much time surveilling Williams, waiting for a guilty move that never came. For all Keane knew, the sister and her PI had already braced their target, maybe spooked Williams into running, or worse, maybe got him talking.

No, Keane couldn't see that happening. Whatever he had done, Williams was a pro. If he believed the Russians and/or shooters from the Company were after him, he wouldn't turn state's evidence. There was no logical percentage in it, since he couldn't make an airtight case on anyone except himself. There were too many cutouts, too much plausible deniability, too many fronts and buffers in the game. What Williams knew and what he could support were two entirely different things.

Which meant that he would run and hide, employing all his covert expertise, spending the money he had skimmed as necessary, going underground. Short term, he had a fairly decent chance of giving them the slip. Over the long run, though, Ted Williams had to know he was dead. The Company didn't forget; the Russian Mafia didn't forgive.

Keane wondered whether Williams had the nerve to deal with Suzanne King and her investigator, maybe take them out himself and dump them somewhere, when he hit the road. That was assuming they had reached him, told their story— whatever that was—and managed to persuade him that his own life was in danger. Given that inducement, Keane believed there was a fifty-fifty chance that Williams may have done them all a favor, without knowing it.

Or, maybe not.

There was a Tucson street map in the glove compartment, and he had the address memorized, no need to write it down. The Browning BDA 9 automatic holstered on his hip featured a muzzle threaded to accommodate the sound suppressor Keane carried in the left-hand pocket of his sport coat. If he had to use the pistol, it would be the third time he had killed a man, his first time in the States. The prospect didn't faze him, one way or the other, since the weapon was untraceable and would be melted down for scrap when he was finished with it.

At the moment, Keane was focused on the hope that they would find Ted Williams waiting at his house, with some entirely logical and unimportant explanation for his failure to pick up the telephone.

In fact, if the Spook was home, Keane knew he wouldn't even ask. Why bother?

The house was small, poorly maintained and its location near the Air Force base told Keane it had most likely been a bargain. No one with half a brain would listen to the scream of jets around the clock, wake up at 3:00 a.m. with windows rattling from the passage of a Hornet F-18, if they could swing the price for better digs.

That was the beauty of it, Keane decided, as they parked out front. Williams was showing off his poverty, taking his licks, and who would ever guess the tenant of a dump like this had stashed away sufficient cash to live in something close to luxury? As covers went, the dump on Escalante Road wasn't half bad.

They walked up to the front door like they owned the place—which, in a sense, they did. Williams was a creature of the Company, his name and prefab life created for him when he took the bait and signed over his soul to Uncle Sam. They didn't have a key, but that was a formality. They formed a skirmish line across the tiny porch, screening Kropotkin from the view of any passing motorists or neighbors, as he gave the door a kick and bulled his way inside.

The living room was spotless, not a *Guns & Ammo* magazine or coaster out of place, except for several articles of clothing that were piled up in the middle of the floor. Keane noted them with interest, though he made no effort to hypothesize. If they found Williams, which he still regarded as unlikely, Keane could always ask. With so much money missing, rumpled shirts ranked low on Keane's list of priorities.

"In here," one of the long-haired men called, poking his head around the corner of a doorway leading to the kitchen. Keane followed Kropotkin through the door.

At first glance, it was just a kitchen, somewhat on the small side, in need of some air freshener. Keane didn't find what he was looking for until one of the Russians stepped out of the way and let him see a pair of desert boots attached to denim legs, protruding from beneath the dining table.

"So," Keane said, "what have we here?"

None of the Russians answered him, but that was fine, since he hadn't expected a reply. All three spoke English, he was fairly sure, but there was no need to solicit their opinions in a situation such as this one. Keane would be well satisfied if they could simply do as they were told.

"Touch fabric only," he instructed them, "and drag him out from under there."

Kropotkin hooked one foot behind a chair leg, easing back the chair that Keane surmised the dead man had been sitting in when he'd collapsed. That done, the Russian bent and grabbed two handfuls of the corpse's shirt. A button popped before he got the body clear, but that would make no difference. Another tiny mystery to keep the local cops confused.

Keane recognized the dead man instantly, despite the blue-gray tint of his complexion. It was Williams, looking vaguely stunned and just a little frightened, his eyes locked open, staring at some point beyond the ceiling overhead.

He crouched beside the body, bracing knuckles on linoleum—no fingerprints, that way—as he bent closer, checking out the stiff. There were no signs of violence, though he had expected strangulation marks, considering the facial hue. A whiff of something reached his nostrils, and he leaned in closer, sniffing. Was it...? Yes!

His eyes trailed down the dead man's torso, found the belt buckle that seemed askew, but which had actually sprung open on a tiny hidden spring, spilling its contents into eager hands.

"I didn't know they made those anymore," he told the corpse.

Rising, Keane scanned the body and the kitchen one more time, searching for any clues that would explain the suicide. Had Williams known that they were coming for him? It was possible, but why would he check out this way instead of simply splitting with his stolen cash for parts unknown? And if he chose to use the cyanide, why here, instead of sitting in his favorite chair, stretched out in bed, or lounging in the bath? Why did the small, untidy pile of clothing in the living room nag so at Keane's suspicious mind?

"Well, shit!"

He had it now, or thought so, anyway. It all made sense if Williams had been braced by someone else, interrogated to a point where he decided it was best to simply die. They hadn't roughed him up at all, which meant that something in the questions they were asking had to have tipped him over, made him realize that he had nothing left to live for in this world, regardless of the choice he made.

As for the laundry in the living room, it smacked of hasty packing—or unpacking? Right! Suppose Williams was packed and ready for the road when he was cornered. One of the intruders found what they were looking for inside his bag and dumped the nonessentials, carrying the rest away.

And what would *that* be? If the prize was only money, Keane could recommend they cut their losses, drop the chase and let it go. Unfortunately, there was no way to be certain without tracking down the folks responsible for Williams checking out so unexpectedly.

Bad news. It meant that his boss would be disappointed, and Pruett had a tendency to kill the messenger. Not literally, of course—at least, not often—but the end result of this snafu was bound to be more overtime, more hanging out with Russian thugs who never spoke, more living out of suitcases and hotel rooms until Keane wrapped it up.

"We're finished here," he told Kropotkin, as he stepped back from the blue-faced corpse. "I need to find a telephone."

4

"Why Los Angeles?" Johnny asked. "Why not San Diego, where it started?"

The motel air-conditioning made Mack Bolan's skin feel dry and tight. He fiddled with the knobs, fine-tuning it, and finally gave up. Returning to his chair, he sat heavily. The chair had been positioned so that he could face his brother and Suzanne, each seated on a corner of the motel's midsize double bed.

"It didn't start in San Diego," Bolan said. "That's where Suzanne ran into it and put you on the scent. It's not the heart of this."

"Where, then?" his brother asked.

On leaving Tucson, they had convoyed south until they reached a town whose name—Green Valley—had no more connection to reality than had the name of Many Farms.

"I don't know, yet," he told his brother honestly. "The fact is, we may never know. If it's the Russian Mafia we're up against, they're scattered far and wide. You name a major city in the States or Canada, you'll find the Russians digging in like there was no tomorrow."

"That's what I hear," Johnny replied. "So, why L.A., again?"

"By most accounts, it's their HQ on the West Coast."

"So, you think my brother's in L.A.?"

The question stood between them like an obstacle. There was no graceful way to get around it.

"I was thinking more in terms of finding someone who can tell us what's become of him," Bolan replied. "I have no reason to believe we'll find your brother there. In fact, Suzanne, I think you should prepare yourself—"

"For the worst," she interrupted him to finish the warning. "I know that. Johnny's been reminding me enough, I can't forget." It could have sounded harsh, but Suzanne smiled at Johnny as she spoke. "I can't help hoping, though."

"No harm in optimism," Bolan said, "unless it starts conflicting with reality. That happens, when you're playing with the Russians, you could find yourself in major trouble."

"I'm not playing," Suzanne answered back, sounding offended for the first time since he'd met her. "This is deadly serious to me. I think I proved that back at the motel in Aztec."

Johnny met her gaze and nodded confirmation. "That's a fact," he said. Then, to his brother, "Suzanne did all right."

"All right's not good enough in this league," Bolan said. "You can get by a while on luck and do all right, until you go down for the dirt nap."

Suzanne blinked at him, as if he had reached out and slapped her face. It was a wounded look, but if she felt like crying, she was able to contain it.

"I'm sorry you don't like me," she told Bolan, "but—"

"I like you fine," he cut her off. "I just don't want to see you or one of us dead because you didn't know what you were doing in the crunch."

"Hey, Mike—"

"Hey, nothing," Bolan said to Johnny. "This is life-and-death from here on out. The Russians and the Company won't cut us any slack for having untrained noncombatants on the firing line."

"What company?"

The question from Suzanne made Bolan recognize his error. It was too late to retract the words, and she wasn't the kind to simply let it pass. A clumsy brush-off wouldn't do the trick. He met his brother's eyes, saw Johnny shrug, as if to say it was his call.

Bolan bit the bullet. "It was something Williams said before he took the cyanide," he told Suzanne. "'You guys aren't from the Company,' or words to that effect. He was surprised by that, I think."

"I still don't understand."

"'The Company' is what insiders sometimes call the CIA," Johnny explained.

"You said your brother told you Williams was connected to intelligence," Bolan reminded her. "You remember that?"

"Of course," she said, "but this is still unreal." Her sudden laughter took him absolutely by surprise. "*My* brother and the CIA? I figured he was talking through his hat, you know? Or else this Williams was, to make himself sound big. The only intelligence my brother managed to display was very limited," Suzanne replied. "Billy wasn't even very good at stealing—which was strange, with all the practice that he had. I have to tell you, anyone who thought that Billy would be any good at spying needs to have his head examined."

"It wouldn't be like that." Johnny slid closer to her as he spoke and placed a gentle hand on Suzanne's shoulder. "The different agencies aren't spying all the time, and even when they do, it's not like James Bond in a tuxedo, sipping a martini."

"What's your point?"

"From time to time," Bolan explained, "the Company makes contracts with civilians for specific operations, frequently illegal. During Vietnam, the CIA imported heroin to the United States on Air America, part of a deal with warlords in the Golden Triangle to fight the Vietcong. More recently, they were involved in cocaine traffic from Colombia, selling the drugs to purchase weapons for a coup against the Nicaraguan government."

"I've heard about this stuff," Suzanne acknowledged, "but I still don't see where Billy would fit into anything like that. I'm sorry, but my brother didn't have the money or the brains to be a drug lord. He was basically a petty thief, and not very good at that. It was a wonder that he didn't spend more time in jail."

"We don't know that this deal has anything to do with drugs," Bolan replied, "but let's hang on to the analogy. A drug lord, by himself, is powerless. It doesn't matter how much cash he's sitting on unless he's got accountants, lawyers and lieutenants, soldiers, drivers and gofers. It's the same thing with intelligence. The chief can't do a thing without his agents, his technicians, operators on the telephones, a secretary he can trust to shred those memos, janitors to take the garbage out at night."

"So, you think Billy stumbled into something that was happening between the CIA and Russian Mafia?" The tone of Suzanne's voice told Bolan she was still incredulous.

"We don't know that for sure," he said. "But I'm convinced Ted Williams was connected to the Company. You say he was your brother's friend. If they spent any length of time together, there's at least a fifty-fifty chance he may have put your brother on the payroll, even in some menial capacity. And if he didn't, who's to say the Russians or some other faction wouldn't think he did?"

"That's more like Billy," Suzanne said. "Fall into something that he didn't understand, or get hung up because somebody thinks he's part of it. No damn luck at all."

"It happens," Johnny said. "The Company has tons of cash to throw around, and with the Russian Mafia, they're into everything from gambling and dope to...other things."

"Hookers?" Suzanne asked, forcing a smile at Johnny's obvious discomfort. "No need to blush. I know about the birds and bees."

"The point is, they can reach most people, one way or another, sometimes without being recognized."

His brother's words set off a faint alarm bell in the back of Bolan's mind. He had been vaguely troubled, ever since he spoke to Hal Brognola on the telephone. The big Fed hadn't seemed himself. He was more reticent than usual, for one thing, verging on evasive. If he hadn't known the gruff Fed better, Bolan might have thought that Brognola was trying to discourage him, perhaps to put him off the scent.

But, why?

"Mike?" Johnny's voice cut through his reverie, recalling Bolan to the here and now.

"Sorry," he said. "I missed that. Say again?"

"Just wondering if you had any special contacts lined up in Los Angeles," his brother said.

"I'm waiting to hear back on that," he said. From Brognola. "Meanwhile, we've got some driving time ahead of us, and it's a good idea to look around the place, check out the action, get a feel for things."

"Let's say the guys who tried to kill us back at the motel were Russian Mafia," Suzanne remarked. "And just to make it worse, let's say they really are connected with the CIA, somehow. You don't think guys like that will answer questions, do you?"

"That depends a lot on how you ask them," Bolan said.

"Okay, you've lost me, now."

It was just as well, he thought, but knew that if he simply left her hanging, none of them would know a moment's peace. "You want to find out where your brother is, what happened to him. Am I right?"

"Of course."

"Some men you never saw before have tried to kill you once already, just for asking questions."

"So? Your point is...?"

"My point," Bolan said, "is that if we pursue this game, it won't be anything but rough, from here until the end. I don't know what the end will be, but I can guarantee you that more people will get hurt."

"I told you once," Suzanne replied, "it's not a game to me. I understand my brother may be dead, all right? It's all I think about. But thinking isn't knowing, and I need to know. If Billy's dead, if someone killed him, then they need to pay for that."

"It's good to think about your brother," Bolan said, "but if he's really all you think about, you place yourself—and us—at risk. From this point on, you need to think about survival, too. Make that your first priority. You can't know anything or settle anything, if you're already dead."

"You talk about a game," she said, "but now it sounds more like a war."

"You're catching on," the Executioner replied.

"YOUR FRIEND'S intense," Suzanne remarked, as Johnny walked her to the separate motel room where she would spend the night. It was adjacent to the room he shared with his brother, no more than half a dozen paces in between their doors, but he had felt like stretching, sharing Suzanne's company.

And his brother had seemed to need some time alone.

"Intense would sum it up as well as anything," he said.

She took a key out of her pocket, recognizable by its red plastic tag. "Come in, for just a minute?"

"Well…"

"To put my mind at ease," she said. "Check out the room, you know? And maybe talk."

"For just a minute."

"Great!" She led the way inside, flicked on the lights, not seeming worried that some adversary might be lurking in the room.

Johnny went through with it, a quick look in the bathroom, then the empty closet. "Looks okay," he told her.

"That 'HQ' thing, from the military."

"Yeah?"

"Is that where you met Mike? I mean, the two of you together in the Army?"

Johnny smiled and shook his head. "I've known him since I was a kid."

"Big brother, like?"

"You could say that."

"You're close," she said. "I see that. Even if you weren't together in the service."

"We had separate wars," he said.

"And now," she answered, leaning back against the wall, "both of you are fighting mine."

"It may not be that bad."

"You think my brother's dead, right?"

"It's a possibility you need to face," he said.

"That isn't what I asked you, dammit!"

Johnny paused, then leveled with her, meeting Suzanne's eyes. "I think it's probable."

"Okay." Her lower lip was trembling, and he wondered why that made her even more attractive. "I've been sort of preparing myself, just like you said. The trouble is, I still can't give up on him, Johnny."

"No."

"You wouldn't, right? If it was your brother?"

"No, I wouldn't."

"But here's the thing. If both of us agree that he's most likely dead, I have to ask myself, why am I risking someone else, two total strangers, just to prove a point."

"You hired me to find out—"

"That isn't good enough!" she snapped. "I didn't buy your life, for God's sake! I was thinking you could find him, or find out what happened to him, and we'd take it back to the police, with evidence enough to make them listen. Now, there are people dying left and right—I shot a man, already!—and I get this feeling that I haven't seen the worst of it."

"You need to trust that feeling," Johnny said. "It

wouldn't be a bad idea for you to step aside, Suzanne. We'll find someplace for you to stay, where no one will come looking for you, and—''

"And what?" she challenged him. "If I run off and hide somewhere, then what? Will you and Mike step out of it?"

He shook his head, but said nothing.

"No. I didn't think so." When she smiled this time it didn't strike him as a forced expression. "So, it's settled, then. I'm sticking with you, and I don't want any lip about it. Right?"

"That may not be the best idea you ever had."

"You don't think so? Okay, the truth is, I wasn't entirely honest."

"Meaning…?"

"What I said, just now, about not wanting any lip."

The fingers of her left hand grazed his cheek before slipping around to cup the back of Johnny's head. Her right hand found his waist as Suzanne stepped into him, rising on tiptoe, and her lips met his. There was a spark of static from the motel rug, replaced immediately by a surging heat that sped through Johnny's veins and brought his own hands up around her waist, in reflex action. He felt her ripe breasts swell deliciously against his chest, her thighs pressed tight against his own through layers of denim. Suzanne's tongue flicked out to beckon his, and for a moment, Johnny pressed her back against the wall, one of her slim legs hooked around the back of his, as if to hold him prisoner.

They broke the kiss by mutual consent, when both of them were nearly starved for oxygen. Up close, he saw the invitation in her eyes and felt her hand begin to edge around his left hip, slipping farther down.

"Suzanne, I don't think—"

"Good. Don't think. Just feel."

"—that we have time for this, right now."

Her searching hand withdrew—reluctantly, he thought—

and she slumped back against the wall. "Right now?" she challenged him. "Or, not at all?"

"Right now."

"You know, it isn't nice to string a girl along. You get her hopes up, then you let her down, it could get ugly."

"That's one thing I can't imagine," Johnny told her.

"What?"

"You, being ugly."

"Hey, you haven't seen me first thing in the morning," she replied.

"I'm looking forward to it, though."

"But right now, you've got business with your friend. War games, and all."

"You hit it on the head."

Her hand came back, a teasing stroke. "My specialty," she told him, beaming.

"I'll remember that."

"See that you do." Suzanne was misty-eyed, but smiling. "Better run along now, soldier. Get yourself a good night's sleep."

"I won't be taking any bets on that."

Returning to the next-door room he shared with his brother, Johnny took time to wipe the lipstick from his mouth and readjust his jeans, which had somehow shrunk a size within the past ten minutes. With his key, he let himself into the room and found his brother seated at the small vanity table, staring at an Auto Club map of L.A.

"You missed a spot," Bolan told him.

"What?"

His brother raised an index finger to the corner of his mouth and smiled. "Pink Passion, is it?"

"Very funny."

Bolan made no attempt to hold the smile. "That could be dangerous, you know. A personal involvement slows you down and clouds your thinking."

"Really? Is that how it was with Val?"

The brothers seldom spoke of Valentina Querente, the woman Bolan had learned to love during his first campaign against the Mafia, in his hometown of Pittsfield, Massachusetts. Later on, the Mob had kidnapped Val and Johnny, using them as bait to draw the Executioner, but it had backfired in a Boston blitz that still rated special "anniversary" stories in the *Globe*. Later still, Val had married an FBI agent, Jack Gray, adopting orphaned Johnny Bolan in the process.

"I suppose it varies, case to case," Bolan said, then turned back to his map.

"Look, this is—" What? Johnny asked himself.

"Nothing?"

"I didn't say that."

"It's not my business," Bolan said, interrupting him. "I just don't want to see you lose your focus when you need it most. I haven't got all kinds of relatives to spare, you know?"

"I know. It's cool."

"All right, then."

"Scoping targets?" Johnny asked him, keen to change the subject.

"Nothing special, at the moment. I still need to talk to Hal again."

The way Bolan said it, concentrating so intently on the map, gave Johnny pause. "Is something wrong?" he asked. "Hal come up short this time?"

"Still waiting," Bolan replied. He raised his eyes—but not to Johnny, rather staring at the mirror mounted on the vanity, as if his own reflection held some secret he couldn't divine.

"Because, if something's wrong…"

"We need to watch our step on this," Bolan said. "Between the Russians and the Company, we could be in a world of shit."

"I brought my waders," Johnny said, smiling.

"That's good. About Suzanne…"

"I talked to her. She won't bail. Feels like she owes her brother something, if you can imagine that."

"The odds of finding him alive are next to nothing," Bolan reminded him.

"She understands that, too. No blinders. She just wants to know, and see the end of it."

"Two different things," Bolan said. "No guarantee she'll be around for both."

"I'll talk to her again, okay? No promises."

"There never are."

"How sure are we about the Company involvement?" Johnny asked.

"You heard the same thing I did," Bolan replied. "The guy expected Russians or a visitor from Langley."

"Right, but what did Hal say, when you told him?"

It seemed to Johnny that his brother's face grew darker for an instant, some kind of a shadow there and gone, almost before it had a chance to register.

Almost.

"He couldn't think of anything, right off the top," Bolan said. "We did the basics, how the Company has always fudged its charter, running covert operations in the States, and how they've tried to work with certain Russian elements, the past ten years."

"There's work, and then there's work," Johnny remarked.

"Agreed."

"I'm trying to imagine what the Russian Mafia could possibly contribute to the CIA in Southern California, and I come up blank. I mean, unless the Company's still running shit at home to finance black ops somewhere else."

"It doesn't feel like dope," Bolan said. "But I've been wrong before."

"What does it feel like?" Johnny asked. "Because I have to tell you, I've been hitting brick walls every time I try to think it through."

"We haven't got enough to sketch the outline yet, much

less connect the dots. There's something, but I still can't put my finger on it.''

Johnny sat on the bed. His mind was whirling with the possibilities, and none were pretty. Members of the Russian Mafia had started infiltrating the United States during the Reagan years, either illegally or in the guise of refugees from Communist oppression. After the 1991 Soviet collapse, the trickle had become a flood. Travel restrictions were relaxed, if not abolished absolutely, and the mobsters who had built illicit fortunes in Moscow, St. Petersburg and Chechnya fanned out across the globe, establishing alliances with thugs in Western Europe, the Americas, North Africa, and Asia. Everywhere they planted flags, the Russians turned a profit, moving drugs and weapons, human sex toys and illegal immigrants. Some operators specialized in moving nukes, stolen from stockpiles in the former Soviet republics, auctioned to the highest bidder in a world where *terror* was a common synonym for *strength*.

"It may be something on the side," Johnny suggested. "Even if Ted Williams was connected to the Company, it doesn't mean that everything he did came out of Langley. Maybe he was running something on the side. Moonlighting, perhaps?"

"It's possible," Bolan said. "In that scenario, he might even employ connections that he made while on the job."

"Russian connections?"

"How it looks right now, I'm not dismissing anything. The only way that I can think of to find out is to get in among the Russians, shake them up and see what happens."

"Or Hal might still come up with something?" Johnny suggested.

The same uneasy shadow fell across Bolan's face, or maybe it was just a trick of light combined with Johnny's own imagination.

"I should call him back," Bolan said. "He's had enough time, if there's anything to find."

The Executioner was on his feet and moving past his brother, toward the door, when Johnny asked, "What's up?"

"Pay phone, next to the Coke machine outside," he said. "I don't want this call going through the motel switchboard."

"Right."

Alone inside the cheaply furnished room, Johnny was anxious to accept the explanation, hoping there was nothing wrong between his brother and the man from Justice. Hal Brognola had supported Bolan almost from the beginning of his one-man war against the Mafia, in the grim days after their parents and sister were buried in Pittsfield. At first, the collaboration between Fed and fugitive was strictly covert, a violation of "The Book" that could have sent Brognola to prison for the rest of his life, as an accessory to multiple murder and sundry other crimes. Later on, after Mack Bolan "died" and was reborn as Colonel John Phoenix, a fully sanctioned—although strictly unacknowledged—agent of the U.S. government, Brognola had been placed in overall charge of the operation, coordinating field operations with the project's nerve center at Stony Man Farm, in Virginia.

Brognola had always been a part of it, always a friend.

If that was jeopardized, if that had changed, what could it mean?

Johnny dismissed the morbid thought, convinced that he was jumping to conclusions. Switching on the television, he began to surf the channels, pausing when he came upon an adult movie, naked bodies writhing on a rumpled bed. Nothing he hadn't seen before, of course.

Suzanne was right next door.

Stop that!

Their kiss had been electric, in a sense that had no link to scuffing shoes on nylon carpeting. Suzanne had wanted him, from all appearances, and it had taken Johnny by surprise. There had been nothing to suggest desire in any of their dealings, heretofore. Some casual remarks, perhaps, that might have passed for lightweight flirting under other circumstances, and while Johnny was attracted to Suzanne from their first meeting back in San Diego, he had done his utmost to remain professional. She was a paying client with a problem, and it was his job to find her missing brother if he could.

Before the fight in Aztec, when he clapped a hand across her mouth to keep Suzanne from crying out, alerting their potential killers, Johnny Gray had never touched the lady, other than to shake her hand. He hadn't propositioned her, nor had he seriously entertained the thought.

Until this night.

This was a problem, Johnny thought.

He had dismissed putting Suzanne into federal protective custody as soon as he discovered that the CIA might be involved in whatever had happened to her brother. Even as a long shot, it was still too dangerous to risk. If Billy King had vanished on an errand for the Company—or while attempting to outwit its agents—it would be impossible to guard Suzanne from spooks in any federal safehouse. A determined hitter would get through somehow, if he was so inclined.

The next best thing would be to park Suzanne in a hotel somewhere, well off the beaten track, and leave her there until the game had played out to its finish, one way or another. With a false ID, perhaps a marginal disguise from makeup and hair color, she should be all right. The Russians and whoever else was backing them would be distracted, anyway, once the brothers hit Los Angeles.

It was the smart thing, but Johnny knew Suzanne would never go for it, and there was no way to confine her without bringing in the Feds they needed to avoid.

Catch-22.

Besides, if he was honest with himself, it pleased Johnny that he would see Suzanne, spend time with her. In retrospect, he knew that feeling had been with him from the moment they left San Diego, bound for Tucson. He was almost hoping they would miss Ted Williams, have to chase him for a while around the great American Southwest. Not for the money extra days would bring, but for the simple pleasure of Suzanne King's company.

Except, it wasn't simple anymore.

Johnny wasn't naive enough to tag his feelings with the L-word. He believed that love took time to grow, required encouragement and work by parties on both sides of the occasion. Locking eyes across a crowded room and falling into bed an hour later was another thing, entirely. He was well acquainted with infatuation from his youth, and recognized the warning signs on sight.

But this felt different.

It was one thing to identify a feeling, analyze it and dissect it, put it underneath a microscope. To act upon that feeling was a very different thing, particularly when the act meant casting caution to the wind and jeopardizing lives.

Johnny had a responsibility to Suzanne King, his paying client, to behave as a professional. Now that his brother was involved, responding to a plea for help, Johnny had a responsibility to him, as well. And, finally, there was the matter of survival, a responsibility he owed himself.

"Cold shower time," he told the rutting couple on the screen, and switched off the television.

There might be something with Suzanne, but it would have to wait until their lives weren't at risk—and if it couldn't wait, it wasn't real. Right now, he had to think about the Russians, Langley and the kind of thought process that made a man take cyanide before he even heard a single question from the mouths of his interrogators. Was that fear, defiance, or a simple act of resignation? What had Williams known, or guessed, that ranked above his own survival instinct in importance?

Johnny knew that he would have to answer that before the case was solved—unless somebody killed him first. One thing the younger Bolan knew, beyond a shadow of a doubt:

if he went down, it wouldn't be by his own hand, and he would take some of the other bastards with him.

Stripping down, he left his Glock within arm's reach, atop the toilet tank, and turned the shower on full-blast, ice cold. An image of Suzanne, stark naked in the shower stall, flashed through his mind, and Johnny mouthed a curse before he stepped into the stinging spray.

There is no Russian enclave in Los Angeles, per se. It isn't like Koreatown, South Central, Chinatown, or Little Tokyo, where members of a given ethnic group are concentrated in a certain neighborhood by economics, racism, or natural selection. Russians are among the relatively new arrivals in L.A. They are Caucasian, often affluent, and if some of them speak accented English, they are still a jump ahead of those who speak no English whatsoever. If anyone has trouble with the accent, money speaks up loud and clear, the universal language of Los Angeles.

Brognola had supplied a list of targets in L.A., including businesses that fronted for the Russian Mafia, some offices, a handful of expensive homes. The list had been provided with reluctance, bracketed in warnings that the Russian Mob was strong and well-armed in Los Angeles, perhaps with certain mercenary friends in local law enforcement. There had been no word on a working CIA connection, no word on Ted Williams, not a whisper on the fate of Billy King.

Mack Bolan had made a conscious choice to put Brognola out of mind, as he began the battle in Los Angeles. It was essential that he focus, concentrate on what was coming, what he wanted to achieve.

This wouldn't be a war for turf or territory. He wasn't naive enough to think that he could drive the Russian Mafia out of L.A. all by himself, or even with his brother's help. His goal was information, something that would put them on the track of King or, failing that, expose any existing links between the Russian Mob and agents of the CIA. To that end, he would have to question some of those he faced, instead of simply killing them.

And he would have to leave a message for the men in charge.

It was a risky game, but every game was risky when the stakes were life and death.

Bolan's first target on that Friday night was a strip club christened Lubyanka, after the infamous Moscow political prison. He guessed the name was someone's notion of a joke, perhaps even a homage to a former home away from home. Most of the Russian mobsters in America had been locked up at one time or another, prior to going international. New names and bogus paperwork gave them free access to the world at large, while Moscow stalled on giving rosters of convicted felons to the FBI and Interpol.

Club Lubyanka was located on Wilshire Boulevard, just east of the artsy Miracle Mile. The galleries were closed when Bolan made his drive-by, but the flesh trade was going full-blast. Hookers parading on the street outside the nudie bars left potential johns hungry for something more substantial than a wink and wiggle on the runway. Bolan guessed the street girls would be working for the men who ran the clubs, fat cats who covered all their bets, but he wasn't concerned about that at the moment. This wasn't a vice raid. It was time to rattle cages, knock on doors and see if there was anybody home.

"You know the drill," he said, as Johnny swung the Audi left, into an alleyway that ran behind the Wilshire clubs.

"I still think—"

"We've already covered this," he said, cutting off his brother's protest. "Somebody has to watch the car. You're it."

"And what about next time?"

"We'll see."

He left the Audi, stepping out into the warmth and air pollution of a Southern California evening, waiting while his brother cleared the alley. Bolan wore a charcoal-gray Armani suit, the jacket cut a half-size large to cover any hardware that a special outing might require. This night, since he didn't anticipate confronting many troops, the Executioner was traveling light. He wore the Beretta 93-R in its standard shoulder rig, two extra magazines in pouches underneath his right armpit and carried two standard smoke grenades clipped to his belt, one canister on either side. If anyone was eyeing Bolan from behind, they might have been mistaken for love handles, but he had no audience as he approached the Lubyanka's back door.

He half expected the back door to be locked. It was a pleasant surprise, therefore, when the knob turned easily in his hand, admitting Bolan to the backstage quarters that were standard for a strip club. On his left, what looked to be a storeroom for the liquor and assorted packaged snacks; immediately on his right, a Spartan cell reserved for janitorial equipment and supplies. Next up, two doors marked Private. Standing with his ear pressed to each door in turn, he picked up female laughter on the right and pegged it as the dancers' dressing room. The muffled *click-clack* of a computer on Bolan's left told him that he had found the office, someone working while the customers enjoyed themselves out front. The last two doors before he reached the main room of the club were rest rooms, ladies' on his right, men's on the left.

Bolan emerged into the Lubyanka's showroom, took a look around and saw that someone had invested major rubles in the club. The lighting was professional, the sound system impressive in its volume and the naked girls on stage high-class, as far as strippers went. He watched them for a moment, spotting none of the usual bruises, cellulite, or spaced-out looks that were a standard feature in the low-rent nudie bars. Whoever did the hiring at the Lubyanka liked his women young, athletic and enthusiastic.

Bolan checked the room for bouncers, spotted two of them in muscle shirts near the main entrance, neither of them armed with any weapons he could see, aside from bulging arms and fists. The bartender was thirty-something, slim, with shoulder-length black hair. If he was armed, it had to be some kind of weapon stashed under the bar.

Bolan reached underneath his jacket and removed both smoke grenades, hooking a thumb through one pin, then the other, holding down the safety spoons. No one had spotted him as yet, all eyes on the young women who were riding metal poles—and one another—on the stage. He pitched one canister behind the bar, off to his right, and lobbed the other toward the middle of the room, waiting for thick white smoke to burst from both before he shouted, "Fire! Clear out! The club's on fire!"

Retreating toward the office as all hell broke loose, he drew his pistol, stepped into the office, closed the door behind him on the racket from outside. The guy behind the desk regarded him with small eyes planted in the middle of a moon-shaped face, deep acne craters on both cheeks completing the illusion. He was half-turned toward a Macintosh computer that occupied the left side of his desk, his jacket off, no hardware visible.

"What's this?" he asked, the accent telling Bolan he had struck paydirt.

"Ted Williams sent me," Bolan said.

The Russian blinked at him, uncomprehending. "Who? Ted Wilson?"

Bolan didn't know the guy from Adam—or from Ivan— but if he was faking it, he had rehearsed the dumb act to perfection. "Never mind. Who runs this show?"

"I am the manager," the Russian said.

"That wasn't what I asked you." Bolan thumbed back the Beretta's hammer.

"I have partners, but—"

"One name is what I'm looking for."

Just then, the door burst open and a suit he had to have missed barged in, blurting a warning in Russian. Halfway through his spiel, the new arrival noticed Bolan and the pistol in his hand, digging for something underneath his jacket, on the left-hand side.

The 93-R spit a sound-suppressed Parabellum round into the young man's face and slammed him back against a filing cabinet, pinning him until his knees turned into rubber and he slithered to the floor.

"About that name," Bolan said, turning back to face the man behind the desk.

"Tolya Valerik."

"When you see him," Bolan said, "tell him that this was from Ted Williams." Thinking fast, he added, "And from Billy King."

"Da."

"You'd better split now," Bolan said, when he was satisfied. "Word has it that the joint's on fire."

Johnny was waiting when he hit the alley, one door east, lights off, a micro-Uzi resting on the console in between their seats.

"You get a name?" Johnny asked after they were well away.

"Tolya Valerik," Bolan said.

"Was that one of the names Hal gave you?"

Headlights splashed across his face gave Bolan's frown the aspect of a grimace etched in granite.

"No," he said.

SUZANNE WAS RESTLESS, pacing in her Hollywood motel room, two blocks south of Sunset Boulevard. Two hours in the room, and she had given up on television, showered, washed and dried her hair—done everything she could think of to distract herself, and she couldn't sit still.

It was the waiting, she decided, the not knowing that propelled her into restless pacing, like an animal unused to being caged. The danger to herself was merely background noise, a kind of static in her mind. She understood that someone she had never met wanted to kill her, had already tried it once, but Johnny and his friend were adamant in their assurances that she was safe at the motel, for now.

She had signed in as Mike Belasko's wife, while Johnny waited in the car, outside. The logic: if her stalkers knew Suzanne's name and had traced her to the Desert Rose Motel in Arizona, they would probably know Johnny Gray's name, too. Belasko was a "wild card," as he phrased it, coming out of nowhere, unknown to the enemy. Unless they canvassed every motel in L.A. with photographs, the odds of any hostile snoopers finding her were virtually nil.

And if they did come, she was armed. Johnny had left the pistol she had used in Arizona, cleaned and freshly loaded since the last time she had fired it, plus a heavy sawed-off shotgun.

"Here's the safety," he had told her. "All you have to do is press this button, here, until it shows red on the left. It's cocked and loaded now. You heard how loud it is at the motel. Make sure you hold it tight against your side, like this—" his strong hands guided hers "—and point it toward your target. You don't really have to aim. Just pull the trigger. You've got six shots. The slide locks open when they're gone, and then you'll need the Glock, if anyone's still standing."

Right. He was mistaking her for Lara Croft...or, was he? She had shot one man who tried to kill her, and had no doubt she could do the same again, if cornered. Truthfully, the fear she felt wasn't evoked by any thought of enemies discovering her hiding place. She was afraid for Johnny Gray, and for his friend.

And for her brother. She couldn't forget Billy.

Except, she hardly thought of Billy anymore, at least in terms of finding him alive. In Suzanne's heart, she knew he would have called her, left some message, if he had been able to. The possibility that he was being held somewhere against his will evoked such terrifying images of pain and degradation that she almost found the notion of his death more comforting. As far as Billy turning up alive, she knew it would require a miracle, and she had given up on such nonsense when she was still a child.

Pacing, her thoughts came back inexorably to Johnny Gray. When they had kissed—when she kissed him, she silently corrected—Suzanne's surprise had almost been the equal of his own. She hadn't expected to be so aroused, so overwhelmed, by the result. When he had begged off going any further at the moment and retreated to his room, her disappointment had been strangely mingled with relief, a sense that once they were in bed together, she would have no choice but to surrender the control she valued so much in her life.

Next time, perhaps.

If he survived the night.

She hadn't pressed Johnny or Belasko for the details of their plan, but they had gone out wearing guns, with extra weapons in a duffel bag Belasko carried. Suzanne didn't know what all the hardware was, but she had recognized something that looked like a machine gun, and the chunky metal eggs that had to be hand grenades.

So, they were out there making war in the City of Angels, presumably against the Russian Mafia, and Johnny's life would be at risk until he walked back through the door to Suzanne's motel room. When she could see him for herself, and only then, would she be able to relax.

Thinking about the Russians brought her mind back to the question of her brother's theoretical involvement with the CIA. Despite the one-time casual remark from Billy, it still seemed preposterous, but Suzanne supposed she couldn't absolutely rule it out. Williams was the link, if Belasko was correct, and Suzanne knew no more about the dead man now than she had known three months ago when Billy first described him as "a guy I met in Vegas." Was it possible that Williams had seduced her brother somehow, used him in some convoluted plot that Billy never fully understood?

No more implausible, she thought, than Russian gunmen trying to assassinate her at the Desert Rose Motel.

Suzanne forced herself to sit on the bed, her hands clasped with fingers interlaced. The full impact of what was happening had struck her like a slap across the face and left her stunned.

She had supposed, when Billy disappeared, that he had gotten into trouble with the law and felt a need to get away from San Diego for a while. When time went by without a call, she had begun to think that something bad had happened to him, one of his "arrangements" with assorted low-life operators had to have blown up in his face. When she hired Johnny Gray, Suzanne was torn between dual fears that he would find her brother dead, or locked up somewhere, maybe in another state, awaiting trial on some new felony indictment. Either way, she knew, he would be lost to her.

But this was something else. By hiring Johnny and pursuing it alone, she had disturbed a hornet's nest—or, worse, a hive of killer bees. Instead of simply losing Billy, now, she had to think about the possibility that she would also lose her own life in the bargain.

"Dammit, Billy! Damn you straight to hell!"

It took perhaps two seconds for the guilt to hit her before she doubled over, sobbing in her bitter grief and shame.

LOS ANGELES POLICE and prosecutors liked to say that their city was free of organized crime. It had never been true, but the myth still lived on, grim-faced detectives from the LAPD "hat squad" driving gangsters from the city, beating them in cheap motels, or pitching them off cliffs like the notorious "Mulholland Falls." In fact, crime in L.A. was organized, to some extent, before the city had its own police force, starting in the 1880s, and there had been no cessation since that time, in terms of vice, narcotics and assorted other rackets. Police were often paid to look the other way, exactly as they were in New York City, in Chicago, in St. Louis, and ten thousand other towns across the continent.

Casino gambling was a case in point. The Vegas-style casinos were outlawed in California, but exceptions had been made for "poker rooms," and half a dozen operated within fifteen miles of downtown L.A., mostly in suburban Inglewood and Gardena. Each casino was limited to thirty-five poker tables with eight seats each, and bets were limited by law. The house provided dealers and charged each player a predetermined fee, ranging from one dollar to twenty-four dollars an hour, depending on the stakes at a given table. Card rooms also featured restaurants and cocktail lounges where the players could refresh themselves with drinks both overpriced and watered down.

The Tiger's Cage, a poker room bankrolled by members of the Russian Mafia since their arrival in L.A., was situated near Normandie Avenue and Redondo Beach Boulevard, in Gardena. The decorators had gone all out, Bolan saw, to capture an ambience halfway between a Vegas carpet joint and a New Orleans brothel. Somehow, they had just missed both, resulting in a motif that was gaudy, yet without any distinctive sense of style.

Bolan counted heads while he was circling the room. The tables looked to be at full capacity, and there were easily another hundred players and their women killing time in the café and bar, all waiting for a seat to open. Even if they played it straight, the owners would be making money, but the skinny had it that the men behind the Tiger's Cage were less concerned with poker than they were with other services. The place was said to deal extensively in heroin and cocaine for an upscale clientele. The "hostesses" and any number of the unescorted ladies in the bar were also rentable if any of the gamblers chose to scratch a different itch and still had cash on hand.

One of the heads he counted, moving through the room, was Johnny's, playing five-card stud with four hard-bitten men and two drab women at a table near the entrance to the bar. Examining their faces as he passed, Bolan decided none of them would be selected for a TV spot that advertised the joys of gambling in Gardena. Win or lose on any given hand, his brother's fellow cardplayers wore grim expressions, as if they despised their lives and had been beaten down one time too often for their mental health.

Johnny was gambling money from the Tucson stash, keeping an eye out on the room at large. They had already noted the surveillance cameras, ceiling-mounted at each corner of the room, with others in the bar and restaurant, remote-controlled from somewhere in the back, behind the scenes. Bolan was headed for the men's room when he detoured, veering through a doorway marked Employees Only, to investigate that portion of the Tiger's Cage the average player never got to see. Johnny would cover him if anything went wrong. If it was quiet when he left, Johnny would say goodnight, cash in his chips and follow Bolan outside.

Security was on his right, a quiet room with stale smoke in the air and half a dozen TV monitors stacked up behind a cluttered desk. The guard on duty was a bullet-headed character, almost as wide as he was tall.

"What the fuck you want?" he challenged Bolan.

"Men's room?"

"Shit. You missed it. Back that way." He fanned a big hand vaguely, in the general direction of the poker room.

"Well, how about if I just piss on you, then?"

"What? You lousy fu—"

The hulk was on his feet, prepared to charge, but Bolan met him more than halfway, shooting out an open palm that flattened the man's nose and snapped his head back, hard enough to rattle anything inside that passed for brains. The guy pitched over backward, banged his head against the desk as he was falling and collapsed facedown, limbs splayed like a skydiver hurtling through space.

The man was probably alive, but Bolan didn't stop to check his pulse. The door had a push-button lock, and he thumbed it down before he exited. The guy could still get out, if he woke up, but no one else would find him now unless they had a key or broke down the door.

He passed the service entrance to a busy kitchen, found the office all the way in back, as if the manager was fond of slipping out unseen by his employees. Then again, it could be more convenient for an off-the-books delivery, or for a pickup by some customer who didn't care to try his or her luck at cards while waiting to get high.

Bolan listened at the door before he turned the knob and entered, the Beretta 93-R leading. There were two men in the room, both seated, one behind the desk, the other to his right. Both wore tailored suits, one navy blue, the other chocolate brown. The guy behind the desk had ten or fifteen years on his companion, though he tried to hide it with a hundred-dollar haircut and a sun-lamp tan. The facelift would presumably come later, if he lived that long.

"Ted Williams sent me," Bolan said, the Russians blinking at him as if he were speaking Japanese. "With a message for Tolya Valerik," he added, watching their mouths tighten into thin, bloodless slits.

"I'm afraid you are mistaken," said the older man, behind the desk. "There is no Tolya here."

"I didn't figure he'd be slumming," Bolan said, and watched the younger man flush rosy pink with rage. He moved around the desk, still covering his hostages, and ripped the phone cord from the wall. "When that gets fixed and you call Tolya, tell him there's a price to pay for Billy King. Maybe he wants to split it with his friends at Langley. That's his choice. You got that?"

"I'll remember," the older man said.

"Good deal. Now, strip."

The Russians looked confused, until he pumped a sound-suppressed round into the trash can standing near the young one's feet and snapped, "Take off your clothes!"

They undressed, the younger of the two muttering in Russian. When they were done, he gathered the clothes and took them with him as he left the office. Pausing at the swing door to the ladies' room, he chucked the suits and underwear inside, then made his way back through the poker room and out. The doorman either didn't notice he had spent no more than fifteen minutes in the club, or didn't care.

After another five minutes, Johnny joined him in the parking lot. "Twelve dollars up," he said. "Is that a winning streak, or what?"

"Know when to fold 'em," Bolan said, and wheeled the Audi out of there.

"IT'S NOT YOUR average crack house," Johnny said.

"It's not supposed to be," Bolan answered, rummaging around inside the duffel bag until he came out with a Spectre submachine gun.

"Got another one of those in there, by any chance?"

"Never leave home without it," Bolan replied.

The Spectre SMG was made in Italy, a compact double-action weapon that fired from a closed bolt, thus allowing shooters to carry a live round in the chamber, safety off, with no fear of an accidental discharge. Its unique four-column, 50-round box magazine gave it an edge over any other modern SMG, in terms of firepower, while the folding stock and forward pistol grip provided excellent stability, even with a full-auto cyclic rate of 850-rounds per minute. Weighing in at close to eight pounds, fully loaded, it was lighter than an Uzi, even with the extra eighteen rounds.

"All set," he told Bolan, when the SMG was locked and loaded.

"Right. Let's go."

The drug house was in The Valley—San Fernando, that

would be, but if you had to ask which valley, you were definitely out of step with L.A.'s "happening" environment. In point of fact, the place was in North Hollywood, off Laurel Canyon Boulevard, some three miles west of Disney, NBC and Warner Brothers. There was gold in those hills, true enough, and some of it was crystal-white, packaged in nickel bags.

The drug house stood on six or seven wooded acres, well back from the street. The brothers left their Audi on an access road nearby and hiked in from the south, black-clad and armed as if they thought an army would be waiting for them when they reached their destination.

Anything was possible, of course, and it was always best to be prepared.

The house was quiet when they got there, Johnny counting two cars parked in front: a jet-black BMW and a cherry-red Mercedes-Benz. They circled toward the rear and found the first sentry back there, reclining in a deck chair by the swimming pool. There was an AK-47 on the ground beside him, but he never had a chance to reach it, or to recognize his danger. Bolan produced the 93-R, aimed and capped the soldier with a silenced Parabellum round from thirty feet, the dead man going limp and slouching lower in his seat.

No one had bothered locking the back door, presumably because the guard was trusted and he might need access to the house from time to time, throughout the night. The brothers entered through a utility room, washer and dryer on one side, a stainless-steel sink on the other. It led to a kitchen, where they found a second shooter standing at the open fridge, selecting items for what looked to be a killer sandwich. Silently, they waited until he had closed the refrigerator door, turned and noticed them. His eyes locked on the sleek Beretta with its custom sound silencer.

"The lab," Bolan said. "Where is it?"

Glancing toward the riot shotgun he had left atop the

kitchen counter, near the sink, the Russian sneered and said, "Fuck you."

"Wrong answer," the Executioner replied, and shot him in the face. The fixings for his sandwich scattered as he fell, Johnny relieved to find the jar of mayonnaise was plastic, bouncing twice instead of shattering on impact with the floor.

It still made noise, though, coupled with the dull thud of the body dropping, and he knew that they were swiftly running out of time. They split up, searching empty rooms, and wound up back together in the kitchen moments later.

"Nothing," Johnny said.

"It has to be here," Bolan replied, "unless—"

"What's this?" Johnny asked.

He had dismissed the door at first glance as a broom closet, but when Johnny opened it, he saw a flight of wooden stairs and lights below. A basement, shadows moving. He had one foot on the top step when a shooter moved into his field of vision at the bottom of the stairs. The guy was tall and muscular, long hair tied back, the shoulder holster dark against his pastel shirt.

He blurted something in Russian, reaching for the weapon slung beneath his arm, and Johnny fired without thinking, the Spectre sending half a dozen rounds to close the gap between them. Where the gunner's shirt had once been pastel pink, it flowered sudden crimson, rippling with the impact of the hollowpoint rounds. His target lurched and staggered backward, stumbling, going down.

Johnny didn't pursue him. Someone in the basement lab had grabbed a weapon and was firing up the stairs, wasting his bullets on a brick wall, since he had no targets. Someone else was shouting, an excited, frightened voice...or, was it two?

"Cocaine, you said?"

"So I was told," Bolan answered him.

"That makes it volatile." As Johnny spoke, he found the thermite canister beneath his jacket, stripped the pin and made his pitch. The fat incendiary bomb bounced once on the concrete, then spun and wobbled out of sight around the corner. Someone yelped a warning, and the unseen shooter pumped a few more rounds into the wall.

"Stand clear!"

The thermite charge was chemical, not high explosive, but its white-hot flash ignited ether and the other chemicals involved in the refinement of cocaine. A shock wave rippled through the kitchen floor beneath their feet. Screams from the basement were muffled by the blast and sudden rush of flames that filled the stairwell, leaping from the open doorway to ignite the wall and ceiling.

"That's a roger," Johnny said, retreating toward the exit that would put them on the patio beside the swimming pool. The dead man hadn't moved, still lounging in his chair and staring off across the water with his sightless eyes. They left him to it, racing down the hill through trees that plucked at Johnny's clothing, urging him to stay a while and watch the pretty fire.

Johnny had no way of calculating how much had gone up with the lab, but with the drugs, dead men and the house, now burning fiercely in the night, he estimated their visit had to have set the Russian Mob back several million dollars. There would be more trouble when the blaze was finally extinguished, and investigators started picking through the rubble, counting guns, identifying any bits of lab equipment that had managed to survive the blaze. Detectives would be checking out the owner of the house, the BMW and the Benz. There might not be enough for an arrest, but they were turning up the heat.

He wondered how Tolya Valerik would react, if he would reach out to his friends, and whether any of his friends were found at Langley.

But most of all, Johnny wondered what Suzanne would say when he informed her they were still no closer to her brother. Getting there, perhaps, but still not in the home stretch.

Johnny hoped all three of them would be alive to see the finish line.

6

Hal Brognola stripped the plastic wrapper from another pair of antacid chewables and popped the cherry-flavored tablets into his mouth. His stomach was in turmoil, the insistent pain reminding him of his last adventure with Cajun cuisine. At least, that time, the spicy food had been appreciated, going down. This morning, after skipping breakfast, he had no legitimate excuse for heartburn.

None, that is, except the bad news from Los Angeles.

It wasn't all bad news, of course. According to the fax the big Fed had received from his connection in the FBI's Los Angeles field office, there had been several strikes the previous night on establishments known to be owned and operated by the Russian Mafia. He scanned the list: a strip club, a gambling parlor and a drug lab in the suburbs. There were seven dead so far, one injured, and the drug lab had been razed by fire, recorded logically enough as an apparent act of arson. There had been no damage to the gambling hall, although at least one shot was fired inside the office, and the manager was "visibly disturbed." The strip club would be shut down for a day or so, while they were airing out the place. Smoke bombs could leave a certain resonance behind.

"Persons unknown" were listed as responsible for the attacks, but Brognola wasn't deceived. He recognized the Bolan touch from personal exposure, could have guessed who was behind the raids even without a warning from the Executioner that he was heading for L.A.

Brognola checked his watch and wondered when the antacid tablets would kick in. Not that it mattered, when he thought about it, since the real source of his agitation—part of it, at least—was twenty-seven hundred miles away, beyond the reach of medicine that he could swallow to alleviate his pain. And there was worse in store, no doubt about it.

His gut ache was only a foretaste of things to come.

Brognola didn't come into the office on a Saturday very often, but he had told his wife he had an operation running that required some personal attention. That had been a lie, of course. If he had sent the Bolan brothers to Los Angeles, perhaps he also could have called them off.

Perhaps.

The big Fed never really knew what Bolan did. Part of their deal left Bolan with the liberty to pick and choose assignments, though in practice, it was rare for him to turn Brognola down on any job where the big Fed believed his intervention would be beneficial. On the flip side of that coin, Bolan was also free—at least, in theory—to go after targets of his own, without approval from Brognola and without involving Stony Man Farm. This also happened rarely, but with greater frequency than Brognola appreciated. Any time that Bolan took the field, he was at risk, and every time could be his last. Now, with his brother in the mix, the risks were multiplied. If anything went wrong…

That wasn't all of it, unfortunately. Any threat to Bolan and his brother constituted only half Hal Brognola's present stress.

The Company, for Christ's sake. Reaching for his coffee cup, Brognola stared at it a moment, thinking better of it as his stomach churned, and left it where it was. Why did it have to be the goddamned CIA?

They had a history, to say the least. The rivalry between the CIA and Justice, more specifically between the Company and the FBI, actually predated the CIA's creation. Bureau Director J. Edgar Hoover, a champion at taking petty grudges to the grave had despised "Wild Bill" Donovan, wartime leader of the Office of Strategic Services, and that hatred had spilled over when the CIA replaced the OSS, two years after V-J Day. If personal animosity wasn't enough, Hoover—and, by extension, the personal lackeys who served him—resented the CIA's monopoly on foreign intelligence gathering, while suspecting that the Company would never be content with simply spying overseas. Hoover had fought the CIA tooth and nail until his death in 1972, and that need-to-know guerrilla war still echoed through the halls at Langley, and around the murky basements of the Justice Building, in D.C.

That was a part of it, but there was more. Brognola's personal collisions with the CIA had nearly trashed the operation that he ran from Stony Man Farm. Granted, that particular conflict—and a couple more similar, if less sanguinary clashes—had resulted from the operation of rogue agents in the Company, but you could never really tell, with Langley, if the buck stopped anywhere. The Company was literally built from the ground up on lies, deception and concealment. Nothing could ever be taken for granted, even when—or, maybe, most particularly when—you had it written down in black and white.

As for the Russian Mafia...

Brognola sighed and shook his head. As with the FBI feud, CIA involvement with the underworld dated from World War II, when it was still the OSS and Donovan's cowboys were calling the shots. Operation Underworld, conceived in 1942, had signed on thugs like "Lucky" Luciano to protect the New York docks and pave the way for an Allied invasion of Sicily. Around the same time, Corsican gangsters were hired to collect wartime intelligence in Vichy, France. Years later, when the Company desired to kill Fidel Castro, they farmed the contract out to mafiosi who despised "The Beard" for closing their casinos in Havana. As for drugs, the trail led back to Sicily and France in 1945, wound on through Turkey and Iran, through Vietnam and Bangkok, through Bolivia and

Mexico. If there were off-the-record dollars to be made and right-wing "freedom fighters" to be served, chances were good the Company would be there with its hand out, cashing in.

Brognola scanned the fax from L.A. one more time, his face as grim as Death. Indeed, it felt like he was *holding* Death. How could a flimsy sheet of copy paper jeopardize so many lives?

The bulk of them were strangers, granted. He would never know their names or see their faces, never fully realize that they had ever lived. They would be digits on some other field report, faxed in from God knew where, and he would promptly shred his copy, leaving the filing chores to Barbara Price, at Stony Man.

There were a handful he would miss, though, and Brognola wondered if—

The ringing of the red telephone distracted him, but didn't wholly break his train of thought. As he reached out for the receiver, he told himself there was nothing that he could have done. It wasn't his fault.

If he could only start believing that, Brognola reckoned he would have it made.

"YOU HAD A BUSY night," Brognola said.

"We hit some parties, just to say hello," Bolan replied. "If you're in L.A., you make the scene."

"You made quite a splash," the big Fed said. "Some people felt it all the way back here."

By L.A. standards, it was cool and reasonably clear this Saturday, at 10:19 a.m. In meteorological terms, that meant the air was breathable, light beige instead of smoky gray. A few miles inland from the great Pacific, the humidity had peaked at forty-two percent, which made it muggy, even as it ruled out any prospects for a cool, refreshing rain. The public telephone was mounted on a wall, outside a pharmacy on Sunset Boulevard, where privacy was minimal but none of several hundred people traipsing by appeared to care much for a stranger's conversation.

"Did you find out anything?" he asked Brognola.

"Yes and no," the big Fed answered. "Which, first?"

"The negative."

"Okay." From where he stood, Bolan thought he could hear some paper rustling, Brognola reviewing notes. "We've got no word at all on Billy King or any variation of the given name, except for confirmation of his California record. That's from NCIC, by the way, with zero from the Company."

"That's a surprise."

"It doesn't prove they had him," Brognola reminded the soldier. "Every now and then, when Langley tells you something, there's an outside chance they're not entirely full of shit, okay?"

"If you say so."

"Anyway, the backdoor scoop on this Ted Williams, courtesy of Stony Man, says he was recruited by the Company out of U.S. Army Intelligence, circa 1978, apparently more of a contract fixer-upper than a full-time agent. He left tracks in South America and Africa, maybe in Asia."

"Where in Asia?" Bolan asked.

"If it was really him, Hong Kong and Bangkok."

"Nothing out of Eastern Europe?"

"Not that we can access," Brognola replied. "Of course, that doesn't mean he wasn't there. Your Teddy got around, and some of it was on his own. The profit motive, if you get my drift."

"A mercenary?"

"Not front line," Brognola said. "More like a spook for hire. I can't tell if he ever worked the other side, but some of it was definitely borderline. When he was in Algiers—"

"That doesn't put him with the Russians," Bolan said.

"You noticed that," Brognola stated. "The more I think about this gig you're on, the more I feel like you should walk away. At least until we have more information on the table."

"I'm already into it," the Executioner replied. "The ball's in play."

"So, call time-out, for Christ's sake! What's the rush?"

"Did we exhaust the negative?" Bolan asked.

"Not entirely," Brognola replied. "Predictably, there *have* been overtures between the Russian Mob and certain front men for the Company. Officially, the talks haven't resulted in significant collaboration. If you buy it, that would mean they're swapping recipes and feeling one another out, but haven't really started doing business yet."

"It's been ten years," Bolan said.

"I'm just telling you—"

"What about Valerik?"

"Right." Brognola shuffled papers for another moment, killing time. "Valerik, Tolya. Born in Moscow, August 13, 1962. He's Chechen, on his mother's side, if that means anything. Looks like he's been arrested thirty-five or forty times since he was twelve years old, but no one's made a solid case against him since he took a two-year fall for manslaughter in 1983. The story is, a drunken fight got out of hand, and Tolya cracked some other comrade's skull. Sounds like the standard cover story for a turf war, possibly a contract job."

"He's definitely made, then," Bolan said.

"Made in the shade, my friend. If anybody had a Top Ten list for Russian gangsters hanging out in North America, this guy would fall somewhere around number three with a bullet."

"Is he wanted back in Russia?" Bolan asked.

"That's a negative. You know the FBI's been working overtime with the militia over there, to get a handle on the Mob, as well as peripheral problems like serial murders."

"I've heard that."

"Well, everyone knows about Valerik, but proving him guilty just hasn't worked out. That tells me he's been paying the cops, or he's learned how to cover his tracks. Maybe both.''

"So, no warrants," Bolan said.

"And no extradition," the big Fed added. "He's been ret- roactively pardoned on the manslaughter beef—*that* must have cost him—so his adult record's clean in Russia, and he's never been connected to illegal operations here, with anything admissible. We have no lawful cause to yank his visa, as it stands."

"It's just as well," Bolan replied. "I wouldn't want him going anywhere."

"Uh, well...about that...."

"What?" The sudden tightening in Bolan's neck and shoulders was a sure sign of incipient anxiety.

"Your boy blew out of L.A. International first thing this morning. He's already gone."

"Gone where?" Bolan demanded.

"New York City."

Dammit! Bolan understood that New York was the Rus- sian Mob's nerve center in America. The syndicate—or syn- dicates, more properly—had outposts nationwide, but each of the competing Families was headquartered in the financial capital of the United States. It came as no surprise, therefore, that Bolan's quarry would seek cover in New York if he was rattled in L.A., and while the Executioner wasn't averse to traveling, he sensed that leaving the Southwest would sever any slim remaining link to Billy King.

He'd do what he had to do.

"New York," he said. "It's not so far away."

"If anyone asked me," Brognola said, "I'd have to say it's not the best idea you ever had. Between the Russians, their domestic buddies and the local cops, we're talking max- imum risk."

"I've done the Apple," Bolan said. "I know the drill."

He had, indeed, "done" New York City—more than once, in fact, when he was squared off in a one-man war against the Mafia's Five Families, hunted by contract killer, cop and federal agent in the tristate area. He had survived each time, on guts and gall, together with a kind of combat savvy that was only earned through painful personal experience.

"I'm guessing you'd have mentioned any ties between Williams and Valerik."

"There's nothing," Brognola replied. "Or, if it's there, I don't have access."

"Fair enough."

"I have to tell you," Brognola said, "I think tangling any further with the Russians at the present time would be a bad idea. From what I understand there are some diplomatic moves in progress, treaty stuff, that could be very beneficial to both sides."

"And it involves the Russian Mob?"

"I didn't say that. There are times, though, when it's better if we don't make waves. Like wasting Russian nationals in L.A. and New York, for instance, while the White House and a truckload of ambassadors are talking foreign aid."

"I doubt if I'll be meeting any diplomats," Bolan replied.

"Okay. Just bear in mind, I doubt I can be much help to you in New York City or in Washington, with the negotiations under way."

"It's duly noted," Bolan said, in answer to the not-so-subtle kiss-off. "Look, I'd better go. We've already been on the line too long."

"Stay frosty, guy," Brognola said, his tone dispirited.

"The only way to fly."

Ten minutes saw him back at the motel, knocking on Suzanne's door. When Johnny answered, he was carrying a Glock. Suzanne was sitting in a corner, well back from the windows, with a twin to Johnny's pistol in her lap. They both looked anxious, furtive, but when Bolan checked his brother's mouth for telltale lipstick traces, he was clean.

"How'd it go?" Johnny asked.

"We got quick results," Bolan replied, "but not what I was looking for."

"How's that?"

"Valerik left L.A. this morning on the first flight he could manage to New York."

"New York?" Suzanne pronounced the name as if it were entirely new to her, some foreign place, exotic and mysterious. "What's in New York?"

"The hard core of the Russian Mafia," Johnny said. "Sanctuary. He can go to ground and hide there."

"He can try," Bolan corrected.

"What happens now?" Suzanne inquired.

"We follow him," the brothers said in unison.

"Hold on a sec," she challenged them. "My brother's definitely not in New York City, okay? Alive or dead, I guarantee you that."

Johnny read Bolan's mind and fielded the complaint. "We lost our only firm connection to your brother when Williams died," he said. "Our next best hope of finding out what happened to him would be questioning Valerik. Anyway," he added, softening his tone, "you have to know it's gone beyond your brother now."

"What's that supposed to mean?"

"The Russians have already tried to kill you once," Bolan pointed out, picking up from Johnny, "so we have to take for granted that they see you as some kind of threat. Which means they'll try again, and won't give up until you're dead...unless we find a way to stop them first."

"And stopping them," Johnny added, "means we have to find out what they're up to, what it is they think you know, or might find out."

"It's like we're giving up on Billy if we go."

"Suzanne—"

"All right!" she said. "I know the chances that we'll find him still alive are next to zero. I've accepted that. But even if he's...even if he's not alive, I still believe he's here, somewhere in Southern California, maybe Arizona or Nevada. I could lose my real shot at finding him if I run off to New York City now.''

"About that," Johnny said. "It might be better if you didn't come."

"What?" The color rising in her cheeks was echoed by taut anger in her voice.

"Come to New York," Johnny said.

"It's a whole new theater of operations," Bolan added, "and the risks are multiplied tenfold, at least. It won't be just the Russian Mob we're up against. We're closer to the CIA back east, and if their people are mixed up in this somehow, they could decide to lend a hand. Whichever way that goes, we'll definitely be in conflict with the NYPD and the FBI."

"Why's that?" Some of the color had already drained from Suzanne's cheeks. "Can't we just tell them that we're looking for my brother? You don't have to go in shooting, right? I mean, these Russian characters are criminals, for God's sake! The police and FBI are paid to deal with guys like this."

"I wouldn't count on any help from that direction," Bolan said.

It was his brother's turn to frown. "You talked to—" Johnny caught himself before he spoke Brognola's name. "I mean, you called that friend of ours. What did he say?"

"He said what I've already told you," Bolan answered. "There's no record of a link between Williams and the Russians, nothing on the books connecting Williams or the Mob to Suzanne's brother."

"Nothing from the Company?"

He saw no harm in sharing what Brognola had disclosed, as meager as it was. "Ted Williams was a contract agent, off and on. He also worked some angles on his own, four continents and counting. Hey, for all we know, he could have drawn a paycheck from Saddam Hussein."

"I'm more concerned about the Russians," Johnny said.

"Me, too. There's just no way to pin it down, so far."

"And if there was," Suzanne asked, "what would it be?"

"Tolya Valerik," Bolan said.

"In New York City."

"Right."

"You're going, then?" she asked them both.

"I don't see any way around it," Bolan said. His brother simply nodded.

"All right, then. I'm coming, too."

"Suzanne, I told you—"

"I know what you told me," she said, cutting Johnny off. Suzanne was on her feet, pacing, dangling the Glock in one hand, at her side. "I won't just run and hide somewhere, waiting for one of you to call and fill me in on what's been happening. If it's as bad in New York as you say, you may not get a chance to call. You could be…someone might…I'd never even know, goddammit!"

Bolan caught his brother staring at him, met his gaze and shook his head. "I'd vote against it."

"No one asked you!" Suzanne said. "Look, this all started when my brother disappeared and the police saw fit to blow me off. I started it by hiring Johnny. He called you for help, and that's okay by me, unless you try to cut me out. I won't sit still for that, you hear me? Billy's my responsibility, alive or dead, and you can both go straight to hell if you think I'd abandon him."

"It isn't that, Suzanne."

"Okay, I'll tell you what it is," she said. "I can't force either one of you to travel with me or report on what you find out in New York, but you can't stop me flying back there on my own. I guess I wouldn't stand much chance, from what you've said. You make Manhattan sound like Kosovo, some kind of war zone, but I'll have to take my chances if you cut me loose. That's it. With or without you, if the answer's in New York, that's where I'll be."

Bolan imagined Suzanne dead, or worse. She wouldn't be

the first young woman who had come to grief from meddling in his business, dancing too close to the flame. But she was right, of course; it wasn't really his business, so much as it was hers.

Granted, when Suzanne started looking for her missing brother, when she hired Johnny to help her, she had had no thought in mind of tangling with the Russian Mafia, much less the CIA. Things changed, however, as her very life itself had changed, the past few days. She was a hunted target now. Johnny had feelings for her, and the heat was mutual from all appearances. If they simply abandoned her in Southern California, even if she didn't trail them to New York, Bolan suspected that her days were numbered.

And what would happen if she joined them in New York? How would they manage to protect her there when they were on Tolya Valerik's trail, faced off against the Russian Mafia and anybody else who chose to join the action on Valerik's side?

"It's your choice," Bolan told her, "but we won't have time to baby-sit." His last words were directed more to Johnny than Suzanne, reminding him of the inherent danger.

"I don't need a baby-sitter," Suzanne answered. "I can take care of myself."

"I hope so," Bolan said. "Because we've just been paddling in the kiddie pool. New York's the deep end, sink or swim."

"I'm in," she stated. "When do we leave?"

"Start packing," Bolan said. "Johnny and I have some things to do before we fly. We won't be long."

"I'd hate to think that you were ditching me," she said suspiciously.

He nodded toward their bags lined up beside the chest of drawers. "You've got our clothes and hardware," he reminded her. "If we're not back inside an hour, you can start to execute my shirts and slacks."

"Don't think I won't," she said, but Bolan picked up on a measure of relief in Suzanne's voice.

As they were waiting for the elevator, Johnny asked, "Where are we going?"

"Nowhere special," Bolan said. "A little walk around the neighborhood. We need to talk."

Johnny was silent until they hit the street, then cut directly to the chase. "That thing you said about the FBI. What's up with that?" he asked. "I thought Hal had your back?"

"I thought so, too," Bolan replied.

"Can't say I like the sound of that."

"It may be nothing," Bolan said, trying to radiate a confidence he didn't feel. "Bad timing."

"Bad timing? Can you vague that up a little for me?"

"Hal thinks it would be inadvisable for us to track Valerik in New York right now. Something about diplomacy and treaty talks, no details. Bottom line—his hands are tied. If we go to New York, we're on our own."

Johnny was quiet for another half-block, then he said, "You know, I'm thinking maybe it was a mistake for me to call you in on this."

"Oh, yeah?"

His brother nodded. "Yeah. I mean, your gig with Hal and Stony Man, it's more—"

"Forget about it, Johnny. I'm already here."

"But I can do this on my own."

"I wouldn't be surprised," he said. "Thing is, you won't be doing it alone."

"Look, Mack—"

"Don't waste your breath. You couldn't bluff Suzanne, you damn sure can't bluff me."

"*I* couldn't bluff Suzanne?" Johnny was grinning now, despite his mood. "Who was it trotted out NYPD, the FBI and CIA? I didn't see her backing down."

"You like her, don't you?" Bolan asked.

"That's irrelevant."

"Just thought I'd check. It's a relief, if you want to know the truth. The other night, I thought you might have started wearing lipstick. Not that it's a bad thing, but the shade was terrible. I really think you're more an earth tone, if you want to know the truth."

"Har-har. My brother, the comedian."

"It changes things, you know."

Johnny made an exasperated face. "Okay, if I start wearing teddies, I'll make sure they're done in camouflage. That put your mind at ease?"

"I'm serious," Bolan said. "If you care about somebody, and they're on the firing line, you need to be prepared for loss."

"No reason it should play that way," Johnny replied.

"Except it does," Bolan reminded him.

"You mean, with April." Johnny was referring to April Rose, Bolan's one great love since Val Querente, who was murdered when a hit team, sponsored by a traitor in the Company, had raided Stony Man Farm. Some scores were never settled, even when you stacked the bodies up like firewood.

"Not just April," Bolan said. "It nearly went that way with Val, and more than once."

"I know that."

"You don't know the half of it." This sudden anger startled Bolan, all the more so since it was directed at himself. "There was a time, it seemed like everyone I touched went in the ground. It wasn't quick and clean for any of them. I don't want.... You shouldn't have to go through that."

"Who says I will?"

"We're asking for it, both of us, if Suzanne tags along."

"And if we try to ditch her, she'll go in alone. You heard her, Mack. What chance would she have, then?"

"Just so you know. Don't count on any happy endings."

"I gave up on those when I was fourteen," Johnny said, referring to the massacre that nearly claimed his life and left the brothers orphaned. "These days, I just take what I can get."

"Well, if we're doing this," Bolan said, "we should do it like we mean it."

"Now you're talking."

7

New York, unlike Los Angeles, did have a Russian immigrant community. In fact, predictably, the nation's largest city, gateway to the continent for millions of arrivals from the Old World, boasted not one, but several neighborhoods where settlers from Russia had found homes and put down roots. The old White Russian enclave on the Upper East Side of Manhattan had dispersed with time, but St. Nicholas Russian Orthodox Cathedral remained as a landmark on East 97th Street, with mass performed in Russian every Sunday. More recently, Ukrainian immigrants congregated in the East Village, while other Russians—many of them Jewish refugees from anti-Semitism in their homeland—transformed Brighton Beach into "Little Odessa by the Sea."

Tolya Valerik wasn't Ukrainian, but he found the East Village district renowned as "Little Ukraine" a convenient hideaway, whenever he was in New York. Granted, his penthouse flat on East Seventh Street was only half a block from Little India, across Second Avenue, but the people kept to themselves. Valerik still couldn't deny a certain fascination with the vast melting pot that was New York. In truth, he didn't see much "melting," but diversity—even antagonism—could be useful to a savvy businessman.

So many different tastes. So many vices.

So much money to be made.

This morning, just in from La Guardia, Valerik had more pressing matters on his mind. His flight from California had

GET FREE BOOKS
and a
FREE GIFT WHEN YOU PLAY THE...

LAS VEGAS
GAME

*Just scratch off the gold box
with a coin. Then check
below to see the gifts you get!*

YES!

I have scratched off the gold Box. Please send me my
2 FREE BOOKS and **gift** for which I qualify. I understand
that I am under no obligation to purchase any books
as explained on the back of this card.

◄ DETACH AND MAIL CARD TODAY! ►

366 ADL C6RD

166 ADL C6RC
(MB-OS-03/01)

NAME   (PLEASE PRINT CLEARLY)

ADDRESS

APT.#   CITY

STATE/PROV.   ZIP/POSTAL CODE

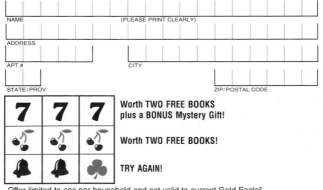

| 7 | 7 | 7 | Worth TWO FREE BOOKS plus a BONUS Mystery Gift! |

Worth TWO FREE BOOKS!

TRY AGAIN!

Offer limited to one per household and not valid to current Gold Eagle® subscribers. All orders subject to approval.

The Gold Eagle Reader Service™ — Here's how it works:

Accepting your 2 free books and gift places you under no obligation to buy anything. You may keep the books and gift and return the shipping statement marked "cancel." If you do not cancel, about a month later we'll send you 6 additional novels and bill you just $26.70* — that's a saving of 15% off the cover price of all 6 books! And there's no extra charge for shipping! You may cancel at any time, but if you choose to continue, every other month we'll send you 6 more books, which you may either purchase at the discount price or return to us and cancel your subscription.

*Terms and prices subject to change without notice. Sales tax applicable in N.Y. Canadian residents will be charged applicable provincial taxes and GST.

BUSINESS REPLY MAIL

FIRST-CLASS MAIL   PERMIT NO. 717   BUFFALO, NY

POSTAGE WILL BE PAID BY ADDRESSEE

GOLD EAGLE READER SERVICE
3010 WALDEN AVE
PO BOX 1867
BUFFALO NY 14240-9952

NO POSTAGE
NECESSARY
IF MAILED
IN THE
UNITED STATES

been first-class all the way, but he had been unable to relax, despite the courtesy champagne, the airline's version of a "gourmet" meal, and pretty flight attendants who seemed perfectly susceptible to Russian charm.

Another time, perhaps. Another flight.

"Tell me," Valerik said. "What have you learned?"

Anatoly Bogdashka, his second-in-command for operations in America, put on a somber face and took a long drag on his panetela. "Very little, I'm afraid," he answered.

"Very little." When Valerik spoke the words, he made them sound as if they were entirely new and strange to him, their meaning hopelessly beyond his grasp. Reclining in his wingback chair, Valerik pinned his first lieutenant with a stare that had been known to break down hardened killers, prompting them to weep and babble filthy secrets all night long.

"By all means," Valerik urged, "share with me the *little* information you have gained."

There was a tremor, barely visible, in Bogdashka's hand as he stubbed out the slim cigar and left its twisted remnants in a crystal ashtray. "The fact is, Tolya, we've learned nothing since you left Los Angeles."

"Nothing."

Again, the word seemed strange to him, but anyone who knew the Russian mobster well—as Bogdashka had come to know Valerik in their fifteen years of daily interaction— would have recognized the cutting edge his voice had suddenly acquired.

"That is to say," Bogdashka hastened to amend, "we have alerted all our law-enforcement contacts in the area, instructing them to forward any information they receive, without delay. So far, beyond a body count speculation on the types of weapons used, however, they have nothing to report."

"Are they our only eyes and ears?"

The question was rhetorical. Like any other syndicate engaged in full-time violation of prevailing law, the Russian

Mafia maintained a network of informers in each city where it operated, ranging from the gutters of Skid Row to city hall. For such a task as this, Valerik understood, the lower echelons would likely be more useful. Someone on the streets, or in the smoky dives where criminals were prone to congregate, had to know something about a sudden, violent move against the Russian outfit in Los Angeles.

"No, sir," Bogdashka said, willing to play along with the charade. "As in the other case, we've offered bonuses for information leading to the men responsible for the attacks. So far..."

Bogdashka didn't have to finish. So far, they had come up empty, looking foolish. And Valerik had been forced to run away.

But that wasn't what troubled him the most.

"They asked about Ted Williams," he reminded his lieutenant. "Twice."

"At Lubyanka and the Tiger's Cage," Bogdashka said. "Yes, sir."

"Was that coincidence?" Valerik asked sarcastically. "A name picked from the air?"

"I wouldn't think so, Tolya."

"No. I wouldn't think so, either."

"They won't find him, though," Bogdashka added cheerfully. "Kropotnik found him dead."

"I know that," Valerik said. "I am not some senile idiot."

"Of course not! I didn't mean to imply—"

"Ted Williams sent me."

"Sir?" Bogdashka was confused, and he couldn't hide the fact.

"It's what the bastard told Stolichkin, at the Lubyanka," Valerik said. "'Ted Williams sent me.' Don't you see, Anatoly?"

"Um..."

Valerik slammed his open palm against the polished hardwood of his desk. It pleased him not to show the burning pain that gesture cost him. He considered it a very minor victory.

"If Williams *sent* them, they weren't *looking* for him!"

"No. Of course. But Williams—"

"Killed himself, I know. Do you remember what Kropotkin said? What Keane said?"

"They thought someone had been in the house with Williams," Bogdashka replied. "Perhaps someone had tried to question him."

"And maybe took the money that the two-faced bastard stole from us."

"The money, yes." Bogdashka nodded, but his frown bespoke confusion. "Tolya, if they took the money, why—"

"Why flirt with death, disrupting our investments in Los Angeles?"

"It makes no sense."

"When we have answered *that*," Valerik said, "then we will know our enemy. What of the woman, Suzanne King, and her accomplice?"

More bad news. Bogdashka pulled another sour face and said, "No word since the unfortunate mistake in Arizona. I had planned to punish those responsible for her escape, but with the recent trouble in Los Angeles, I thought we might have need of soldiers." Bogdashka suddenly hunched forward in his chair. "You don't suppose the woman was behind what happened in Los Angeles?"

"Behind it?" Tolya shook his head. "I doubt that very much. Involved, perhaps, but that's an entirely different matter, and I don't believe much in coincidence. Consider this, Anatoly—Williams hired her worthless brother, yes? And both of them were stealing from us, yes? The woman seeks her brother, and we try to stop her, but our soldiers are defeated. Two days later, we find Williams dead, a suicide, with indications that he may have been interrogated. One day after that an unknown enemy begins to raid our operations in Los Angeles. All chance?"

"It is unusual," Bogdashka said.

"Unusual? Unusual!" This time, Valerik slammed both meaty fists down on his desk. "A birthmark shaped like Stalin's profile on your mother's ass would be unusual, Anatoly. This is more than just unusual."

"Of course, Tolya. But, what I meant to say…I mean, the woman…" There, Bogdashka faltered, visibly reluctant to provoke another outburst.

"Well? Go on! Speak up, for God's sake!"

"It's simply that the woman has no contacts or resources, Tolya. How could she arrange such things?"

His second-in-command had a point. "Perhaps her hired man is responsible," Valerik said.

"He is simply a window peeper," Bogdashka replied. "His kind are sometimes foolishly romanticized in the United States, I grant you. They have great adventures on the television and in cinema. In real life, Tolya, what they do is hide in closets and watch strangers fucking. They take pictures for divorce court. Now and then, they find a missing poodle."

"Still, this bedroom peeper and his female client managed to defeat your soldiers, killing half of them, disabling both their vehicles." Valerik chose his words deliberately, dumping the full responsibility for that screw-up into Bogdashka's lap. "What is this poodle hunter's name, again?"

"John Gray."

"What do we know about him?"

"He is licensed in the state of California as a private investigator, which includes a gun permit."

"American's have guns. It's a fact of life," Valerik said. "Go on."

"His license application indicates a term of military service in the Army Rangers. They are similar, although inferior, to—"

"I know what the Army Rangers are, Anatoly. I watch CNN."

"Of course, Tolya."

"What else?"

"The basics—address, age, birthplace…"

"Where was this one born?" Valerik asked.

"Somewhere in Massachusetts," Bogdashka replied. "I don't recall the town. If it's important—"

"Never mind. He knows the East Coast, too."

Now Bogdashka saw where he was going with it, and he shook his head, unable to repress a smile. "Tolya, you can't be serious. Why would they follow us across the country? How could they find out our names, much less that we had come here from Los Angeles?"

"How did they find Ted Williams?"

"I, for one, am not convinced they did," Bogdashka said. "We can't be certain *anyone* interrogated Williams, but assuming someone did, there's nothing to suggest it was this woman and her private eye."

"Who, then, Anatoly?"

"Why not Pruett?"

"No. Noble Pruett sent Keane to help Kropotkin question Williams and dispose of him. Why do that if he knew the man was dead?"

Bogdashka's shrug was just a hair too casual. "Perhaps," he said, "to keep you from suspecting him."

Valerik frowned at that, unhappy that it echoed a suspicion he had tried to shelter, even from himself. If Pruett had betrayed them and was keeping secrets to himself, Valerik would be forced to reconsider their agreement. That could be expensive and potentially disastrous.

"You're giving me a headache."

"I'm sorry, Tolya."

"Don't apologize," Valerik said. "It's what I pay you for. To give me headaches, and to make them go away."

"What would you have me do?"

"Make sure the usual defenses are in place, with no one

sleeping on the job,'' Valerik said. "Meanwhile, I think it's time I had another little chat with our associate.''

ON SATURDAY, if he wasn't required to visit Langley on some special errand, Noble Pruett liked to relax at his home outside Falls Church, Virginia, four miles from CIA headquarters. On Saturdays, Pruett sometimes slept in until 8:00 a.m., sometimes 8:30, dawdling over a breakfast that he had prepared himself with the same attention to detail that marked his work at the office.

Pruett wasn't married, had no live-in "significant other," and he kept no servants at the split-level house he had built from the ground up, on thirteen acres of prime Virginia real estate. The cleaning lady who came in to tidy up twice a week had been vetted by the Company before she got the job. She also understood that her inflated paycheck was contingent on discretion, much as her continued residence in the United States was dependent on her loyalty to her employer. While the cleaning lady did her thing twice weekly, an entirely different team of cleaners also swept the house three times a week. In place of brooms and dust rags, they employed the latest electronic gear for spotting taps and bugs.

Pruett wouldn't be angry if he found a spider in the bathroom, or a roach beneath the kitchen sink. If he should find a hidden microphone, however, it was safe to say that heads would roll.

This Saturday, Pruett was working on an omelette: cheese, diced ham, red peppers, just a smidgen of cilantro. It was nearly finished, fluffing nicely, when the phone rang, and he pondered for a moment whether he should simply rip the damned thing off the kitchen wall. Instead, he turned the heat down on his omelette, snaring the receiver on the second ring.

"Hello?"

"Is this line safe?"

Tolya Valerik always asked the same thing, apparently

conditioned by the bad old days in Moscow, when a person couldn't even use a pay phone on the street without a risk of talking to the KGB.

"If anybody's tapping it, it would be me," Pruett replied. "What do you want?"

"We need to talk," the Russian said.

"So, talk."

"I don't trust the telephone."

"Are you outside my door, by any chance?"

"Of course not." Vaguely scornful, now.

"Then, either trust the telephone or leave me to my breakfast, Tolya. You could always write a postcard, send a fax, or—"

"Have you heard what happened in Los Angeles last night?"

"Can't say I have. Another earthquake? Please don't tell me O.J.'s acting up again."

"This is not funny. Three of my business enterprises were attacked," Valerik told him. "Several of my men were killed."

"You're in a risky business," Pruett said.

"The gunmen mentioned your Ted Williams. Twice."

"Is that a fact?" Using a spatula, he turned the omelette over, noted its perfection and reduced the heat beneath the skillet. "Are you certain of your facts?" he asked.

"There's no mistake."

"I beg to differ, Tolya. You've made one mistake already. The unfortunate in question was not 'mine,' in any sense."

"You picked him," Valerik continued.

"Once again, you're incorrect. I delegated that responsibility to my subordinate."

"Does Keane not speak for you?" Valerik asked him, going heavy on the sarcasm.

"Why quibble, Tolya? We're all in this together, yes?"

"You call it quibbling. Keane, on your behalf, invited Williams to participate in our arrangement. Williams then employed a man named King. The two of them conspired to steal from me.''

''From us,'' Pruett corrected him.

Valerik let it pass, continuing his recitation of complaints. ''King's sister has been searching for him. When I tried to stop her, several of my men were killed.''

''I don't see how that—''

''Six weeks,'' Valerik cut him off, ''had been wasted before you finally agreed to deal with Williams as I wanted to in the beginning. Thanks to the delay, some unknown person had an opportunity to question him, resulting in his death.''

''That hasn't been established,'' Pruett said.

''It was your own subordinate's assessment,'' Tolya countered. ''Are you telling me he was mistaken, now?''

''The very fact that Williams took his own life suggests to me that he gave nothing up to anyone,'' Pruett replied. ''He wasn't bound, or he couldn't have reached the capsule. There were no apparent signs of violence, and toxicology reports found nothing in his system, other than the cyanide. If he was questioned—and it's still an *if*, in my mind, I'd say they got nothing for their trouble but a corpse.''

''Why, then, are gunmen in Los Angeles dismantling my businesses and leaving messages behind that say 'Ted Williams sent me'? Would you dare suggest it's a name someone has picked out of the air?''

''I'm not suggesting anything,'' Pruett said. ''With all due respect, I don't have many facts to work with.''

''I've told you—''

It was Pruett's turn to interrupt, and it felt good. ''But I'll look into it immediately, Tolya. Keane's in Phoenix as we speak, waiting for new instructions. I can have him in L.A. this afternoon. You two can put your heads together, and—''

''I am no longer in Los Angeles.''

''I see. Where are you calling from?''

''A safe place,'' Tolya said, stonewalling him.

''All right, then.'' Stupid bastard, thinking Pruett couldn't trace the call in minutes. "Give a shout to someone you can trust out west, and tell them to watch out for Keane at LAX. I'll have him on the ground as near as possible to noon, Pacific time. If your people cooperate—"

"We have done nothing but cooperate."

"—I'm confident that we can wrap this matter up in no time and get back on track."

"I hope so, Pruett. These events are most disturbing. They suggest I may have been too hasty in agreeing to collaborate with you."

"Before you start to come unglued, remember Krestyanov. He brought you into this, not me. You feel like bailing out, you need to take it up with him."

There was a momentary silence on the line, Valerik mulling over options and deciding not to press his luck. "That will be satisfactory," he said at last. "For now."

"We're all in this together, Tolya. Take a little breather. We'll get this thing cleaned up." As he returned the handset to its cradle, Pruett made a sour face and growled, "You stupid schmuck."

And realized he wasn't even sure whom he was talking to.

Enlisting Williams had been Christian Keane's idea. Pruett himself had never met the man, and was increasingly grateful for that small favor, as the ripples from Williams's betrayal continued to spread. Still, it was his responsibility to see that everything ran smoothly, that there were no critical snafus before their operation finally bore fruit.

Too late.

Already, they had Williams and his flunky sidekick in the ground, close to a million dollars in black money missing, and the Russian Mob was fumbling efforts to assassinate the flunky's sister, traveling around the country somewhere with a half-assed private eye, for God's sake. Now, this bloody business in Los Angeles was dumped on top of everything, like frosting on the cake.

Keane would be livid when he heard about the side trip to

L.A., and that was tough. In Pruett's view—though he had offered no objection at the time—recruiting Williams was the cause of all their difficulties to the present day. If Keane wasn't able to clean it up, then maybe it was time for Pruett to go shopping for another Number Two.

That would be perilous, of course. So many secrets were locked up inside Keane's head, and while he could be silenced with a phone call, finding a replacement might be difficult. It would, if nothing else, be hazardous in the extreme. So much would have to be revealed, so many confidences shared. And all for what?

Pruett was reaching for the telephone again when he remembered breakfast and decided the call could wait a while. His omelette would be getting cold, and there was nothing he despised so much as waste. He could reach out to Keane as easily in an hour as he could right now. And if his aide was forced to scramble for the next flight out of Phoenix, it would do him good.

Keane had been getting careless lately. He could use a good, long run, Pruett thought. If he missed the noontime flight into L.A., then he could always catch a later one, and offer his apologies.

As for the Russians, they could sit at LAX and wait.

THE IN-FLIGHT MOVIE was a comedy about a mafioso plagued by fits of weeping and anxiety attacks, who sought relief with a psychiatrist and wound up acting crazier than ever, while the shrink began to take on gangster traits. Ten minutes into it, Bolan regretted shelling out three dollars for the earphones, switching over to an audio track that was advertised on the airliner's plasticized menu as "easy listening." Apparently, that meant they stripped the lyrics from assorted vintage tunes, slowed the beat and played it back with strings. Bolan, getting a headache, took off the earphones and stuffed them in the seat pocket before him.

He had a window seat, no one on his right. His brother

and Suzanne were seated just in front of him, both dozing now, from all appearances. He wished them pleasant dreams and raised his plastic window shade, searching the tattered clouds for any omen that might help him be prepared for what was coming in New York.

Aware that they couldn't discuss their business on the plane, they had made plans before they caught the flight out of Los Angeles. The stopover in Houston was behind them, and three more hours should see them on the ground in Newark.

Bolan had selected the New Jersey airport as a hedge, in case Tolya Valerik's Russian goons—or someone else, perhaps—was watching out for Suzanne and his brother at the New York City airports. It would mean a slightly longer drive, but that was better than an ambush on the concourse, when their guns were traveling as check-through luggage in the cargo hold.

The New York battle plan was rudimentary, designed with flexibility in mind. They would find someplace safe to stash Suzanne, where they could keep in touch, and then begin to work the streets. Bolan had several targets spotted, going in, and he was sure that others would suggest themselves, once things got rolling in the Apple. More than racking up a body count, however, he was interested in getting to the bottom of whatever scheme Ted Williams had been trying to protect by taking cyanide. He had to know what was at stake, and who the players were.

And why Brognola had been so averse to Bolan coming east.

A part of Bolan's mind told him it was ridiculous to even think about the big Fed turning on him, after all the action they had seen together, all the secrets they had shared. About the time that part of him was getting sentimental, though, another part spoke up, reminding Bolan that Brognola was a bureaucrat who stayed alive in Washington by playing politics and juggling his priorities. If there was something in the works that Brognola found more important than his friends...

What would it be?

Not family. Brognola had already passed that test, with Bolan's help, when covert enemies in government had grabbed his wife, demanding Brognola's conspiratorial cooperation under threat of death, or worse. There had been death that time, all right, but the big Fed had come through like a champ.

What, then?

Something political, perhaps? Not in the ordinary sense, of course. Brognola had abandoned party politics years before Bolan met him, convinced that any group of humanoids pursuing public office desired the same thing: namely, power. In pursuit of that ultimate goal, they would lie, cheat and steal without compunction.

There were some officeholders Brognola respected. He wasn't a total cynic after all, just ninety-nine percent. When he found someone he trusted, that trust and respect were strictly personal, without endorsement of a given campaign platform. If a heroine or hero let him down, Brognola took the blow in stride and edged a little closer to the point of abject cynicism, even though he never quite went all the way.

Was that the key? Had Brognola found something larger than a politician or a party? Something international? If so, what could it be?

What would it take to woo and win Brognola on the global scale, to make him crawl in bed with both the CIA and members of the Russian Mafia? The very notion seemed ridiculous, but there was no denying the big Fed's initial reticence when Bolan asked about prospective links between the Russians and the Company, the sense that he was holding something back, his effort to dissuade the Bolan brothers from pursuing Tolya Valerik to New York. The nagging bits and pieces added up to...

What, goddammit?

Staring out the window, Bolan was reminded of the classic "Twilight Zone" episode, wherein William Shatner saw a gremlin tearing at the engine of an airliner in flight. His efforts to alert the crew were fruitless, prompting everyone aboard to think he was insane.

It would be much the same, thought Bolan, if he started asking questions, airing his concerns to any member of the crew at Stony Man Farm. They were his friends, and some of them had displayed a willingness to die on his behalf, but Brognola had called the shots at the Farm from the beginning. In a sense, Brognola *was* the program, having lobbied for its institution, built it from the ground up, handpicked personnel, selected missions and absorbed the heat in Washington when anything went sour. What would induce the man to throw it all away and turn his back on—

Bolan caught himself before his paranoia ran amok. He had no evidence that Brognola was throwing anything away, that he had turned his back on anyone. It was a certainty, in Bolan's mind, that the big Fed was sitting on some kind of secret that involved the Russian Mafia and CIA. As to the nature of the secret and its import, though, he was entirely in the dark. There was no prima facie reason to suppose Brognola's motive sprang from any sinister—much less, apocalyptic—urge.

Except, of course, that people had been getting killed.

Brognola had been angry when he heard of the attempt to murder Johnny and Suzanne in Arizona. Bolan didn't question that emotion. He had no good reason to believe it was an act, put on by Brognola for his benefit. He knew Brognola cared for Johnny like a brother—or a son—but there were times in each man's life when heart and mind collided, and a cruel choice was required. Sometimes, he understood, you had to make that choice and go ahead, regardless of the cost.

Jumping the gun, he thought. There was a difference, he realized, between Brognola's begging off from any action in New York and actively supporting Bolan's enemies. The

Fed's very reticence was so unusual, however. It would be easy to interpret Brognola's withdrawal as a hostile act, itself, and go from there.

But would it be correct?

If Brognola had turned against them, or was somehow in the process of conversion to the other side—whatever that turned out to be—the consequences would be grim indeed. Losing the steady flow of information and the technical support from Stony Man was bad enough, but that would be the least of it. In theory, if worse came to worst, Brognola could start hunting them himself. Bolan didn't believe the men of Able Team or Phoenix Force would join the hunt, unless they were somehow convinced that Bolan had turned traitor to the cause, but Brognola's resources weren't limited to the Farm. He had the FBI and U.S. Marshal's service standing by, along with sundry military units. And if he was acting in collaboration with the CIA...

Worst-case scenario, it could be like the bad old days when Bolan had been ranked as the most-wanted fugitive in the United States and half a dozen foreign countries. There would be no Wanted posters, if that happened, no TV spots with his mug shots on display, since Washington had publicly announced Mack Bolan's death some years before. The down side of his anonymity: there would be no attempt to capture him alive for trial.

Slow down.

The curse of an imagination was its tendency to run away, sketch morbid fantasies and populate the world with lurking monsters, where there might be none at all.

His problem, at the moment, was twofold. First, he had to keep both eyes wide open for his coming contest with the Russians—and, perhaps, with agents from the Company. At the same time, he had to narrow his focus, try to penetrate the wall of secrecy that Brognola had raised between them, without losing track of those he knew to be his mortal enemies.

And if Brognola stood among their ranks, what then?

Bolan was pledged to never kill a lawman, even if the cop in question was a criminal. His long friendship with Hal Brognola made that promise to himself doubly imperative. And yet, this time, it wasn't simply Bolan's life at stake. His brother's life was riding on the line, as well as Suzanne King's.

The final question, then: If Brognola *had* turned, would any of them manage to survive?

8

Viktor Seriozha didn't understand what all the excitement was about. There had been fighting in Los Angeles, some property had been destroyed and certain people had been killed—though none of them were personally known to him.

So what?

Seriozha was a soldier. He had grown up brawling in the streets and alleyways of Moscow, breaking heads, arms, legs. There had been fighting in his life since he had learned to walk. In time, hard-knuckled fists had given way to blades, and later to guns. The simple fact that someone had been killed three thousand miles away was no cause for alarm, in Seriozha's eyes.

Because he was a soldier, he did what he was told. His orders, at the moment, called for him to guard a loft on Wooster Street in SoHo. What mattered to him was his mission and the Uzi submachine gun slung across his shoulder on a canvas strap.

Two others were assigned to help him guard the loft, with one downstairs, the other, named Pavel, was presently engrossed in thumbing through a *Penthouse* magazine. Seriozha could hardly blame him, since the job was boring, and he couldn't very well complain, in any case, since Pavel had been left in charge.

The loft was primarily used for storage space. At present, there were several crates of new Kalashnikov assault rifles stacked against one wall, destined for sale on the American black market, but the loft was also sometimes used for drugs in transit, stolen merchandise or new arrivals in the country, waiting for their ID and assorted travel papers to be forged. Seriozha wasn't convinced the crates of rifles needed three men to protect them, but he didn't question orders.

It wasn't a healthy way to live.

Seriozha had eaten Chinese food for lunch, a little place on Mott Street, just a short walk from the loft, and he was suffering the consequences now. He always liked the spicy dishes—hot-and-sour soup, the kung pao chicken, sizzling garlic beef—but none of it liked him. His favorite dishes made him sweat while he was wolfing down the food, and later on came heartburn. Each time, he vowed that he wouldn't repeat the same mistake, but Seriozha was a slave to carnal appetites. He liked his vodka and cigars, the spicy food, and sex with no-holds-barred. He reckoned one of his addictions would eventually kill him, but what better way to go?

Right now, the only place he had to go was to the toilet, and he took the Uzi with him, telling Pavel he wouldn't be long.

The loft had never been designed for residential purposes, and so the bathroom was an afterthought, with nothing but a sink and toilet walled off in one corner, and smaller than your average walk-in closet. Seriozha hung his SMG on a coat hook beside the door, lowered his trousers and was seated. On the floor beside the toilet, shoved beneath the sink, he found a stack of girlie magazines.

The first gunshot made him drop the magazine.

He wondered, for a heartbeat, whether Pavel might have switched on the television, but then Seriozha remembered that there was no television in the loft. He lurched erect, yanked up his shorts and slacks in painful haste and fumbled with his belt. No time to think about his zipper, as the gunshots started going off like fireworks, Pavel shouting something that he couldn't quite make out, with all the racket.

He ripped the Uzi free from the coat hook and thumbed off the safety. Emerging from the tiny bathroom, Seriozha caught a glimpse of figures moving in the dim light, near the couch where Pavel had been seated earlier, and he cut loose instinctively, the Uzi rattling off a burst in their direction, bullets peppering the walls.

An instant later they were firing back at him, at least two guns, and Seriozha found himself in desperate need of cover. That was yet another problem with the loft: so little furniture, that there was nothing much to hide behind. There were some standing pillars though, one of them close enough to save him as he ducked behind it, bullets spraying plaster dust on either side.

Who were these bastards? He assumed they had to have killed the guard downstairs, and it was troubling to Seriozha that he couldn't instantly recall the dead man's name. He shrugged it off and concentrated on the sound of footsteps, stealthily advancing on his hiding place. They would fan out, surround him, if he didn't head them off. The only exit from the loft was fifty feet away, through the hostile gunfire.

No choice. He had to go for it, then.

He burst from cover, firing from the hip, and saw one of them recoiling, reeling backward. For a moment, Seriozha thought the other man was hit, exhilaration soaring in him, but he had no time to relish the sensation. Something struck him in the ribs, low down, with all the power of a mule's kick, and he lost the submachine gun as he fell.

Seriozha was fumbling for his pistol underneath his jacket when they reached him. Someone flipped him over on his back and slapped his hand aside, while someone else stepped on his wrist—the backup gun forever out of reach. Two faces loomed above him.

Could there be only two? he thought.

"Tolya Valerik," one of them was saying. "If you tell us where to find him, you can walk away from this."

But Seriozha wasn't walking anywhere. He couldn't even feel his legs. What did he have to lose?

He sneered at them, tried laughing at them, but it hurt too much, and he was forced to compromise on cursing them in Russian.

Viktor Seriozha was still muttering his imprecations when he closed his eyes and slipped into the waiting darkness.

THE TOBACCO SHOP on East Sixth Street wasn't what it appeared to be. It sold tobacco, true enough, but its significance to the Ukrainians who occupied the neighborhood had nothing much to do with nicotine. In fact, the shop had served for years as an informal—and unlicensed—lending institution. Ready cash was made available to anyone in need, at standard interest rates of twenty percent per week.

Such terms, while stringent—and illegal—were the best available to many recent immigrants. Most of them lacked collateral to satisfy a bank, and some of them didn't even possess a green card, granting them permission to remain in the United States. Beggars couldn't be choosers in America, especially if they were dodging Immigration while they tried to pay their bills and feed their families. If someone fell behind on payments, there were ways to make it right. Some errands to be run, perhaps a nubile daughter who could work the streets from time to time. If all else failed, a nice vacation in the hospital. Of course, that would generate new bills.

Bolan was painfully familiar with the pattern. It was such an operation that had torn his family apart and left the brothers orphaned, Johnny barely out of junior high school at the time. Loan sharks had rated high on Bolan's list every since, along with pimps and pushers, for their tendency to victimize the helpless. Hit men, by contrast, were almost paragons of virtue in the underworld, most often killing other thugs or fat cats who had prospered through corruption of their fellow man. It took a special breed of scum to prey on working parents and their children. Bolan, for his part, would never miss a chance to take down a loan shark.

Scorched earth.

"You ready?"

"As I'll ever be," Johnny replied, seated at the wheel of the Infiniti J30 they had purchased with a portion of the cash obtained in Tucson. It was safer than a rental car, and they could always score new license plates from any parking lot or residential street in town.

Parking in New York City was a challenge at the best of times, and while he didn't like it, Johnny had agreed to serve as wheelman this time out, remaining with the car while Bolan went inside the shop. If anything went wrong, he would be close enough to help. If it went seriously wrong, he could escape, pick up Suzanne from the hotel and figure out the next move on his own.

"Just drive around the block like we agreed, okay?"

"You got it, bro."

The shop was three doors from the corner of East Sixth and Second Avenue. As Bolan made the walk, he automatically checked out the upstairs windows facing him, across the street and scanned the rooftops. Would the loan shark have a sentry or a guard outside? If so, the guy was well disguised as one of several old women or a child on roller skates.

A large, old-fashioned cowbell clanked above his head as Bolan entered, then again, when he allowed the door to close. At first he thought the shop might be deserted, as improbable as that would be, but then he heard footsteps approaching from the back, somewhere behind a curtain hung to screen the shop's rear quarters from its public area. He counted two, perhaps three pairs of scuffling feet, but only one man showed himself, emerging from behind the drape to meet his would-be customer.

"I help you find something?"

The man was in his fifties, gray hair in retreat from a

scarred, freckled forehead. He was average height, but his barrel chest made him look shorter, almost freakish. The long sleeves on his white dress shirt were rolled up elbow-high, revealing tattooed forearms.

"I'm a little short of cash," Bolan replied. "Word has it you're the man to see."

The older man regarded Bolan with a frown, then shrugged. "I sell tobacco here," he said. "For money, you go to the bank."

"Word has it that you are the bank around this neighborhood."

"What word? Who've you been talking to?"

"Your satisfied customers," Bolan remarked with a smile. "Are we dealing or not?"

"You've made a mistake," the Russian said. "I'm a busy man, got things to do. You go, now."

"Not without my cash."

The loan shark shrugged again, spoke Russian to the curtain on his right, and two young men emerged from hiding, armed with baseball bats.

"Okay," the Russian said. "Now, you *can't* go."

The first punk came across the counter like a gymnast, with the loan shark yelling at him, "No! The glass! You go around!" His partner took the long way, giving Bolan ample time to ease the 93-R from underneath his jacket and dispatch two silenced rounds that turned the first punk's kneecaps into bloody porridge. With a shriek, the guy went down, his bat forgotten as it wobbled off across the floor.

His backup saw the pistol rising, read the look on Bolan's face and cocked his arm as if to pitch the bat from where he stood. Another Parabellum round from the Beretta took him in the upper chest and slammed him back against the precious counter, cracking glass, unleashing a small avalanche of stacked cigars.

The loan shark had one hand beneath the counter when he froze, already framed in Bolan's pistol sights. "I hope you've got a weapon under there," Bolan said. "Anytime you're ready, make your move."

The hand was empty when it surfaced, rising up to join its mate, hoisted above the Russian's head. "You've robbed the wrong place," he suggested, without much conviction.

"No, I think I've got the right place," Bolan said. "Let's see the safe. Be cool, and you might just come out of this alive."

"IT'S HARD to picture sixty grand in cash lying around a place like that," Johnny remarked as they were wheeling down Sixth Avenue, approaching Greenwich Village.

"It's a cash-and-carry business," Bolan reminded him. "Nobody wants a paper trail."

"Like us. They've got the cash, we carry it away."

"I thought the name was Johnny Gray, not Dillinger."

"My friends all call me Baby Face."

"I'll bet."

"So, what's up in the Village?"

"Dope. Unless I'm misinformed, they're dealing from a gay bar that the Russians own on Barrow Street."

"Is that from Hal?"

Bolan hesitated just a second, but it seemed to stretch forever. "No," he said at last, "this came from someone else."

"Look, maybe this is none of my business—"

"Sure it is," Bolan interrupted him. "You're on the line, the same as I am. I just don't know what to tell you, honestly. Hal's acting…strange."

"That's it? I mean, should we be worried?"

"No." Bolan shook his head. "Concern would be appropriate, I think, but worry is a waste of time. It slows you down, distracts you, makes you lose your focus."

"Jesus." Johnny had a sinking feeling in his gut. "I never thought that Hal—"

Bolan cut him off again. "We don't know anything, okay? Turn right up here."

Greenwich Village was teeming with locals and tourists alike. The real action wouldn't begin until sundown, but the shops and coffeehouses were doing brisk business. The grunge look might be in for starving artists and musicians, but most of the strollers seemed to prefer bright colors. Most of them seemed cheerful, too. It almost felt as if they had been teleported to another city, or another time.

Their target was the Pump House, halfway down the block from Redford Street. The neon Open sign didn't appear to have much influence on passersby. Perhaps it was too early in the day for beer and bondage, Johnny thought.

And as they motored past, he said, "I'm going in."

He was expecting static from his brother, but instead, Bolan simply said, "You sure?"

"Next loading zone you spot, sing out. I'll hop out there, and you can take the wheel."

"Have you got everything you need?"

"I will if you reach back there and grab a couple of those phosphorous grenades."

"The whole block doesn't need to go," Bolan said.

"I hear you. Just the dope stash, right? And maybe our good friend Valerik's personal investment in the property."

"Remind me not to piss you off."

"I'll make a note." He spied a loading zone, blue-painted curb the only space in sight, and nosed in with the shiny new Infiniti. Bolan had already slipped the thermite canisters into a plastic shopping bag from Saks Fifth Avenue.

"I'm stylin' now," Johnny remarked and flashed a grin.

"Just come back in one piece," Bolan said. "Watch six."

"I've got it covered."

Johnny sauntered back in the direction of the Pump House, merging with the weekend crowd. Outside the bar's entrance, he put on a show of indecision, glancing up and down the street, then slipped inside.

The place was cool and dark inside, reminding Johnny of a visit to the London Dungeon, several years before. There were no implements of torture dangling from the walls or ceiling here, but Johnny still experienced a sense of going underground, encroaching on a world that outsiders weren't supposed to see.

In fact, he knew, it was his expectation that produced the feeling. At this hour on a Saturday, nothing was happening inside the Pump House to betray the nature of its standard clientele. There were no same-sex couples dancing, holding hands, or doing much of anything. Two young men clad in leather jackets had a booth staked out in back. Their heads were shaved, but Johnny took for granted that the two weren't Nazi skinheads from their choice of drinking spots.

He had the bar all to himself, setting the Saks bag on the stool beside him as he settled in. The bartender, he noticed now, had also shaved his head. Johnny began to feel like someone from the ''After'' shot in a commercial for Rogaine.

''What'll you have?''

Instead of ordering, Johnny inquired, ''Are we alone?''

The barkeep flicked a glance in the direction of the leather boys and asked, ''What did you have in mind?''

''I thought I'd set the place on fire and burn your dope stash. How's that sound?''

The man behind the bar blinked twice, then broke into a smile. ''That's pretty rich,'' he said.

''The rich part is, I'm serious,'' Johnny said, showing him the Glock.

The barkeep raised his hands, though Johnny hadn't asked him to. He shot another glance in the direction of the clean-heads, Johnny picking up vague movement in the long distorting mirror mounted on the wall behind the bar.

He moved as if the leap had been rehearsed a hundred times, grabbing the Saks bag as he vaulted off his stool and rolled across the bar. The leather boys cut loose with semi-auto pistols as he dropped from sight, and Johnny heard a stray round slap the bartender. When he collapsed against the knee-high fridge, the barkeep had a hole below one eye and he was weeping crimson tears.

No time to think about the back rooms now. Johnny would trust the sudden gunfire to alert and scatter any loiterers who didn't want to die. He pulled one of the fat incendiary canisters out of his shopping bag, removed the pin and lobbed the grenade blindly toward the center of the room.

The shooting had subsided for a moment, and he clearly heard one of the skinheads ask his buddy, "What the fuck is that?" No Russian accent Johnny could detect, but that wasn't his problem. At the moment, he was focused on the task of getting out of there alive.

The phosphorous grenade exploded with a *pop-whoosh*, its white-hot tendrils snaking out across the room in all directions from ground zero. In the aftermath of the explosion, Johnny heard the skinheads shrieking, and he came up in a fighting stance, the Glock extended in both hands.

Two flaming scarecrows danced and capered in the middle of the room, emitting whoops and squeals of agony. He gave each one a double tap and put them down, retrieved the second thermite bomb and made his way around the bar, in the direction of the street.

The place was burning, filling up with smoke. There was no way for him to reach the back rooms where the drug stash would be kept, but Johnny primed the second canister and lobbed it back in that direction, hoping for a hit. Whatever happened, by the time the fire department got there, finished putting out the blaze and sent an arson team to make the rounds, Tolya Valerik would be looking at red ink.

A tentacle of smoke trailed Johnny to the sidewalk, but he shrugged it off, picked up his pace, and he was half a block down range before somebody started shouting, "Fire!" Ten seconds later, his brother pulled up in the Infiniti and tapped the horn.

"No problems?" he inquired.

"A couple guys wanted to dance," Johnny said, "but I told them I didn't have time."

"Hey, they'll get over it."

The younger Bolan frowned and said, "I don't think so."

BOLAN'S SECONDARY contact in New York was an Italian gangster, never "made" as an oath-bound member of the Cosa Nostra, who wasn't averse to selling information that would damage his competitors—assuming he was guaranteed full anonymity, of course. Sounding impressed by news of Bolan's alias "Mickey Brasko's" daylight moves against the Russian syndicate, he volunteered the information that a group of Chechen shooters were collecting at a Lower East Side warehouse, suiting up in preparation for a countermove against the guys who had been raising hell among their comrades. All they needed was a name and address, the informant said, and they were primed to rock and roll.

Bolan decided there would never be a better time for a preemptive strike.

The warehouse was on Water Street, a short block distant from the same East River where the likes of Albert Anastasia and Dutch Schultz once dumped their victims in the murky water, clad in proverbial "cement kimonos." Johnny made a casual approach, and Bolan counted nine cars in the parking lot. If their opponents carpooled, Bolan estimated they could count on thirty guns or more inside the warehouse, every shooter psyched for battle, ready for a taste of blood.

"This may not be the best idea I've had all day," he told his brother.

Johnny flashed a grin while he was parking the Infiniti. "I'd disagree with you on that," he said, exuding confidence. "We've barely scratched the surface, and we have to thin the herd sometime. Besides, there must be someone in this dump who knows where we can find Valerik."

Bolan nodded, swallowed his uncertainty and started getting ready for the strike. This thing with Brognola, combined with his concern for Johnny's life, was threatening to put him off his game. The best thing he could do right now was to put all such distractions well behind him and get on with business in the classic Bolan style.

They each drew Spectre submachine guns from the OD duffel bag, with ammo belts supporting extra magazines in canvas pouches. Each took a pair of frag grenades and clipped them to his belt. The rest of it—enough to arm a front-line rifle squad—was left behind for later use.

Assuming they survived.

It was a short walk to the warehouse, and they circled to the rear. The access door was locked, and Bolan picked them both in eighty seconds flat, with Johnny covering his back. They eased inside and left the door unlocked behind them, a potential exit route.

The warehouse smelled of age, as if it hadn't been aired or fumigated since the Nixon era. Bolan led his brother past a single lavatory—women weren't expected here—until they reached a point where they could stand in shadow, checking out the warehouse proper.

It was still in use, from all appearances, but only just. Away to Bolan's left there were some crates, perhaps one decent tractor-trailer load, that looked as if they had been standing in their present ranks for months, if not for years. A shiny, brand-new forklift parked beside the cargo seemed out of place. What Bolan chiefly registered about the crates and forklift, though, was that they were positioned too far away to serve as cover, once the battle began.

The gunmen he had come to kill were congregated in the middle of the warehouse, milling around two long tables that supported coffee urns, a washtub filled with bottled beer on ice, and a buffet of cold cuts, bread, apples and pears in plastic bowls. He counted thirty-two and glanced at Johnny without speaking.

"Thirty-two," his brother whispered in confirmation.

There was no way in the world to pull it off, except by

absolute surprise. If they could hit the gunners hard enough and fast enough, before their adversaries worked out what was happening, they had a fighting chance. No more, no less. It was impossible to drop all thirty-two of them at once, and Bolan still had hopes of grilling a survivor. In any case, it meant a dirty fight.

Without a word, Bolan unclipped the frag grenades from his web belt, the Spectre dangling from its shoulder strap, and saw his brother do likewise. He dropped both safety pins, but held the safety spoons in place until the kid's grenades were likewise primed. From this point on, it would be each man for himself.

"I'll see you on the other side," he said and made his pitch.

All four grenades were airborne in the next two seconds, wobbling through the air and dropping in the midst of gunmen. He saw one strike a Russian on the head, the impact stunning him. The guy went down, but there was no time to observe his progress, as the charges started going off in rapid fire, spraying the ranks with shrapnel as they blew.

The rest was nothing short of butcher's work. The brothers opened up with SMGs from fifty feet away, Johnny strafing the Russians from left to right, Bolan working in the opposite direction. Smoke and blood were everywhere, men cursing, screaming, in the aftermath of the explosions that had nearly deafened them. One of the coffee urns went over with a crash, the other sprouting leaks that gave it the appearance of a pop-art fountain. Fruit was spattered into pulp across the buffet table, cold cuts sliced and diced by flying Parabellum rounds.

But even caught flat-footed, dying where they stood, some of the Russians managed to fight back. Each man was armed, and even when a wounded soldier dropped his automatic weapon, there was still a side arm to fall back on. Some of them fired wildly, without marking targets, but a handful of the best picked out the source of that incoming fire, returning it as best they could.

A couple of them ducked behind the table, turned it over, spilling what was left of the buffet in their attempt to find some cover for themselves. The table hadn't been designed for stopping military rounds, of course, and bullets found them in their makeshift hideout, ripping through the fiberboard as if it had been tissue paper.

Others tried to run, three of them breaking for the crates and forklift, hoping to find cover there, but Johnny cut them down before they reached half the distance to their goal. They fell together, as if they had passed out in the middle of a drunken game of Twister, nothing but the spread of crimson ripples on the concrete floor to indicate that they were dead, instead of merely dozing.

One man, strangely, ran directly toward the brothers. He had no gun in his hand, but rather held an open wallet in front of him. A shrapnel cut above one eye had bathed the left side of his face in blood, and he was shouting, "Don't shoot me! I'm not with them!" Before Bolan could make the choice, a shotgun blast from somewhere in the ranks surprised the runner with a swift kick to the spine and sent him sprawling, facedown on the floor.

The Russians weren't quitters. They fought on until not one of them was left alive. By Bolan's watch, the slaughter had consumed three minutes and eleven seconds from the time the first grenade exploded, to the echo of the final gunshot in the charnel house.

He moved among the bodies, looking for survivors, finding none. Behind him, Johnny called, "We've got a ringer, here."

It was the runner who had his ID in place of hardware, calling out for mercy in the midst of death. Johnny had rolled the dead man onto his leaking back and found the wallet underneath. Behind a shield of plastic flecked with blood, a laminated card identified the corpse as Walter Graham, until very recently an agent of the CIA.

"Bingo," Johnny said, noting the expression on his brother's face.

"Bingo," Bolan repeated.

And wondered why he felt as if he had just lost the game.

9

Hal Brognola hated JFK. The airport, that is, not the president. He dreaded getting off the flight from Washington, D.C., and merging with the crowd that seemed to pack the terminal regardless of the hour, day or night. Arrivals and departures out of Kennedy, unless he had the rare good luck to be escaping on a private charter flight, were always chaos.

In other circumstances, he would normally have called ahead, to have a car and driver waiting for him, courtesy of the FBI's field office in New York. This errand was a private matter, though. Strictly off the books. He hadn't wished to talk about it any further on the telephone, and he most definitely didn't want the FBI to know he was in town, discussing tactics with the man who was about to stand the city on its ear.

The trouble had already started in New York, and that was bad enough. If it continued—which it would, unless Brognola found a way to call the Bolan brothers off—the end result could be calamitous. Brognola wasn't one to panic, but from what he knew already, Bolan's intervention in this particular game could be global bad news.

The trick, if Brognola could manage it at all, would be to ease the brothers out of it, persuade the two of them to disengage, without revealing what he knew or what he half suspected. It would be no simple task, and might well prove impossible. In all the time that he had known Mack Bolan, the big Fed had never talked the warrior out of anything, once Bolan's mind was set on a particular desired result. The battle didn't always play as Bolan hoped it would, but he had never backed away from danger in his life, not even when the odds against him seemed impossible.

It took Brognola twenty minutes to complete the rental paperwork and find his car, another twenty-five to make his way out of the airport traffic snarl. JFK International was located in Queens, fifteen miles southeast of Manhattan, and the best part of another hour had been lost before he crossed the Queensboro Bridge, winding his way toward Central Park.

New York's "backyard" had been constructed in 1858, ten million cartloads of fill dirt dumped into 843 acres of quarries, hog farms, swampland and squalid shanties. The end result was a panorama of scenic hills, lakes and meadows, half a million trees and shrubs, an ice rink, a zoo and a castle—but the mean spirit of the great park's beginning seemed to fester under all that soil, refusing to dissipate over time. Locals and tourists might enjoy the park by day, but come sundown, the predators took over, nominally human, and the Apple's vast backyard belonged to them. Most cops wouldn't go in the park alone at night, and any foolish jogger who decided on a midnight run along the Ramble would be lucky if he only lost his wallet and his watch.

Sundown was still some hours away when Brognola found a public parking garage on East 81st Street, left the ticket stub in plain view on the rental's dashboard and walked two blocks west to the park. It seemed to take forever crossing Fifth Avenue, the stretch they called Museum Mile, but Brognola knew his main problem was nerves.

Relax, for Christ's sake!

He had no fear of being mugged or otherwise molested in the city. On his hip, he wore the Smith & Wesson .40-caliber autoloader that had been standard-issue at Justice for nearly a decade. He had badged his way around the metal detectors at Dulles, and he would do the same thing at JFK, going home. In between, any low-life son of a bitch who felt lucky was welcome to take his best shot.

His mood wasn't entirely Bolan's fault, although the last call from New York had prompted Brognola to go back on his word. He had already cautioned Bolan that he couldn't help with any move the brothers made against the Russians in New York, and Bolan had to understand that Brognola was also speaking for the team at Stony Man. A week ago—hell, yesterday—Brognola would have laughed at anyone who told him he would ever speak those words, but circumstances altered cases. He had been prepared to sit it out, and live on Pepto-Bismol if he had to, but the last phone call had put him on the next flight out of Dulles, into JFK.

"We've got a dead spook on our hands."

Not *maybe* there's a Company involvement with the Russians, or the grapevine says there *may* be spooks in town. They had an agent down, ID and all, in with others who were absolutely, positively Russian Mafia.

Brognola could have blown it off, of course. It was the perfect opportunity for him to say, "I told you so. See what you've done? Can't help you, buddy. Better luck next time." If he had been the heartless bastard some folks back in Washington believed he was, Brognola would have done and said exactly that.

But some folks back in Washington were wrong about the man from Justice. More or less.

Brognola made the hard decisions when he had to, which was often, but he'd never left a valued friend exposed if there was any way around it. He was hoping that he might still find a way around it in the present case. If not...

They had agreed to meet at the Metropolitan Museum of Art, in the sculpture garden, on top of the Twentieth Century wing. It was supposed to cut down on confusion, wasted time and aimless wandering around the park, but as he started up the broad front steps of the museum, rummaging inside a pocket to come up with the admission charge, Brognola wondered if the meeting might turn out to be a trap.

He had no fear of Bolan turning on him—not yet, anyway—but Brognola wasn't inclined to underestimate the Russian Mob, much less the CIA. The Bolan brothers had gone head to head with soldiers from Tolya Valerik's Family on both coasts now, and they had been seen in Los Angeles by living witnesses. More to the point, if Bolan's estimation of the setup was correct, Valerik's people had IDs on Johnny and the woman going in, before the Executioner became involved. What would prevent them from establishing surveillance, maybe even trailing Bolan to the Met, to see if he was meeting someone on the sly?

Brognola felt as if he had a giant bull's-eye painted on his back, but that was simple paranoia talking. He was unknown to Valerik's people, and shouldn't be recognizable at first sight by a team of spotters from the Company. He could turn back, right now, and simply skip the meeting. Why take chances, jeopardize his pension and the whole program at Stony Man?

Get real.

Without Mack Bolan, Stony Man wouldn't exist. The men of Able Team had been allied with Bolan since the early weeks of his original campaign against the Mafia—and two of them before that, from his military days. If it came down to choosing sides, Brognola had no doubt which way they would go, and Phoenix Force would almost surely follow suit. Back at the Farm, he would lose Barbara Price, for sure, and probably Aaron Kurtzman. More importantly, however, if he turned his back on Bolan now, without another try at putting things to rights, Brognola stood to lose his self-respect.

The big Fed bought his ticket, entered the museum and moved directly to the stairs, ascending to the second floor. The Twentieth Century wing was situated at the massive building's southwest corner, its rooftop sculpture garden accessed via elevator or another flight of stairs. Brognola made his way past various exhibits without seeing them, his marginal everyday interest in art entirely suppressed at the moment. Passing Rembrandts and Cézannes, Van Goghs and Picassos, he was focused on the people around him rather than the paintings. Any one of them, he realized, could be a watcher, maybe an assassin with a silenced pistol or a hypodermic filled with some exotic toxin cooked up in a lab no one outside of Langley even knew about.

He was getting too damned old for this, Brognola thought, casually slipping the button on his jacket, thereby shaving half a second off his time, in case he had to reach the Smith & Wesson in a hurry.

He ignored the empty, waiting elevator, climbed the stairs and stepped out into daylight, at one corner of the rooftop garden. The sculptures here weren't on permanent display. New ones were brought in every year, the old ones trundled off to who knew where. Brognola moved among them, judging each piece in its turn for the potential cover it would offer, if he had to duck below some crazy shooter's line of fire.

There were no more than half a dozen browsers in the garden when he got there, none of them the man he'd come to see. Brognola guessed the crowds were often thin this time of day, with most New Yorkers busy at their jobs, the tourists dawdling over an extended lunch or working up to happy hour. Either way, the crowd was thin. Brognola felt exposed, imagining a thousand unseen faces in the windows of the distant skyscrapers all turned in his direction, maybe one guy watching from a rooftop or an open window, through a telescopic sight.

He was supposed to be exempt from fieldwork, at his rank and age, but here he was in freaking New York City, standing on a rooftop, pitifully exposed, and waiting for—

"You made it," said a voice behind him, and Brognola nearly jumped out of his skin.

BROGNOLA TURNED to face him, putting on a smile that wouldn't have convinced a blind man. "Made it, right," he said. "We had some kind of cheerleaders convention on the flight. No uniforms, just yak-yak-yak, the whole damned way."

"Let's walk," Bolan said, as a pair of women in their early sixties drifted closer, whispering as if they were in church, instead of standing on an open rooftop in the middle of New York.

Brognola checked out the women, then fell in step beside Bolan, slowly circling the sculpture garden, keeping to the outer edge. "Wide open spaces, here," Brognola said. "Could be a sniper's paradise."

"Somebody follow you?" Bolan asked.

"Me?" Brognola frowned and shook his head. "No way. I would've seen them. Coming in from Queens, *I* didn't know where I was half the time."

"You didn't tell the Bureau you were coming into town?"

"Nothing to do with them," Brognola said. "I'm on my own time here."

"And no one could have spotted you at JFK? They didn't have a chance to mike your car before you picked it up?"

Brognola blinked at that, then shook his head. "When did the Russian Mob start going in for tricks like that?"

"I wasn't thinking of the Russians," Bolan said.

"Okay, let's talk about this so-called spook."

Bolan produced the dead man's wallet, handed it to him and waited while his old friend studied Walter Graham's laminated ID card. "Can I keep this?" Brognola asked.

"You might as well. The owner doesn't need it anymore."

"Okay." Brognola hesitated before asking, "Do I want to know what happened to this Walter Graham?"

"He was hanging with some of Valerik's soldiers when I happened by without an invitation."

"You and Johnny, that would be."

Bolan ignored his comment. "Graham tried to badge his way out when the shooting started, but he didn't make it."

"Look, I hate to ask you, but—"

"It wasn't me. One of the Russians took him down. It may have been an accident."

"That's something, anyway."

"It doesn't make much difference," Bolan told him, "when you're stuck on the receiving end."

"It might to Langley."

"That's if somebody told them, right? Who'd want to do a thing like that?"

"It might be helpful down the road," Brognola said. "In terms of extrication from a no-win situation."

"Defeatist thinking can be dangerous. You start out backing up a step or two, next thing you know, you're running for your life."

"They never talked about retreat when you were in the Special Forces? Live to fight another day, that kind of thing?"

"It rings a bell," Bolan replied. "We were encouraged to assess all aspects of the situation first, and do our best with what we had."

"Makes sense," Brognola said. "Have you assessed the situation here?"

"I'm working on it. When you told me you were flying in, I thought you might have something I could use."

By this time, they had reached the northwest corner of the sculpture garden. There was only one small piece of statuary close at hand, no one to overhear them as they spoke. Brognola turned his broad back to the New York skyline, facing Bolan, with his face in shadow from the brim of his hat.

"I'm not exactly in the loop with CIA."

"You hear things, though. We both know that."

"You're right, I do. But what I hear on this is nothing. Are you reading me?"

"I guess you'd better spell it out," Bolan said.

"I've got eyes and ears at Langley," Brognola replied, "but only to a point. When I need information, there's a deputy director over there who's helpful when he wants to be. That's mostly when the Company runs into something it can't handle with the oversight committee breathing down its neck."

"This deputy director knows the score on Stony Man?" Bolan asked.

"No." Brognola was emphatic as he shook his head. "He understands I know some guys who know some guys. That kind of thing. If somebody asks, the only one that he could point a finger at is me."

"Okay."

"They've also been doing some hacking at the Farm, of course," Brognola said.

"Akira and the Bear?"

"Right. Between them, they can eavesdrop on the Company from time to time. We don't have constant access, though. We don't know everything the spooks are doing, and never will."

"Cut to the chase," Bolan suggested.

"I already did. My contact in the shop knows squat about any connection with the Russian Mob."

"Or he's not telling you."

"Or that," Brognola granted. "He's held out on me before, God knows. It wouldn't be the first time."

"And there's nothing in the system?"

"Nothing that we've been able to uncover in the past two days," Brognola said.

"So, what we've got is two dead spooks, in Arizona and New York, plus one ex-con still missing, out of California. On the spook side, Walter Graham had a definite connection to the Russian Mob. It got him killed. Ted Williams was expecting Russians or a contact from the Company, before he killed himself. Meanwhile, the Russians come gunning for the ex-con's sister just because she tries to track him down. Call me a head case, but that smells like a conspiracy.''

''To what end?'' Brognola asked.

''That's what I'll be trying to find out.'' When Brognola said nothing, Bolan prodded him again. ''You mentioned some kind of diplomacy that's in the works. What's that about?''

''The usual,'' Brognola said. ''I mean, a little bit of everything. You know the way it's been in Russia, since the old regime collapsed. They've got recession, runaway inflation, shortages, their crime rate's through the roof and half the former soviet republics have guerrilla armies raising hell. The Reds are trying for a comeback, and you've got a nationalist movement that makes Hitler's gang sound liberal. On top of that, you've got a large part of the former Russian arsenal for sale to anyone with cash on hand.''

''A mess, in other words.''

''That fairly sums it up. As far as the negotiations go, the State Department is talking over everything from human rights and foreign aid to mutual disarmament, deactivation of the Russian nukes—you name it. We've got people from the Bureau helping with the Russian Mob, and getting nowhere fast, as far as I can tell. The CIA had people trying to buy secrets from the what everyone refers to as the 'former KGB,' but whether it paid off, I couldn't say.''

''Put all of that together,'' Bolan said, ''and it explains the sensitivity.''

''In spades,'' Brognola readily agreed.

''And if the Company had something going with the Russian Mob, they'd want it buried deep enough that no one could uncover it, regardless of the goal they had in mind.''

Brognola frowned. ''That's one interpretation,'' he said cautiously.

''You have another one?'' Bolan asked.

''It could just as easily be something totally legit,'' he said. ''By which, I mean, cleared from the top.''

"Top-level clearance doesn't mean an operation is legitimate," Bolan replied. "Remember Air America? The shit they smuggled back from Nam wound up on the streets. I know you haven't forgotten Iran-Contra, or—"

"Top-level clearance," Brognola said, interrupting him, "means one thing only, in my book. It means that if the Man approves an operation, and he doesn't clue me in, I'm being kept out for a reason. That, in turn, tells me that if I start to sniff around too much and rock the boat, I'm jeopardizing everyone connected to the Farm, along with everything we've managed to accomplish since the operation went on-line."

"Priorities," Bolan said.

"That's the word."

"In which case, if you knew about the operation we're discussing, it would be a critical mistake for you to fill me in."

Brognola looked away from Bolan, staring off across the park. When he turned back, his jaw was set, and there was something very much like sadness in his eyes.

"I've told you what I know," he said. "If you want to assume I'm lying to you, that's your call.

"It wouldn't be my first choice," Bolan said.

Brognola chewed that over for a moment, finally nodding. "Shall I check this Walter Graham out, or not?"

"I'll be in touch to see what you find out," the Executioner replied.

"Okay. Well, Striker, if there's nothing else..."

"Can't think of anything."

"I guess there's no way I can talk you into stepping back from this, at least until we find out what the story is?"

"From where I stand," Bolan said, "pushing on would seem to be the only way we'll ever know."

"Sometimes I hate my job," Brognola said.

"I know the feeling, Hal. It doesn't mean we get to lay it down."

"Guess not. Just play it out, huh? Let the chips fall where they may?"

"Right now, that seems to be the only game in town."

"I'll see you, then."

"I'll see you," Bolan said, and they shook hands, before his old friend turned and walked away.

Bolan gave Brognola five minutes to clear the building, before he left. He made his way downstairs and out, remaining in the massive building's shadow for a moment, checking out the street, before he started to descend the stairs.

He turned right on Fifth Avenue, in the direction of the traffic flow, and made no effort to spot Johnny on patrol in the Infiniti. When he had covered maybe half a block a horn beeped twice behind him, and the sleek J30 passed him, swung into a bus stop up ahead, just long enough for Bolan to catch up and slide into the shotgun seat.

"He show?"

"Yeah," Bolan replied.

"What's the word."

"The word is that there *is* no word."

Johnny was silent for a block until they reached East 79th Street and he made a left-hand turn, cruising eastward with no destination in mind. "What's that really mean?" he asked at last.

"It could mean one of two things," Bolan said. "If everything Hal said was true, he has no access to the information that we need. He's frozen out. His contacts at the Company are either frozen out, or else they don't know squat. The techs at Stony Man can't get a line on anything by hacking into Langley, either."

"Is that even possible?"

The soldier nodded. "Sure it is," he said. "The Company has been caught with its pants down, now and then, but if they screwed up every time, they wouldn't have survived for over half a century. For every Bay of Pigs or Aldrich Ames, you should assume there have been several hundred ops that never made the papers. Keeping secrets from the FBI is second nature to the Company.''

"So, there's a chance that Hal was coming clean, is what you're saying.''

Bolan nodded grimly. "There's a chance,'' he said.

"But you don't think so, right?''

He cast a sidelong glance at Johnny. "When did you start working for the Psychic Friends?''

"I don't need crystal balls to read your mind, Mack,'' Johnny said. "This thing with Hal has got you worried, or concerned, I should have said.''

The kid was right, of course. It wasn't simply Brognola's unprecedented claim of total ignorance that was disturbing Bolan. Everyone who worked intelligence was bound to come up empty, now and then. Bolan had pumped dry wells himself, from time to time, and had to blast bedrock before the treasured secrets flowed.

There was no sin in ignorance, no guilt...unless, of course, the ignorance was willful and deliberate. In that respect, it was Brognola's attitude, his hesitance, that jangled Bolan's nerves. The big Fed may as well have worn a sandwich sign around his neck, bearing the schoolyard taunt of "I know something you don't know!''

"I am concerned,'' he told his brother finally. "The trouble is, I'm not sure why.''

"Um, let me guess on that one,'' Johnny said. "Is it because you're thinking there's a possibility Hal may have turned?''

"I don't buy that,'' Bolan replied emphatically, and hoped that it was true.

"But, if he's lying to you—''

"Holding something back,'' Bolan corrected him.

"Come on! You wouldn't let me get away with splitting hairs like that. If Hal has information that you need to stay alive and he sits on it, it's the same as lying through his teeth. Or maybe worse, because he's conned you into giving him the benefit of some unrealistic doubt.''

"You don't know Hal the way I do," Bolan replied.

"I know him well enough to hear alarm bells going off when he starts playing deaf and blind. I'm guessing he still wants us out of town?"

Bolan didn't reply, his silence passing for assent.

"So, he's not only cutting off the flow of information," Johnny said, "he's also lobbying for you to let the Russians slide on whatever they've cooked up with the Company? What's up with that? Does that sound like the Hal you know?"

It didn't, but agreeing with his brother, saying it out loud, made Bolan feel as if his world had tilted on its axis. Brognola had been a constant in his life for so long now, always supportive, even in the early days when there was little he could do aside from lending an appreciative ear. Bolan had realized that Brognola had to drop out of his life one day— either retired or dead—but he had never counted on the man from Justice pulling down a screen between them.

"Do you want to know what I'm concerned about?" his brother said into the silent void. "I can't help thinking that if Hal's already cut you off, in terms of battlefield intelligence, and if he's warned you to stand down, his next step could be more extreme."

"Meaning?" It was a wasted question. Bolan knew what Johnny meant, but he couldn't admit it to his brother, much less to himself.

"I mean that if he wants you off this operation, and you won't agree to bail, he could take steps to make you quit."

"I don't believe that," Bolan said. "Hal wouldn't run that game on either one of us."

"You want to bet your life on that?" Johnny asked.

"I already have."

Of course, it had occurred to him that Brognola might take proactive steps against his campaign in New York, but Bolan didn't want to think what that would mean, in terms of testing loyalties and drawing battle lines between his friends in Washington, or at the Farm. Would Leo Turrin side with Hal if it came down to hunting Bolan? Jack Grimaldi? Able Team? Phoenix Force?

He was appalled by what that kind of internecine war would mean for Stony Man, and likewise by the fact that it would totally derail his effort to decipher what was happening between the CIA and members of the Russian Mafia.

And that, he realized, would be the point of any hostile moves Brognola made. Was the big Fed prepared to sacrifice his brainchild, watch the program he had fought and bled for in a hundred backroom skirmishes go up in smoke, to help protect a criminal conspiracy he should have been the first to rail against?

"I just don't see that happening," he told his brother.

"Well, you need to think about it seriously," Johnny answered. "By the time you see it happening, the chances are, it will already be too late."

"I'll think about it," Bolan promised. Great. That's all he needed right now on top of everything.

"Meanwhile…" His brother left it dangling, waiting for instructions.

"Meanwhile," Bolan said, "we need more information. If we can't rely on Hal, we need to try another route."

"What did you have in mind?"

"If something big is cooking, you can bet there's more than one chef in the kitchen," Bolan answered. "That means, more than one brain we can pick. Now, all we have to do is get it right the first time, no mistakes."

"We'd need a pretty decent lead for that," Johnny observed.

"I've got one," Bolan said. "I need a telephone."

10

Bolan's connection was in the Angellela Family of the Cosa Nostra. A call came in from "Mickey Brasko" at 5:00 a.m. on Sunday morning.

"No fucking sweat," he said. "I just got in myself, Mickey. I had a busy night and all."

"I heard that," Bolan told him. "I been keeping busy, too. You maybe heard about it on the news or something."

"Heard about it?" There was sharp, appreciative laughter on the other end. "Damn right I heard about it. You got people talking, Brasko. That's a fact of life. We've had these Russian bastards nosing into everything we got for two, three years, now. Seems like nobody's got the balls to draw a line, know what I'm saying? Jesus H., it does me good to see them get their asses kicked. It does a lot of people good."

"I'm doing what I can," the Executioner replied.

"You're doing good. If there's something else you need, off the record, just ask."

"I could use one more piece of information," Bolan said.

Despite his confidence and praise, there was a note of caution in the man's voice as he replied, "I'm listening."

"I still can't put my finger on Valerik or his Number Two," Bolan explained. "There's got to be someone around who has that kind of information, right? Like a consigliere or some kind of elder statesman in their crew."

"Hang on a second. Let me think." Dead air for close to half a minute, Bolan checking out the traffic flowing past the empty parking lot of the all-night convenience store where he had found the public telephone, until his source spoke up again.

"There is this guy," the soldier said. "Nikita something— Stroganov, Stravinsky, I don't know. No, wait! Stureyev! That's the ticket."

Bolan waited while he spelled it out phonetically. "You got an address on this guy?" he asked.

"He lives out in Queens, but he won't be there, right now."

"Why's that?"

"Because it's Sunday morning. You forget your catechism? Every Sunday, rain or shine, this guy heads over to St. Nicholas to make his peace."

"East 97th Street?" Bolan asked.

"That's the only one I know about," his source replied.

"How will I know this guy?" Bolan asked.

"Easy. He's like five foot nothing, with this pile of snow-white hair. Looks like some kind of sawed-off gospel singer from TV or something. Always carries an umbrella with him everywhere he goes, no matter what the weather's like."

"Thanks a million," Bolan said. "My people won't forget it. I won't forget."

"All for one," the mobster said. "You mind my asking, are you going to clip this guy, or what?"

"I thought we'd have a little talk," Bolan said. "See the way it goes from there."

The mafioso was still laughing when Bolan cradled the receiver, walking back around the corner to the point where Johnny waited in the car, concealed from traffic passing on the street.

"So, what did he say?" his brother asked, as Bolan closed the door behind him.

"Word is," Bolan replied, "we go to church."

He briefed his brother as they were driving north along Third Avenue. It ran one-way, and while the stores were all shut down—even the ones that sold their wares on Sunday closed until the stroke of noon—there was a steady flow of traffic on the street.

How many bound for church? he wondered. In a city like New York, perversely proud of its bloody, decadent reputation, there were thousands—make that tens of thousands—who maintained their faith. How many of them truly lived their faith from day to day might be debatable. In Bolan's view, it was a minor miracle that anyone in New York City even gave a nod to any power greater than the teeming megalopolis in which they lived.

St. Nicholas Russian Orthodox Cathedral was a landmark of the Upper East Side. A Muscovite Baroque masterpiece, it boasted five onion domes surmounted by crosses, with blue-and-yellow tiles on a redbrick and white stone facade. For years, after its erection in 1902, the cathedral had been a focal point of "Moscow on the Hudson," a White Russian community that swelled with refugees from communism following the Bolshevik revolution of 1917. That community had long since dispersed, but St. Nicholas remained in many hearts, attracting new devotees over time, as perestroika and the ultimate collapse of Soviet rule.

Bolan experienced a nagging sense of déjà vu as they approached St. Nicholas, with a clear view of Central Park across Fifth Avenue. Some eighteen hours earlier and sixteen blocks away, he had been talking life and death with Hal Brognola in the middle of a rooftop garden. Now, with gray dawn filtering to Earth between the high-rise buildings flanking 97th Street, Bolan had come in search of someone else, the same agenda on his mind.

"Nowhere to park," his brother said. "Can you believe this? Not a single space."

"It's just as well," Bolan replied. "Once we make the pickup, we don't want to sit around the neighborhood."

"Okay. We're looking for a white-haired midget, right?"

"With an umbrella," Bolan said, and mimicked his Mafia contact. "Ya can't miss 'im."

"Unless he's already inside," Johnny said, checking his watch against the Infiniti's dashboard clock. "What time does the early Mass start, and how long does it last?"

Bolan shrugged. "All I know is, they tell me our boy never misses."

"There's always a first time," Johnny said. "Besides, if he's in there already, we could be circling the block for two, three hours here. Who knows how religious he is?"

"Let's give it a while," Bolan said. "If he doesn't show up, I can go in and check out the place."

"Looks like a full house, Mack. You plan to walk around with a collection plate?"

"The shylock covered that already," Bolan said. "I'll have a look and if I don't have any—What's this?"

A Lincoln Town Car passed them in the curbside lane and double-parked a half-block from St. Nicholas, blithely obstructing traffic. Bolan saw the driver step out, move around to open the back door and mutter something to a short man whose most memorable feature was a snow-white pompadour. The short man had a black umbrella tucked beneath his left arm, like a swagger stick.

"Bingo!" Johnny said, as the Lincoln pulled away. He changed lanes with the casual indifference to his fellow motorists that marked a born New Yorker, braking long enough for Bolan to step out and reach the sidewalk, then he started creeping forward, barely touching the accelerator, holding to his brother's pace.

Bolan came up behind the Russian, walked three long strides past the smaller man, then swung around to block his path. "Nikita Stureyev?" he asked.

The Russian stared at him, his head tilted back, a look of bland incomprehension on his face. He said something in Russian, a dismissive tone.

"No sale," the Executioner replied. "We need to have a

talk, and we'll be having it in English—that is, if you wish to make the later Mass alive. It's your choice, either way. A talk, or I can drop you where you stand.''

NIKITA STUREYEV HAD had a birthday coming up. In two weeks' time, he would be fifty-five years old, and who could have predicted he would live so long, with all the hardships he had faced in life? It was a miracle, for which he thanked the Lord each Sunday morning, never failing to display his gratitude with a deposit in the church collection plate.

The struggle had begun when Stureyev was barely three years old. Joseph Stalin had dispatched his father to the gulag, while Stureyev's mother and her three young children were uprooted from their small flat in St. Petersburg and moved to a collective farm outside Murmansk. The frigid winters there began in late September and hung on through April, sometimes into May, when it began to rain and turned the frozen earth to sucking mud. His father died and was presumably cremated, somewhere in Siberia, before his only son was six years old. The month Nikita Stureyev had turned eight, his namesake—Khrushchev, the ''reformer''—had rescinded some of Stalin's arbitrary punishments, at which time the Stureyev family was resettled in a Murmansk tenement. His mother worked ten hours a day on an assembly line, while her son learned to run the streets and steal.

He was in trouble frequently, ''reeducated'' twice before he cleared his teens, but his real education came from others like himself, boys who had seen their families torn apart on orders of the commissars. Stureyev hated communism with a revolutionary's zeal, but he was unencumbered by ideology, preferring to look out for number one and those he counted as his friends. They were a ruthless clique, fighting for turf, and he had killed his first man—well, a boy, in fact—when he was barely eighteen years of age. If fighting failed to do the trick, Stureyev and his cronies would collaborate with other gangs, as smugglers, pimps and thieves have done since time began.

As an adult, Stureyev had several other names, including one which, if examined, would reveal a six-year-prison term for manslaughter. More often, though, he beat the rap and prospered, eluding the dim-witted militia, sometimes selling rivals to the KGB when he ran short of drugs and other contraband to trade. Improved relations with the West had made him fabulously rich, and when the Soviet regime had finally collapsed in 1991, Stureyev knew that it was time to see the world.

He got no farther than New York, with the occasional side trip to Canada, and there put down his roots. The Russian Mafia was already established in the States, but it was long on muscle, short on brains. It needed thinkers, statesmen, who could deal with politicians, judges and police commissioners; men who could negotiate with jealous rivals spawned in Sicily, Colombia, Jamaica, Harlem, or the Golden Triangle. Stureyev fit the bill, and he had served his brotherhood with undeniable distinction, reaping the commensurate rewards. Semiretired today, he left the wet work to a younger generation, men who still took pleasure in the stalk and kill. Stureyev, for his part, would rather sit down over coffee or a glass of vodka and negotiate a treaty than unleash the dogs of war.

And every Sunday, without fail, he went to early Mass.

Stureyev felt the stranger coming up behind him, but he paid no real attention, since it was a public street. Then the tall man reversed direction suddenly and blocked his path, speaking his name. Stureyev answered him with an obscenity in Russian, testing him, in hopes of finding out how critical his situation really was.

"Where would we have this talk?" Stureyev asked.

The tall man nodded toward a car that idled in the curbside lane and said, "Let's take a ride."

"If you're police—"

"We're not."

Stureyev shrugged. "A ride, then."

He was reaching up for the umbrella, tucked beneath his left arm, when the stranger deftly took it from him and informed him, "You won't need that in the car."

So, he wasn't a fool. That could be good or bad, depending on what he wanted from Stureyev in return for letting him survive.

When they were settled in the back seat of the car, the stranger spent a moment studying the black umbrella. When he found the trick, a subtle pressure on the handle instantly released a three-inch spike concealed within the ferrule. It was stainless steel, but two-thirds of the needle's length was amber-colored.

"Ricin?" the stranger asked.

"You study history."

"I keep my hand in." Leaning toward the driver, holding the toxic shaft well away from his face, the tall man said, "Your basic Ricin cocktail is an extract from the castor-oil plant. Supposedly, it's twice the strength of cobra venom. KGB used these trick umbrellas to kill a couple of Bulgarian defectors in London and Paris, back around '78."

And many more, besides, Stureyev thought, but kept it to himself.

"You won't mind if I pat you down," the tall man said, his statement punctuated by a shift of the umbrella's deadly spike in the direction of the Russian's face.

"Go ahead."

The frisk was swift, painless, professional. Stureyev's only weapon, in addition to the Ricin-tipped umbrella, was a two-inch penknife that he sometimes used to clean his fingernails. It struck him as a sacrilege to carry guns in church, although that hadn't stopped him shooting down two men outside St. Vladimir's in Moscow, years ago. What good were scruples, after all, if they were totally inflexible?

When the American was finished searching him, and the

umbrella had been laid aside, Stureyev said, "May I ask what you wish to talk about?"

"Tolya Valerik," the tall man replied. "We've got business to discuss with him, but he's a hard man to pin down."

There seemed to be no point in feigning ignorance. "Tell me your business," Stureyev suggested. "When you let me go, I leave a message for Valerik, and he will call me back."

"I'd like to," the stranger said, smiling, "but if you'll forgive my saying so, there's just an outside chance you might decide to warn him. We've trailed him all the way from California, as it is, and I don't want to make this a career."

"Alas," the Russian said, and offered them an old man's shrug, "if Tolya doesn't wish to see or speak with you, I'm powerless to help."

"We don't require your intercession," his abductor stated. "An address ought to do the trick."

"Tolya Valerik is a man of many addresses," Stureyev said. "His best friends often don't know where to find him on a given day, and I am hardly that."

"You keep in touch, though."

"We converse from time to time, of course. Most often, he calls me when he needs my advice."

"Most often, but not always, eh?"

"I've told you, I can only leave messages."

"How about that contact number, then?" the stranger said.

"I don't have it memorized," the Russian told him, stalling. "If you take me to my home—"

"We don't have time to mess around in Queens," the driver said, speaking for the first time since Stureyev had entered the car. It troubled him that they knew where he lived, more so that they wouldn't fall for his trick and take him to the house where he had armed retainers, weapons hidden all about.

Stureyev realized that he was well and truly on his own.

"You want to take him to the place?" the driver asked his friend in the back seat.

This was the point where they expected him to quail and wet himself, but they had made a critical mistake. Nikita Stureyev had suffered through interrogations in his time, and he had never broken once. It was a point of pride. If he had managed to survive the Soviet militia and the KGB, what could these two limp-wristed Yankees show him that he hadn't seen before?

Still, he considered, there might be a way to spare himself unnecessary pain if he could reason with his captors, make them understand the foolish risk that they were taking. Nothing that they said or did from this point on would save their lives—it was too late for that, the moment they had stopped him on the street outside St. Nicholas—but if Stureyev could persuade them to be reasonable, he might extricate himself with promises he never meant to keep. There would be time to hunt these bastards down and kill them later.

First, he had to find out who they were and what they wanted from Valerik. The attacks that had occurred on Saturday gave him a fair idea of *what,* and yet, the *who* eluded him.

"Perhaps, if I knew something of your purpose," said the Russian, "who it is you represent, it might be possible for me to help you in some way."

The man seated beside him seemed to think about it, shifting in his seat to face Stureyev as he said, "Tolya's been doing business with the company we represent. We've had some problems with his job performance lately, and we need to speak to him about it."

"If he is working with you," Stureyev replied, "then surely you must have a contact number, some means whereby you may get in touch with him."

"We did," the tall man said without missing a beat. "It's funny, though. These days, when we leave messages, he doesn't call us back. It's making certain people nervous, if you get my drift, and now there's this war that's blown up out of nowhere. It's disturbing. Worse, it's bad for business. We've been told to sort it out before somebody gets it in his head to sort out Valerik. That's who we are, and what we need."

Nikita Stureyev considered what he had been told. A master of deception in his own right, he had no good reason to believe the tall man's words, but certain parts of what the stranger said rang true. His reference to a ''company,'' for instance, echoed what Stureyev had been able to discover for himself about Tolya Valerik's latest, greatest business venture. The suggestion of retaliation by that ''company,'' if its commanders thought Valerik had betrayed them, wouldn't be an idle threat. They could attack the Family in any one of several ways, ranging from prosecution to a shooting war.

And speaking of the recent violence in New York City, what if Stureyev's abductors were exactly who they claimed to be? What if their ''company'' wasn't involved in the attacks, but could assist Valerik in repelling them? For all he knew, Valerik might have broken contact with his silent partners in the false belief that they had turned against him, were responsible for the attacks. In that case, it would be no favor—rather, a disservice—for Stureyev to erect more obstacles between Valerik and his allies.

"So," the tall man prodded him, "what do you say?"

The question tipped him over, instantly reminding Stureyev of other times he had been questioned, threatened, pressured to reveal some cherished secret. Logic could be treacherous in such a situation. He preferred to trust his instincts.

"I am sorry," he replied. "Aside from passing on a message, there is no way I can help you."

"That's your call," the stranger said. And told their driver, "Take him to the place."

THE PLACE had been some kind of factory, uncounted years ago, before it had been left to rot. It fronted the East River, facing Queens across a sluggish flow of dark, polluted water, tucked away beneath the vaulting elevated highway, east of the Manhattan Bridge. Urban renewal had ignored this eyesore, featuring its own rough pier that jutted out some fifty feet above the river's murky current. Teenagers partied here sometimes, but there were none in residence as the Bolan brothers led the Russian hostage from their car and convoyed him inside.

The one-time factory had been easy to rent, once Bolan had figured out the address, made some calls. The price was New York steep, despite the property's deplorable condition, but they paid the tab with cash donated by the Russian Mafia. Eight grand got them a set of keys and thirty days to use the dump in any way they chose. If they went nuts and blew it up, the owner's insurance would cover it, and he would have a vacant lot that might prove easier to move. No sweat.

Inside the crumbling hulk, Bolan led their captive to the portion of the factory that overhung the river. Johnny hung back, took his time, uncomfortable with the second act of their unfolding drama. He had hoped Stureyev would come up with something in the car, and they could drop him off somewhere. It had been understood they wouldn't drop him off alive, since he would obviously tip off Valerik before they had a chance to strike, but his brother would make it easy on him, quick and clean.

The factory had been a fallback option, Johnny hoping they would never have to use it, that the eight grand would be wasted money. Stureyev had refused to buckle, though, and they still needed information on Valerik's whereabouts. If it required persuasion, they would play the game his way.

But Johnny didn't have to like it, not even a little bit.

There was a six-by-eight-foot trapdoor cut into the floor, out on the pier, where crates of who knew what had once been winched up from the river, out of barges moored below. The steel hatch had been sold for scrap, leaving an open portal that admitted rancid odors, rats and birds of all varieties. Human intruders looked for other ways to penetrate the place, but some of those who found their way inside had obviously liked the river view. The concrete floor around the trap was blackened by their campfires, littered with their beer cans, broken bottles, fast-food wrappers, condoms, cast-off underwear.

It was a squalid place in which to die.

The present furnishings, if such they could be called, consisted of a single straight-backed wooden chair, positioned near the river trap. Beside the chair had been arranged a corrugated metal washtub and a smaller bucket, a cheap shovel and a bag of ready-mix cement. A coil of nylon clothesline lay inside the washtub like a scrawny, lifeless snake.

"Sit down," Bolan said, and Johnny watched their captive settle in the only chair available. The Russian made no protest as his hands were bound behind him, clothesline looped around his chest and waist, tied off behind to keep him in the chair.

"Is this how you would kill me, then?" he asked, when Bolan had finished binding him.

Instead of answering, the Executioner took the long remainder of the clothesline—ten or fifteen feet, at least, after he cut it free—and tied one end securely to the handle of the plastic bucket. After he had wrapped the free end twice around one hand, he dropped the bucket through the open trap and out of sight. There was a muffled splash below, and when hauled the bucket up a moment later, it was filled with smelly river water, sloshing some across the rim.

"Not clean," Bolan said, to no one in particular, "but it should do."

The water went into the washtub, Bolan repeating his exercise until the tub was roughly one-third full. It seemed to satisfy him, for he put the bucket down and dragged the tub around in front of Stureyev.

"Shoes on or off?" he asked the Russian. "You decide."

Stureyev frowned and said, "These are expensive shoes."

"You want to donate them to charity?"

The Russian stiffened. "Leave them on," he answered.

"Fine." Bolan looped one arm around Stureyev's calves and raised his feet, just long enough to pull the washtub closer. This time, when the Russian's feet touched down, they were inside the tub, with water ankle deep.

"I've seen this in your gangster movie *Billy Bathgate*," Stureyev remarked, attempting to sound casual.

"Think of it as a living piece of history," Bolan said. "Well, maybe *living*'s not the best word to describe it. Anyway, you've got a ringside seat."

As Bolan was speaking, he produced a folding knife and slid the bag of ready-mix across the top. Hoisting the sack, he poured a measure of cement into the tub, then took the shovel and began to stir it, globules reminiscent of volcanic mud staining the Russian's tailored slacks.

"This is the point, I think," Stureyev said, "when you begin to ask more questions."

"Nope," was all Bolan said.

"What is this 'nope'?" the Russian asked.

"No questions," Bolan replied. "We did that number in the car, remember? You don't want to talk, nobody's forcing you. I never cared for torture, if you want to know the truth."

Stureyev clearly wasn't sure what he should make of that. He watched the shovel churn around his feet for several moments, the cement already thickening, like batter for some ghastly cake. "If I may ask you, then," he said at last, "what is the purpose of this exercise?"

Bolan flashed a crooked grin at Johnny. "Jeez, I thought we had a live one here. Turns out he's just a dummy after all." Addressing Stureyev, he said, "It's called a murder, Comrade. You go in the water, and you don't come out. I thought you saw the movie?"

Stureyev seemed to click with understanding now. "But I have information," he told Bolan. "It could prove useful."

"Keep it," the Executioner replied. "I told you, I don't go for torture."

"If I gave the information freely—"

"You'd feel terrible about yourself," Bolan cut him off. "Trust me on this. You'll sleep much better if you keep the faith and take those secrets with you."

Turning to Johnny he said, "Do you think I need more water, here?"

"It looks all right to me," Johnny replied.

"Okay. Your feet may get a little warm in there once it begins to set," he told the Russian, "but the shoes and socks should help. Look at it this way, in a little while you're going for a nice, cool swim."

"This seems a wasted effort," said the Russian, trying to sound calm, collected.

"Have you read your Melville?"

"Melville?" Stureyev appeared confused. "Who is—"

"Call me Fish meal. Get it?" When the Russian simply gaped at him, Bolan shook his head and said, "I didn't think so."

The cement resembled thick, stale porridge now, still far from dry, but getting there. Stureyev shifted in his seat, experimentally, but there was nothing he could do to extricate his feet, bound as he was. What would have been the point, in any case, with his captors standing there?

"All right!" the Russian said. "I tell you what you want to know."

"I can't ask you to compromise your principles," Bolan told him, stepping back, turning away from the pathetic creature in the chair.

"You want to kill me?" Stureyev demanded. "Kill me, then. It makes no difference. You cannot prevent the coming of the new world order that has been arranged...without my help, at least."

"You pick that up from CNN?" Bolan asked, disinterested. "The 'new world order' has been on its way for what?

Ten years? Nobody's seen it yet. I don't intend to hold my breath…but you might try it, when you hit the drink.''

"Tolya Valerik! I can tell you where he is!'' The Russian started blurting out addresses, Johnny wishing that he had a tape recorder, hoping that he could remember half of them.

"I need to ask about a man in California,'' Johnny blurted out, interrupting.

"I don't know anyone in California,'' Stureyev replied.

"His name was Billy King. I think Valerik had him killed.''

Stureyev shrugged, within the limits of his bonds. "He has so many killed, who knows them all? Details, young man. You must forget about details and see the larger picture.''

"What about the Company?''

At that, the Russian smiled. "Tolya is known, I grant you, by the company he keeps.''

Impasse.

Bolan turned to face them both and asked his brother, "Could you go and get my smokes out of the car?''

It had been years since Bolan quit smoking cigarettes, and Johnny understood that he was being sent to wait outside. Instead of arguing the point they had already settled in advance, he simply answered, "Sure,'' and left Stureyev sitting with his feet in cold, gray porridge, Bolan standing beside him, the Beretta showing where his jacket gapped.

Outside, although he knew he wouldn't hear the shot, Johnny got in the car and surfed the radio until he found a station playing good, hard rock and roll. He switched it off when his brother appeared, moving across the parking lot, and climbed into the shotgun seat.

There was no point in mentioning Stureyev. He was history. His death was simple housekeeping, but Johnny wondered how his brother bore the weight of it sometimes.

11

"You're telling me," Tolya Valerik said, "that someone actually saw them take him off the street?"

"Outside St. Nicholas," Anatoly Bogdashka replied.

"And they did nothing? Said nothing to anyone, for all this time?"

"They were old women, Tolya, on their way to church. What do they know? A tall man in a suit invites another well-dressed man into his car. There was no violence, no display of weapons, no outcry for help. The people in this country, they don't recognize a kidnapping unless you have someone throwing a small child in a beat-up van."

"Four hours ago," Valerik said disgustedly.

"At least."

"There has been no demand for ransom."

It wasn't a question, but Bogdashka felt obliged to answer, anyway. "Nothing at all," he said.

"They've killed him, then."

"Unless they're grunting him, somewhere."

The term was Russian slang for torture, often used by KGB interrogators at the Lubyanka, in the bad old days. Depending on your source, "grunting" derived its name either from sounds emitted by the victims of interrogation, or the noises of exertion made by men who beat them until their mothers wouldn't recognize them in their coffins, afterward. It hardly mattered, either way; the end result was all the same.

"Nikita wouldn't talk," Valerik said.

"Who knows?" His chief lieutenant shrugged. "No man is made of iron. With drugs and electricity…"

Bogdashka didn't have to finish. They had both participated in interrogations. Both men had been grunted; they had grunted others, in return.

"What does he know?" Valerik asked.

Bogdashka frowned. "With all respect, Tolya, I should be asking you. Nikita only speaks to me in passing, like a butler. I am sent to fetch the vodka, while you talk about your plans."

It wasn't a criticism, not exactly, but Valerik heard Bogdashka distancing himself from what might follow Stureyev's abduction. He was on the record, now. Whatever facts the kidnappers extracted from Stureyev, Bogdashka wouldn't be the source, and he couldn't be held responsible. It rankled Valerik, but he couldn't quarrel with his aide's survival instinct. Bogdashka was the sort who seldom fell, or if he did, always landed on his feet.

"Let us assess potential damage, then," Valerik said. "Nikita has advised us on our East Coast operations for the past five years. He knows about the heroin, cocaine, the guns— most everything, in fact. If he had any questions, there are ways of learning more without confronting anyone inside the Family."

"That makes him dangerous," said Bogdashka. "What of Krestyanov and the Americans?"

Valerik felt a hard scowl tugging at the corners of his mouth. "No names," he said. "I didn't offer details, and Nikita didn't ask."

"Some of it," the second-in-command said, "he would be wise enough to work out on his own, if he had access to a newspaper or television set. As for the rest…he knows the outlines of the plan?"

"Vague outlines," Valerik said. "There was no reason to concern him with the details. I consulted with him on the viability of Krestyanov's design, of course, before I would commit the Family. He was one of our elders, after all.''

"Of course." There was no hint of condemnation in Bogdashka's tone. He had a Russian's skill for being noncommittal, riling no one, drawing minimal attention to himself in crisis situations.

"What efforts have been made to find Nikita?"

Bogdashka spread his open hands, a helpless gesture. "We're looking for a car that may be silver, gray or blue. The model is unknown. Old women aren't the most reliable of witnesses, you understand. They didn't see the driver, but the man who led Nikita to the car was white, six feet or better, neither fat nor thin.''

"You're telling me it's hopeless?"

"If we don't receive some offer to exchange or ransom him, I think it must be.''

"Four hours. If a call was coming, we'd have gotten it by now. I don't care if the bastards drove him to Connecticut or Pennsylvania, they would certainly have been in touch.''

"Agreed.''

"He's dead then," Valerik stated. "Or he will be, soon.''

"Let's hope he is," Bogdashka said. "Let's hope he died without revealing anything about our business.''

"There's a possibility he may have been abducted for some other reason," Valerik said. "Something personal, perhaps. The old man had his share of enemies, you know.''

"It's barely possible," Valerik's chief lieutenant said. "Or would be, if the incident were taken by itself. Combined with the attacks we suffered yesterday, Tolya, I must with all respect say that I see no likelihood of a coincidence.''

Valerik recognized the truth when Bogdashka rubbed his nose in it. Sometimes, that was a chief lieutenant's job, however hazardous it proved to be. He nodded wearily and reached out for his vodka glass. So early to be drinking, but he needed something for his nerves.

"You think it may be the Americans?" he asked his Number Two.

"If you mean Pruett, I think not," Bogdashka said. "What would he have to gain? The only secret he could hope to learn from Stureyev would be if you had some plan to deceive him, and the old man might not be aware of that. He would be better off abducting me."

Valerik nodded. There was simply no escaping it. "It all goes back to California and that bastard Williams, then," he said.

"You think the convict's sister is responsible for all of this?"

"Not by herself," Valerik said. "She hired one man to help her, and the two of them were able to elude our soldiers. Why not hire another, even several more?"

"Such men demand high prices," Bogdashka said. "She's not a wealthy woman. When we checked her bank account—"

"I don't mean contract killers," Valerik interrupted him impatiently.

"Who, then?"

"Someone who would be pleased to see us fail, perhaps. Someone who would be pleased to see our allies fail."

"For that to be the case," Bogdashka said, "these hypothetical opponents first would have to know we were involved, then trace our link to Pruett, even back to Krestyanov."

"They found Ted Williams, don't forget," Valerik said.

"And Williams killed himself."

"But did the bastard do it soon enough? How much did he reveal before his nerve failed and he ate the cyanide?"

"Kropotkin said—"

"There were no signs of violence on the body," Valerik finished for him. "Nothing but the poison in his blood. I know."

"Well, then?"

"He must have told them something." It was all Valerik could do to keep from shouting at his friend and aide. "How else would anyone connect our operations in Los Angeles to Williams? Why else would a gunman speak his name to Constantin Stolichkin, at the Lubyanka? Why repeat it yesterday, to Koba, when he looted the cigar shop?"

"You think it is the same man in Los Angeles, and in New York?"

Valerik nearly lost it, then. "I don't care if it was the same man, Anatoly! Are you so blind that you don't see we are in worse trouble if it's different soldiers taking down our people, asking the same questions in New York and in Los Angeles?"

If Bogdashka was insulted by the outburst, he concealed it well, assisted by experience. "I understand you, Tolya. But it can't be Pruett,"

"Of course, it can't be Pruett! Pruett knew about Ted Williams. Williams worked for Pruett, Anatoly. Think, man! Think!"

"All right," Bogdashka said, still calm, apparently unruffled by the outburst. "Not mercenary killers, then, but still professionals. Soldiers prepared to risk their lives...for what?"

"We don't know yet," Valerik said, "and that's the key. If they want us, that's one thing, possibly another Family."

"Stolichkin swears the man who questioned him was an American. Koba agrees."

"Someone who has it in for Pruett, then. Or, else..."

Bogdashka saw it, then, blinked rapidly before he spoke. "Someone who has it in for Krestyanov?"

"At this point," Valerik said, "we can't rule out anything."

"Someone from home, then," Bogdashka said quietly, as if talking to himself. "But Koba and Stolichkin said they were Americans. A mercenary, after all?"

"Or someone from American intelligence," Valerik suggested. "Pruett also has his secrets and his adversaries, yes?"

"We need to find the convict's sister," Bogdashka said. "But where to start?"

"You still have people searching in Los Angeles?"

"And Arizona. Yes."

"Search here, as well," Valerik ordered. "If we find her, maybe she can tell us something. If we don't, at least we're doing something more than looking for a car of unknown make and color."

"I'll give the order now." He was already on his feet and moving toward the door.

"I'll speak to Krestyanov, meanwhile," Valerik said, "and see if he's heard anything that might be useful."

"I hope it isn't Krestyanov."

"I share your hope. But if it is…"

"What, Tolya?"

"We will do what must be done."

Tolya Valerik drained his vodka after Bogdashka left the room. He could have used another, several more, but it would be the wildest foolishness to fill his belly up with alcohol before he made the dreaded phone call. He would need his wits about him, unimpaired, to deal with Krestyanov.

The man was like a viper, one of those from Africa, whose polished scales made it attractive, while its sluggish attitude encouraged carelessness. A fool would marvel that it was a pretty, placid specimen, and lean in for a closer look, before the viper struck and buried inch-long fangs into his jugular, pumping sufficient venom to dispatch an ox.

Whoever underestimated Krestyanov was doomed to take a screwing, at the very least. More often, he or she would simply wind up dead.

It never crossed Tolya Valerik's mind that Krestyanov himself would shift allegiance and betray them. That was madness. Krestyanov would sooner eat his own young than to subvert the plan which he, himself, had helped devise.

Unfortunately, there were other men like Krestyanov in Russia—and, presumably, in the United States, as well—who didn't share his vision or his goals. Such men would try to stop him, if they knew what he was doing.

"A goddamned war," Valerik told the empty room. "That's what it comes down to."

Disgusted with the turn events had taken, he stretched out a hand across his desk to reach the telephone.

"STUREYEV GAVE ME three addresses for Valerik," Bolan said. "One of them is an Upper Midtown office on East 52nd Street. I'd be surprised to find him there at all, with what's been going on, but if he was, we're talking weekday, nine to five. That means we waste two days, dead time, and put a few hundred civilians in the cross fire."

"Skip the office," Johnny said. Suzanne, seated beside him on the bed, said nothing.

"The remaining addresses are residential," Bolan said. "The first one's Upper West Side, off Columbus Circle on East 58th. A penthouse condominium."

"I think they call them co-ops in New York," Suzanne corrected him.

"Whatever. Number three is on Long Island, north of Calverton, in Suffolk County. Our boy's got twenty, thirty acres fronting on Long Island Sound."

"Sounds like the place I'd go to hide," Johnny remarked.

"Unless he thought he'd have a better chance in town," Bolan said, "with the crowds and cops around him. One thing's definite—"

"We have to get it right the first time," Johnny finished for him. "If we screw up, and he knows we've got his homesteads plotted, he'll be gone before we have a second chance."

"What's the call?" Bolan asked.

"I still say Long Island," Johnny told him. "If Valerik hides in town, he gives up too much combat stretch. Whatever edge he gets from having cops around is more than countered by the hassle when they roll out on a shooting call and want to check his troops for gun permits. The co-op puts him in a high rise where he has to trust the elevator or the stairs, and any dimwit with an attitude can block his limo at the curb just when he needs to split."

It all made perfect sense, and Bolan knew they had to make a choice before the sun went down. "Long Island, then," he said. "Let's talk about our method of approach."

"It's either land or water," Johnny said, "unless you want to split the difference."

"Wait a second, here." The strain was audible in Suzanne's voice. "Where do the Feds and the police come into this?"

"We play our cards right," Bolan said, "they're on the cleanup crew."

"But shouldn't we—"

"Do what?" he interrupted her. "Call up the FBI and tell them everything we know about Valerik? Everything we have good reason to suspect? If they don't know the man already, they've been sleeping on the job. They can't use anything we have without an explanation of the source and circumstances anyway—and that lands *us* in jail."

"But what about the CIA connection?"

"What about it?" Johnny asked. "We've got two passing mentions of the Company from people who are either dead or missing—no specifics on the Russian link in either case—and we've got one dead spook, who may have been consorting with the Russians in his leisure time."

"Assuming he was ever there at all," Bolan amended.

"What?" There was a trace of anger mixed in with Suzanne's confusion. "What do you mean by that?"

"We don't know that he ever made it to the morgue," the Executioner explained. "It wouldn't be the first time that a body disappeared in New York City."

"But you had his wallet with the ID card. I saw it!"

"And it's gone," he said. "I gave it to a friend from Washington. I'm hoping that he'll check it out and tell us something new."

"You're *hoping* that he'll check it out? You can't be sure?"

The fact was that he couldn't. Nothing about Hal Brognola could be treated as a certainty, from that point on. He didn't voice those doubts, because it would have served no purpose at the moment and because he reckoned it would make the slow, dull throb behind his eyes more painful than it already was.

Johnny came to his rescue, tearing grim eyes away from his brother and shifting his gaze to Suzanne. "The ID wouldn't help us, Sue," he said. "If one of us delivered it by hand, he'd be arrested on the spot for murder. If we mail it to the cops or FBI, they'd match it to a body—if there is a body—and they'd hit the same stone wall at Langley."

"Are you telling me the CIA's above the law?" she challenged both of them.

"In theory," Johnny said, "the Company is held accountable for breaking laws, just like the other agencies of government. More so, in fact, since there are special oversight committees in the Congress to prevent abuse of power."

"So?"

"So, like I said, that's all in theory. Ninety-five percent of all the agencies in government are breaking laws, right now. Ironically, the more involved they are with law enforcement or intelligence, the more laws they ignore or circumvent. You hear about policemen getting busted every day, on everything from petty bribes to homicide, but what about the Feds? When was the last time that you heard about a G-man going down?"

Bolan stepped in for Johnny. "It's illegal for the CIA to operate inside the country, period, no matter who they're working with. It's been illegal since the Company was organized, but the only spooks who've ever been arrested in the States were those who doubled, spying for the Russians or some other foreign power.''

''You've seen how these scandals run,'' Johnny said. ''Someone in the media starts picking at it, then the rest of them wade in. A few weeks later, if the story has good legs, somebody on the Hill may call for a committee to investigate. That drags on for another year or so, while all the secretaries, undersecretaries, and their secretaries lie their asses off, and in the end, you get a fifteen-second bite on CNN, together with a fat report nobody reads. The good news is, it's printed on recycled paper, so they're helping the environment.''

''So, they're untouchable,'' she said. ''That's what you're telling me.''

''Not even close,'' Bolan replied.

''They're hard to reach through channels,'' Johnny said, ''but there are shortcuts.''

''More killing?''

Bolan turned from his inspection of their weapons, facing Suzanne squarely. ''You've been marked,'' he said. ''The Russian Mob has tried to kill you once, already. They know who you are, and they apparently have no great difficulty finding you. These aren't the kind of people who forget about a plan to kill someone because they miss the first time out. Aside from the original contract, you also owe them soldiers.''

''I can explain all that to the police,'' she said.

''All by yourself? Without involving Johnny?''

''He's—''

''A murderer,'' Bolan said, cutting to the heart of it. ''The soldiers that first night in Arizona would be self-defense, except a jury may not understand exactly why you ran away. As for the rest of it, since then…well, you could maybe turn state's evidence and plead as an accessory, but Johnny's screwed.''

''And you,'' Suzanne reminded him.

''And me.''

No mention of the fact that he would never stand for an arrest. The Executioner had had his day in court, before he "died," and there was no way to reprise that scene. Besides, he had no reason to believe Suzanne would go to the authorities. He was manipulating her, without apologies, and while she seemed to understand that, on some level, it was working, all the same.

"Hey, Mike."

Bolan ignored his brother, pushing it. "Of course, the real threat isn't the indictment," he informed Suzanne. "I mean, it's not like either one of you would ever go to trial. The Russian Mafia has friends in every lockup from Kiev to California. Protective custody may hold you for a while, but they won't keep you in the hole forever."

"So," she said, "there's no choice."

"We were talking land or water," Bolan continued, as if Suzanne had never interrupted them."

"Or split the difference," Johnny said. "I like the sound of that, myself, if we can get our hands on something seaworthy."

"It shouldn't be a problem. We've got money."

"Um—"

"Not yours," his brother told Suzanne, flashing a smile. "We hit the lottery."

"I'm guessing I don't want to know."

"Okay, then," Bolan said. "You want the water?"

"Might as well," his brother said. "Seems like a shame, letting that amphib training go to waste."

"It wouldn't hurt us if we had a better map," Bolan said. "And a look around the neighborhood, ASAP."

"Suits me," Johnny replied. "We can head out there now."

"Or I can do the recon on my own," he stated. He caught the glance from Johnny. "Just a look around and back. The drive out to the island should take longer than the scouting. I can see about the boat while I'm out there."

"You wouldn't try to ditch a fella, would you?" Johnny asked him.

"Not this time," Bolan answered honestly, although he had, in fact, considered it.

The play was shaping up to be a two-man party, at the very least. Come nightfall, Bolan had a hunch that he would need his brother's help, and then some, just to stay alive.

"ALONE AT LAST," Suzanne said in that smart-ass way of hers that Johnny heard her use most frequently to cover tension.

"Yes, indeed."

As usual, he had escorted Suzanne to her separate room. Next door, a cardboard Please Do Not Disturb sign dangled from the doorknob, just in case a maid should wander by and start to poke her head in, trying to remember whether she had cleaned the room or not. No one beside the three of them had any need to see the weapons laid out on the bedspread.

"All those guns," Suzanne remarked, as if reading his mind.

"They come in handy, now and then."

"For what it's worth, I don't agree with what your friend said earlier."

"About...?"

"That you're a murderer," she said, grimacing as she spoke the word as if it had a sour taste.

"He's right, though," Johnny said. "Just ask NYPD."

"I won't be asking the police," she told him, stepping closer, "and I don't care what it says in some law book. A murder is malicious, something done for greed or spite, maybe revenge."

"And how would you define what I've been doing for the past three days?" he asked.

"I'd say that you were helping me to find my brother and to stay alive."

She was close enough now, that her firm breasts grazed Johnny's chest, a contact both ephemeral and maddening.

"About your brother, Sue…"

"I know." Her eyes were brimming as she spoke. "He's gone. I think I've known it since L.A., maybe since Tucson. He'd have been in touch by now, unless they had him chained up in a dungeon, somewhere. And let's face it, Billy wasn't that important, even when—"

"He was to you."

"I wonder, sometimes. I've been covering his action since the two of us were kids. You know, he never had an older brother to protect him when he got in trouble, and our parents…well…I've told you most of this before."

"No sweat." He didn't want her to stop talking, didn't want her to step back away from him.

"That's where you're wrong," she said.

Another half step closer brought her flush against him. Johnny didn't want to retreat from the warm, insistent pressure of her body. Her hands were on his hips, thumbs hooked inside his belt loops, resting lightly there. It should have been impossible to feel the fierce heat of her touch through several layers of clothing.

"Sue—"

"I'm sweating, Johnny. Feel me?"

"Maybe we should—"

"What?"

He had forgotten how to speak, and it was just as well, because she rose on tiptoe, covering his lips with hers. Again, he felt the sweet invasion of her tongue, teasing his own. She whimpered into Johnny's open mouth, and he could feel the echo of it in his pulse.

His two hands met behind her, fingers lightly tracing Suzanne's spine. No bra. That small discovery produced an instant surge in Johnny's groin, and Suzanne felt it, moving to accommodate him. Johnny closed his arms and clutched her tight against him, trailing kisses from her mouth, across her cheek, down to the pulsing, velvet hollow of her throat.

"There are no guns on my bed," she whispered, reaching down between them, finding him with supple fingers.

"Jesus!"

"You don't have to pray for anything," she said. "It's yours. All yours."

HE CAME OUT on the other side of it an aeon later, lying tangled with Suzanne on bedding snarled by passion. Her eyes were nearly closed; she wore a sleepy smile.

"Be careful, will you?"

"It's a little late."

"Tonight," she said. The smile was gone. "Be careful when you go out tonight."

"I will," he said, but he couldn't bring himself to ask why she was crying.

12

"No word from the city."

It was a pointless comment, wasted breath. Tolya Valerik knew that even as he spoke. There had been no calls from Manhattan since they'd settled into the Long Island house six hours earlier. There would be none, unless there was some new assault upon his soldiers or his property.

"No word," Bogdashka said, automatically agreeing with his boss.

The silence gnawed at Valerik's nerves. He wanted no more trouble, craved no further losses, but it troubled him that all the violence could simply stop, as if someone had pulled a plug and brought the lethal, nameless mechanism to a screeching halt.

The worst of it, he realized, was still not knowing who had done this to him, who had sent him into hiding while his soldiers—his surviving soldiers—roamed Manhattan's streets looking for answers, seeking human prey. There would be no rest, no relief from his frustration and his rage, until Valerik had identified his enemies. No peace for him, until he waded in their blood.

If they could simply strike and fade away without a trace, Valerik knew, then he was powerless to stop them from returning, wreaking havoc with his stateside empire any time they wanted to. He may as well have been some peasant, living at the sufferance of a feudal warlord. What were guns and money for, if not to crush a rich man's enemies?

"You've spoken to the men?" It was another wasted question, but he had to ask. The silence made him thirst for a quart of vodka, and Valerik knew that he could ill afford to fall down in a drunken stupor now, when unknown enemies might well be stalking him.

"The men are in position," Bogdashka said. "Six-hour shifts. I took the liberty of offering a bonus for first blood."

"How much?" It was a good idea, but Valerik didn't want his soldiers pumping bullets into shadows, worrying his wealthy neighbors over nothing.

"A thousand dollars."

Valerik nodded. It was just enough to make the game more interesting, not high enough for any veteran shooters to be giddy at the thought of the reward. And there were only veterans on the property tonight, as per his special order. No one who would hesitate to kill, but no one with an itchy trigger finger, either. Each man chosen for the guard detail had proved himself in action; most of them bore scars that testified to their successful grappling with death.

"How long will we be staying here?" Bogdashka asked. He carefully avoided any reference to *hiding,* made it sound as if their visit to Long Island was an overdue vacation.

"I'm not sure."

The hiding had been Krestyanov's idea. Valerik, for his part, had wanted to remain in New York City, use himself as bait to lure the bastards out put them in his sights, but Krestyanov had vetoed the idea. A diplomat of sorts, he made it sound as if it was for Valerik's good, explaining that they couldn't well afford to lose him at so critical a time, his leadership was too important to the cause, but that was horse manure.

Krestyanov always thought about himself first. It was a trait Valerik recognized on sight, because he shared it with the older man. Krestyanov worried that if Valerik had remained in New York, either one of two things might occur. He could be killed by those who hunted him, perhaps with

Bogdashka, and the operation would be stalled—perhaps derailed entirely—while his various lieutenants fought among themselves to fill the power vacuum. Or Valerik might destroy his faceless enemies, but draw so much attention to himself while doing so that he would then become a walking liability.

In which case, Valerik thought, Krestyanov would take steps to see that he didn't keep walking very long.

This way was best, he told himself, and tried to count the reasons why it should be true. He had removed himself from harm's way and in the process showed himself amenable to the suggestions of his allies. A cooperative spirit earned him "points" with the Americans, and would postpone the grim, inevitable day when Krestyanov began to view him as expendable.

The last thing Valerik needed at the moment was a two-front war, against his unknown stalkers *and* Vassily Krestyanov.

Valerik focused on the night ahead in an attempt to calm himself. With any luck, his faceless enemies would linger in Manhattan, mount some new attack against his property and thereby run afoul of his soldiers or, perhaps, the small army of lawmen that was hunting them by now. He would prefer it if his own men did the honors, silenced his tormentors without giving them a chance to talk in jail or in a courtroom, but he would accept whatever swift solution was available.

"I need a drink," Bogdashka said, already on his feet and moving toward the wet bar. "Anything for you, Tolya?"

He shouldn't, Valerik thought, and as quickly asked himself why not? He was supposed to be in hiding, lying low, while others took care of his problems in New York. It was a kind of unwelcome vacation, when he looked at it that way, and who went on vacation without soaking up the alcohol?

"Vodka," he said. "A double."

"Right."

His study faced a garden that was tended by illegal immigrants with something close to loving care. They were a family and resided on the property, so grateful for their home and the false papers that Valerik had obtained for them that they were pleased to tend his home away from home as if it were their own. It was a minor miracle, he thought, how different people were. One looked at vacant land and dreamed of a potential garden; someone else imagined clearing off the land to build a high-rise office, or an apartment complex; yet another saw the same raw stretch of earth and marked it off with mental chalk lines as a future cemetery.

Valerik's live-in staff had been sent to a hotel in Riverhead, provided with an escort and instructions not to leave their rooms unless the place caught fire. They would return when it was clear—a day or two, at most, he hoped—and all would be as it had been before.

Unless something went wrong.

Valerik sipped his vodka, staring into outer darkness. They had left off the floodlights deliberately; it was one of Bogdashka's stratagems, to give the sentries better cover. He reviewed the preparations he had made. Forget about Manhattan. He had twenty soldiers on the property, with ten outside and five more on alert at any given time. Six-hour shifts, as Bogdashka had prescribed, with five men free to sleep on any given shift, as long as they kept one hand on their guns. His black Mercedes limousine was waiting in the drive outside, the key in the ignition, ready for a hasty exit if the whole thing went to hell.

And there was still Plan X, if all else failed. Six miles away, to the southwest, lay the Grumman-Peconic River Airport, and he had a helicopter waiting there, gassed up and ready to fly on a moment's notice. The pilot was on twenty-four-hour call, with a reminder that his life and the lives of his children depended upon his promise to have the chopper airborne within five minutes of receiving his orders by cellular phone.

All ready, then, Tolya Valerik told himself, and went on staring at the night.

THE NIGHT was quiet. Mack Bolan had already scouted out the grounds of the estate, observed the sentries on their silent rounds and was prepared to make his move.

He was in a blacksuit, his face and hands darkened with combat cosmetics, impervious to blood and water. Bolan's web belt and suspenders, also black, supported frag grenades, a Ka-bar fighting knife, incendiaries, canvas pouches stuffed with spare magazines for the weapons he carried. Chief among them was the M-4 carbine version of the standard M-16 assault rifle, a 40 mm M-203 grenade launcher locked and loaded underneath the carbine's foregrip. Strapped across his chest, he wore a bandoleer of grenades, including high explosive, smoke and antipersonnel. His backup weapons were a .44 Magnum Desert Eagle semiautomatic on his hip, with the Beretta 93-R slung beneath his left arm in its standard quick-draw rig. The pockets of his blacksuit hid stilettos and garrotes, in case the fight went hand to hand.

Like most estates of wealthy persons in this age when "stalker" had become a household word, Tolya Valerik's thirty wooded acres had been walled off from the outside world. The wall was eight feet tall and topped by tangled coils of razor wire. The insulated ground wires taped to metal posts that braced the razor wire in place, each thirty feet or so, told Bolan that the obstacle could fry, as well as flay.

He had observed all that on his daylight reconnaissance, and while he couldn't tell for sure if Valerik's fence would flout state law by carrying a lethal charge, he had prepared himself for anything. His heavy rubber gloves and boots were of the same kind worn by linemen for the power company, when they went out to work on downed high-power lines. He didn't have the hard hat or the insulated overcoat, but he would have to do without—and make damned sure the razor wire didn't slice through the gloves to find his skin.

Mounting the eight-foot wall was relatively easy, though it left him painfully exposed to any soldiers passing unseen on the other side. He chose a point where he could get a hand up, clutching one of the support posts for the razor wire, careful to touch the post and sharp-edged strands with nothing but his gloves and boots. The trick was knowing where to put his left foot when he stepped down on the coils of razor wire, compressing it, before he launched off into space. If anything went wrong now—if he nicked himself, or even snagged a strand and tore it loose as he was plummeting to earth—the game was up. One way, the charge would stun him, maybe kill him where he stood; the other, someone in the house would log the break's location, and the sentries would converge to corner him and hose him down with automatic fire.

His luck was holding, though, and Bolan made the drop without a mishap, tugging off the gloves and bulky boots. Taking another moment, he laced up the jungle boots that he had worn around his neck. Finally, still unobserved, the man in black was ready to probe in earnest.

Bolan thought of Johnny, closing from the north, across the jet-black water of Long Island Sound, and hoped his brother's landing wouldn't turn into another Tarawa. The north edge of Valerik's property wasn't walled, since it fronted the Sound, and logic dictated that it should be patrolled more heavily, against amphibious attacks. Bolan had nearly warned his brother off taking the water route, but in the end he couldn't argue with the kid that it would make more sense to split their force, divide their enemies and chop them up piecemeal.

He pushed through the darkness, heading toward Valerik's house. He took his time, no rush to beat the dawn, since it was barely midnight on Long Island. Moving cautiously on unfamiliar ground, he tested every step before committing to it, listening for any telltale sounds that would betray a human presence in the woods around him. Bolan carried night-vision goggles in a fanny pack, but he had opted not to wear them as he wound his way among the trees. The goggles could be useful, but they also had a crucial weakness, in the fact that any sudden glare of light—from muzzle-flashes to a bank of floodlights blazing on—could lance the wearer's eyes with pain and rob him of his sight, leaving him helpless.

A jungle fighter in the days before high tech allowed a sniper to reach out and count the zits on a potential target's face at 4:00 a.m., Bolan had learned to trust his skills and instincts. He could often hear—and sometimes smell—an enemy before the other man was visible, and the advance warning was critical in any contest to the death.

Like now.

It wasn't raining, but his ears picked out the sound of water droplets falling onto shrubbery, some ten or fifteen yards to the northeast. He veered in that direction, picking up his pace a bit, but not enough for any careless misstep to betray him.

He had time for this one. He would make time.

The young Russian had to have had a full bladder. He was still urinating, his legs splayed, his head back, gazing at the stars, when Bolan spotted him. Three strides would do it, and he chose the Ka-bar knife over the Beretta, since the pistol whispered. But the blade, if used correctly, made no noise at all.

He could have waited for the guy to finish, tidy up a bit, but there was no improving on the angle of his target's head and neck. Besides it wasn't as if dignity would matter to this hired assassin when they put him in the ground.

Three silent strides it was, and Bolan clapped his left hand tight across the Russian's mouth, feeling the sentry's AK-47 wedged between them, bulky on its shoulder sling. He cranked the Russian's head back just another inch or so, to stretch the veins and arteries, esophagus and larynx—all the crucial tubes that let a human being think, breathe, swallow, speak. He drove his blade completely through the Russian's neck and brought it back to moonlight with a twisting, sawing motion. Blood exploded from the sentry's gaping second smile, and after several seconds of frenetic trembling, he went limp in Bolan's arms.

Wiping his blade on the gunner's clothing, he put the knife away and dragged the body into deeper shadows, where it would require at least a second glance to pick it out.

One down. How many left to go?

The Executioner moved on.

THE BOAT WAS nothing big or fancy, but it didn't need to be. It was thirteen feet with an outboard motor that required no special training to manipulate. Johnny gave himself two hours for the trip, because he had to kill the motor early, well before he came in sight or earshot of Valerik's property.

A good mile out, he cut it off and started rowing, no great rush, but leaning into it with everything he had, preferring to arrive ahead of time and lie at anchor than to shave it too close and lose his edge.

They would be waiting for him, Johnny knew. Not literally, but the troops would be on guard, at least a couple of them detailed to patrol the waterline. Johnny was counting on their limitations to betray them, but he had to be prepared for a worst-case scenario, prepared to blitz the beach if necessary.

He didn't own a blacksuit like his brother's, and made do with black fatigues, like those favored by SWAT teams nationwide. His black load-bearing vest was anchored to a pistol belt, the rigging fat with ammo pouches, an inverted trench knife and a cross-draw holster for his Glock. The pistol on his right hip was a Ruger Mark II Target model, muzzle-heavy with a sound suppressor that more than balanced out the ten rounds of .22-caliber hollowpoint ammunition in its magazine. His lead weapon for the strike was a Steyr AUG assault rifle, the bullpup design adopted by armed forces from Ireland to Latin America.

Johnny had fifteen minutes to spare when he marked Valerik's pier and boathouse, a hundred yards off to his right. He shipped his oars at once and hunkered below the gunwale, slipping on his infrared goggles for a quick scan of the shoreline.

As expected, there were sentries on the job. Two by the boathouse, sharing something from what appeared to be an insulated bottle, while a third paced off the rocky beach, perhaps two hundred yards beyond the pier. Johnny had no idea how many troops were quartered on the property this night, but it was clear Valerik's gunners didn't have the blind spot to amphibious assault that he had hoped for.

It didn't matter.

The water side of the estate was some three-quarters of a mile in length, and there were only three men watching it. Assuming all three stayed, that gave him two parked by the boathouse, while a third did all the legwork. Even if the trio struck a sudden vein of energy and fanned out on patrol, Johnny was confident that he would find his way ashore.

Because he had no choice.

Whether the landing went down nice and easy, or played out like something from a war movie, his brother was counting on him, and he wouldn't let him down. Not while he lived.

The extra quarter of an hour helped. One of the soldiers at the boathouse wandered back into the woods, leaving the bottle with his comrade. By and by, the shooter who was pacing off the beach came back to get his share, and Johnny chose that moment to begin his move toward shore.

The pier and boathouse were a good four hundred yards to Johnny's left, due east, as he rowed in to wading depth. The last half of his journey he couldn't see either of the sentries, since the boathouse stood between them, but he kept shooting glances in that direction, even as he scanned the tree line set back twenty-five or thirty paces from the beach.

The worst part of it was when Johnny had to ship his oars again and lurch into the water, thigh-deep in the cold, and drag the boat ashore. He was most helpless then, a perfect target for a sniper in the woods, exposed if either of the sentries chose that moment for a peek around the boathouse, down the shore. When no one opened up on him from hiding, Johnny eased the Steyr off its shoulder sling and held it in his left hand, reaching for the sound suppressor Ruger with his right.

His first job was to neutralize the gunners he could find, while moving toward the manor house, to rendezvous with his brother. He still had time, but it was slipping through his fingers. His brother should be across the wall by now. The silence of the grounds told Johnny nothing, but he prayed it meant good news and not disaster.

Either way, he was committed now. No turning back.

Suzanne's face surfaced in his mind, and Johnny pushed it back. This was no time or place for tenderness, no venue for gentility. A stray thought of her smell, her body, could spell sudden death for Johnny.

He made the boathouse unobserved and flattened against the western wall. Mere yards away, he heard the Russians talking in their native tongue, one of them laughing as the other made a joke he couldn't translate.

They should yuk it up, he thought, die laughing, if they could get the chance.

He came around the corner with the Ruger out in front of him, firing at the startled gunners. On his left, the sentry with the insulated bottle took a hollowpoint slug below one eye and staggered backward, spitting blood and coffee. Johnny swiveled toward the other, the pistol tracking into target acquisition.

Three rounds from less than fifteen feet away, and Johnny put the second Russian down without a whimper, though his heels drummed for a moment on the wooden pier. Ignoring the pathetic little dance, he turned back toward the first man, found him slumped against the boathouse, his slack jaw working silently, his mouth awash in leakage.

Say good-night.

A mercy round between the soldier's eyes, and he had used up half the Ruger's load. Counting the shots as lead well spent, he slipped the pistol back into its holster, left the dead behind and struck off for Valerik's house.

ANATOLY BOGDASHKA was working on his third glass of Okhotnichya—"hunter's vodka," flavored with ginger and cloves—when the shooting began. His head was buzzing lightly, but he wasn't drunk. It took at least a bottle of the hard stuff, shared with no one else, before Bogdashka passed from buzzing into snarling and became the kind of ugly drunk who gets a charge from smashing bottles into strangers' faces. He didn't intend to drink that much this night, of course, since he was still on duty, standing watch over the man who was his master and his friend.

The first staccato sound of a Kalashnikov brought Valerik to his feet, the lemon-flavored Limonaya vodka slopping from his glass and down across his knuckles. To his credit, Valerik didn't ask Bogdashka what the noise had been. Both men had fired an AK-47—and been fired on with them—frequently enough to recognize the sound from any other firearm in the world. There was a certain rough, metallic chatter to the Kalis that was unmistakable, once you had heard it for yourself, up close and personal.

Valerik was moving toward the window when Bogdashka reached him, seized his arm and drew him back. "Be careful!" he commanded, taking over for an instant, knowing that it couldn't last. "A stray round through the window, and we'll have to clean you off the rug."

"How could the bastards find me here?" Valerik asked.

"We don't know that they have," Bogdashka said. "It could be some nervous soldier on the line." But that was unlikely, and the feeble lie was mirrored in Valerik's eyes. "It may have been Nikita, though."

"Nikita?" Valerik seemed disoriented, as if knowing he

should recognize the name, yet still unable to connect it to a living person.

"Stureyev knew about this place, as well as your apartment in the city," Bogdashka said. "It could be he was forced to tell."

"We need to finish it!" Valerik rasped.

"That's why we brought the soldiers, Tolya. Leave them to it, will you? Go into the room across the hall and lock the door." No windows there, no access for a sniper's bullet or grenade. "When I have found out what is happening, I'll come back for you, and we can leave this place."

"The men—"

"Will do as they are told. Now go!"

He herded Valerik out, across the hall, and waited at the door until he heard the lock engage. Bogdashka's next stop was the linen closet armory, deft pressure underneath a shelf of folded sheets releasing hidden bolts, the whole wall pivoting to reveal a well-stocked gun locker.

Outside, Bogdashka heard the sounds of combat escalating, drawing closer, and decided there was no point taking chances. Scooping up a Kevlar vest, he slipped it on and fastened it on either side, beneath his arms. It would stop most small-arms rounds, assuming that they struck him in the torso, without slipping through the armpit gaps. A shot above the shoulders or below the waist would take him down, regardless, but it was the best that he could do.

Bogdashka grabbed his own Kalashnikov, a stubby AKSU "bullet hose," with folding metal stock, and slipped two extra magazines into the pockets of his slacks. He wasn't dressed for combat, in his tailored suit and high-gloss wingtip shoes, but it was nerve that counted in a killing situation, more than any costume. He had once committed murder with a knife, while wearing nothing but a towel around his waist, a fat pig of a heroin importer gutted in a Moscow Turkish bath. Blood on the sweaty tile, so deep it squelched and bubbled up between his toes.

Shutting the closet door behind him, Bogdashka moved along the hallway, picking up three sleepy soldiers who were only now descending from their temporary quarters on the second floor. Their shift wasn't supposed to start for two hours yet. They were a little bleary-eyed, but otherwise alert, each with a weapon ready in his hands. Bogdashka ordered them to follow him, and they fell into step without a moment's hesitation, trooping after him as he proceeded toward the kitchen and its exit facing the yard, the swimming pool, the woods beyond.

"Shall we turn on the lights?" one of them asked him.

Bogdashka thought about it. It was dark outside, the floods left off deliberately. If they were switched on now, would it assist the soldiers fighting to defend the house, or make them sitting targets in the crosshairs of their enemies?

"No!" he snapped, deciding on a whim. A wise man always judged a situation as it was, before he tried to intervene and alter the direction of events. For all Bogdashka knew, his soldiers could be winning. Any move he made without due thought could aid their enemies and shift the balance to their detriment.

The night was warm enough for shirtsleeves, and it smelled of cordite. Bogdashka tracked the firefight by its sound, and by the winking muzzle-flashes in among the trees. The water lay in that direction, yachts and trawlers moving on Long Island Sound. He wondered if the enemy had dared to come ashore that way, or merely crept along the coast, from one direction or the other, to avoid the walls surmounted by high-voltage razor wire.

No matter. If they had their backs against the sea, his men could sweep the woods and drive them toward the Sound, enact a parody of Dunkirk, with no ragtag fleet to save the bastards from their fate. If they—

More firing from his left, westward, told Bogdashka there had to be *two* invading forces, or the first had split to flank the house. That made it worse, his own defensive team divided, fighting in the dark. Against how many enemies? More to the point, what could he do, with only three men at his side?

Making his choice, he pointed to the west and said, "You three, go join the others fighting there. I'll see what's happened at the boathouse and catch up to you. Go, now!"

Good soldiers all, they didn't hesitate. Bogdashka waited until they were out of sight, then turned back toward the house.

He knew where his first loyalty lay. If he did nothing else this night, he had to reach Valerik and remove him from harm's way. If, in the process, Bogdashka also saved himself...well, who could argue that performance of one's duty offered no reward?

IT WAS THE SECOND sentry who took Bolan by surprise. He never saw or sensed the man until it was too late, and even then it was a bit of foolishness that saved his life. The Russian should have dropped him in his tracks, but somehow, in the brooding darkness of the miniforest, he apparently became confused, uncertain as to whether Bolan represented friend or foe.

Instead of firing from the shadows, cutting Bolan down, the sentry stepped from cover, barked a warning in Russian.

Bolan milked a short burst from the M-4 carbine at a range of twenty feet or so, the 5.56 mm tumblers slapping flesh, his adversary dropping in a clumsy yoga squat on tangled legs. The Russian was dead or fading fast, but he had strength enough to squeeze the trigger of his AK-47 with a dying reflex, spraying close to half a magazine straight up before the piece kicked loose and went to ground beside him.

He had blown the precious margin of surprise.

Voices were raised from the direction of the house, and somewhere closer, in the cultivated woods ahead of him. The good news: if the Russians started hunting him, it improved his brother's chances of surviving long enough to reach the house and do some damage there.

Bolan kept moving, heard the shooters calling back and forth to one another as they started quartering the grounds. The smart thing would have been to keep their mouths shut, but he understood the impulse—urban soldiers hunting armed prey for the first time on strange turf, craving the reinforcement of their buddies as they scouted through the dark.

He wished them luck, all bad.

A couple of them were approaching on his right-front, two o'clock or thereabouts. He veered in that direction, paused and waited for them. He couldn't see them yet, and didn't need to. Not for the surprise he had in mind.

When they had closed the gap to forty yards or so, he sighted on a point between their two converging voices, counted off five seconds in his mind and stroked the trigger of his 40 mm launcher. The HE round took flight, describing a parabola that brought it down somewhere between the two approaching gunners, yet unseen. It blew on impact, the bright flash speckling Bolan's vision when he blinked his eyelids afterward.

Instead of calling back and forth, one of the troops was screaming now, the other silent. Bolan couldn't tell if he had nailed them both, nor did he care. Right now, it was enough that he had raised the ante, clearly wounding one of them, and all the other hunters knew there was a big dog in the woods.

Reloading on the move, he fed the launcher with another HE round and locked it down. Some of the Russians had begun to fire at shadows, spooked by the explosion and the screams their comrade wailed into the night. The trees were taking random hits, and stray rounds whispered over Bolan's head, but none of them were close enough to slow him, much less draw blood.

The house lay eastward from the point where he had scaled the razor wall, still more or less directly to his front. Approaching it without a detour meant that he would have to clear the field, kill those defenders who opposed him, or compel them to retreat.

The muzzle-flashes in the darkness helped. Instead of firing back at them with the M-4, thereby revealing his position to the enemy, he trusted the M-203, which gave no muzzle-flash. It was like shooting fireflies with a mortar, no precision to it, but he didn't have to be all that precise. With either high-explosive rounds or antipersonnel, he had a killzone that should cover any standing man within six paces of ground zero. If his shots were even close to the erratic muzzle-flashes blinking in the night, he stood to score more often than he missed.

It was a strange, grim battle in among the trees, defenders firing blindly at an enemy they couldn't see, while the invisible replied with flashing thunderbolts. The angry sound of Russian shouts and curses gradually shifted into cries of pain or panic, warbled warnings, as the walking wounded and the fortunate unscathed began retreating toward the manor house.

They didn't go alone.

Some of the stragglers still sprayed shots into the dark, but Bolan didn't answer, simply keeping track of them by muzzle-flashes, avoiding their wild rounds. He had no wish to slow their progress now that they were in retreat. He let them lead him toward his target, smoking brass instead of bread crumbs scattered in their wake.

Too easy, Bolan thought. This many soldiers, maybe more on tap around the house, they should have mounted a better defense. Was it surprise and Bolan's choice of weapons that had broken them, or was the whole retreat a calculated move, the lure to bait a deadly trap?

It hardly mattered, since he had to reach the house in any case, and Bolan let his thoughts shift to his brother, somewhere in the night. He heard the sounds of yet another clash, ahead of him, and pictured Johnny fighting for his life, but there was nothing he could do about it, yet.

The Executioner went forward, Death incarnate, homing on the kill.

13

The sound of automatic weapons firing from the west, Bolan's chosen angle of approach to the Valerik homestead, drove an ice-cold spike of dread through Johnny's gut. It didn't paralyze him, though. He was too professional for that. If anything, the racket—and the corresponding thought of his brother in danger—liberated him from any inhibitions, canceled any need for stealth.

A blooded former trooper with the U.S. Army Rangers, Johnny still made no more noise than absolutely necessary, as he navigated through the darkness toward his target and the rendezvous with his brother. He held the Steyr ready, though, and let the sound suppressed .22 pistol stay holstered on his hip. From this point on, if he met any Russian sentries, they were going down the hard way, and to hell with the illusion of surprise.

As Johnny had anticipated, most of those assigned to watch the northern quadrant of the grounds, facing Long Island Sound, had gone to join their comrades fighting on the west side of the house. It made no difference whether that was shoddy discipline, or if they had been ordered out; the end result was still the same. Not quite free access to the house, but at least a window of—

He saw the Russian sentry almost as soon as the enemy saw him, the difference of a microsecond, either way. In sudden confrontations, most particularly when both parties were surprised, the end results came down in nearly equal parts to training, skill and luck.

This night, the Russian's luck was running low.

He held a folding-stock Kalashnikov, ready for business, but the sling was tangled around his left wrist somehow, as he swung the piece toward Johnny, and instead of cutting loose despite the snag, the hardman tried to shake it off. It was the kind of understandable but unforgivable mistake that claimed lives every day in wartime.

A swarm of 5.56 mm rounds tore through the Russian's chest, tumbling on impact to rip catastrophic wound channels through heart and lungs. Dead on his feet before he knew it, the sentry slumped first to his knees, then toppled slowly forward on his face. Before he kissed the dirt, Johnny had already jogged around him, moving on.

The sound of even that brief skirmish had alerted several other sentries to the possibility of more than one intruder on the grounds. Johnny kept pushing toward the house, but he was still at least three hundred yards away, the roofline barely visible, when he was ambushed in the woods.

It was a hasty trap, and clearly not the best one ever laid. The simple fact that Johnny came through the initial fusillade unscathed was ample proof of that. They nearly had him, though—three automatic rifles hammering away in an approximation of triangulated fire—and it was close enough to make him keep his head down, creeping on his belly through a mulch of fallen leaves, dead grass and insects, as he sought a better vantage point.

The Russians ceased fire after several seconds, and the silence stretched for maybe half a minute, until their nerves began to jangle. When they started calling back and forth from their respective hides, Johnny believed he caught the gist of what was on their minds, although he didn't speak a word of Russian.

For every ambush that resulted in shooting, there was a

moment when the hunters had to check their kill. They had to find out if those they had shot were dead or wounded, maybe even feigning injury. If visibility was poor to nonexistent, then the shooters needed to check to see if they had hit anyone at all, or if their only trophies would be tree trunks scarred by flying lead.

Johnny was waiting with a frag grenade unpinned, gripped firmly in his right hand, when the chosen spotter grudgingly emerged from cover. There was little to be seen, a silhouette scuttling in and out of shadow, but it was enough for him to make his pitch.

Six seconds later, when the grenade went off, he had his first glimpse of the enemy, airborne, an artless somersault through smoke and flames. He didn't mark the shattered body's touchdown point, rather focused on the darkness where a muzzle-flash should soon be showing—

There! And there!

He had them, firing back with short, precision bursts, using the Steyr's optical sight for better accuracy. One hit was confirmed when Johnny's half-glimpsed target lurched and tumbled backward, firing at the treetops as he fell. The other gave a kind of gurgling, thrashing sound that could have indicated he was hit, or bolting in a panic. Listening, it didn't sound as if the source of the untidy noise was gaining any distance. Grudgingly, Johnny decided he should take the time to check it out.

The guy was gut shot, hunched into a fetal curl and kicking feebly so that he propelled himself in jerky little circles, reminiscent of Curly Joe in an old Three Stooges skit. There seemed to be no fight left in him, and it struck Johnny as a shameful thing to simply leave him in agony.

He drew the Ruger, waited for the grunting man to jerk his way around, until his head was next to Johnny's feet, then stooped and put a hollow point slug behind his ear. The soldier stiffened with a final tremor, then went limp, taut muscles slackening in death.

The fact that gunfire and explosions still reverberated from the west encouraged him, as did the fact that the reports seemed closer now. He wasn't sure if that meant his brother was gaining ground, or simply that his own progress had brought him closer to the firefight. Either way, though, Johnny took it as a sign that his brother was still alive and carrying the battle to their enemies.

But was it moving fast enough?

This kind of D day, hell-on-earth concerto would have every frightened resident within a half-mile of Valerik's property rushing to summon the police. Long Island cops were often viewed as being soft, especially compared to those who worked the Apple proper, but they knew which side their bread was buttered on, and they didn't ignore complaints from wealthy taxpayers, particularly if the calls reported wild men with machine guns and grenades tearing the hell out of a ritzy neighborhood.

So, they were running out of time. No sirens yet, no helicopter searchlights lancing through the trees, but it wouldn't be long. His brother wouldn't fire on the police in any circumstances, Johnny knew, which made it even more imperative that they complete their business and clear out before the uniforms arrived.

The younger Bolan understood his brother's view on the police, and while he hadn't bucked the Executioner's unwritten rule—well, he had knifed a Texas courtroom bailiff sometime back, but it was just a flesh wound, so it didn't really count—but he wasn't inclined toward prison, either. If it came down to a choice like that, he thought, it would be each man for himself. And if his brother's life was riding on the line, it would be no damned choice at all.

Putting one killing ground behind him and proceeding toward the next, he moved on toward the Russian mafioso's home away from home.

THE RAPID KNOCK surprised Tolya Valerik, made him raise his Skorpion machine pistol and point it at the door before he realized that any gunmen bent on killing him would probably fire through the door or simply break it down, without the courtesy of knocking first.

"Who's that?" he challenged, speaking Russian, standing well back from the door, his weapon steadied in a firm two-handed grip.

"Tolya, it's me!"

He felt a sweet rush of relief on hearing Bogdashka's voice. Valerik's fingertips were on the latch before he hesitated, stepping back again, imagining his first lieutenant braced between hired killers, with a gun pressed to his head. Would Bogdashka go along to save himself? Had he sufficient courage to become a human sacrifice?

"Are you alone?" Valerik asked.

"There's no one here but me," Bogdashka said impatiently. "Open the door!"

Of course, he would say that if he was being held at gunpoint, forced to play the traitor. Still, the only way to know for sure was opening the door, and Valerik had begun to feel a trifle idiotic, standing in his half crouch, aiming his machine pistol at nothing.

So, he threw the dead bolt, leaping clear, his free hand coming back to clutch the Skorpion. When Bogdashka cleared the door and closed it, he regarded Valerik with a curious expression. "I'm alone," he said again. "I told you that."

"Of course," Valerik answered, lowering the weapon. "What is happening outside?"

"It's difficult to say, but battle has been joined on two sides of the house. We definitely have intruders on the grounds. You've heard the detonations? Our men weren't issued hand grenades.''

''Not the police, then?''

''No. They come with warrants and with television crews to broadcast their achievements. They don't sneak in at night with high explosives and machine guns. Not in the United States, at any rate.''

''Who, then?''

Bogdashka shrugged. ''I've no idea,'' he answered frankly, ''but I'd rather not be waiting here to introduce myself if they should reach the house.''

''You think that likely?'' Valerik cared no more about the house, per se, than for the other dwellings he maintained at sundry points around the world. He felt a certain rage, however, at the sense of violation that accrued from picturing armed strangers knocking down the door and moving freely through its rooms.

''They're still advancing,'' Bogdashka said. ''It's clear we've lost some men. As to how many, who can say? I have committed the reserves. It may not be enough.''

''To run like this—''

''Is better than to die like this, I think,'' Valerik's first lieutenant finished for him.

Valerik stared into his old friend's eyes, saw the truth there and nodded his head reluctantly. ''You're right, of course. Where's Leonid?''

Leonid Kubichek was Valerik's chauffeur. He would drive the Mercedes limousine and whisk them safely off Long Island.

''He's out with the others,'' Bogdashka said. ''We needed every man to hold the line.''

So much for Kubichek. ''All right,'' Valerik said. ''I still know how to drive, or you can—''

''We should call the helicopter, Tolya,'' Bogdashka interrupted him again. ''The pilot is already standing by. Five minutes to get airborne, and another five or six to put him on the heliport out back. We could be that long getting to the car and driving to the gate—if we get there at all.''

Valerik hesitated, mulling over options. Now that he had made his choice to cut and run, he didn't like the thought of hiding in the house another minute, with his enemies advancing from two sides.

"The car's not bulletproof, remember," Bogdashka said. "The raiders must have driven here. They can pursue us on the highway, but if we were in the air..."

Valerik saw the logic of it, reaching in his pocket for the cellular phone that he carried everywhere. Speed-dialing, he was gratified to hear his pilot answer halfway through the first ring.

"Da?"

"You recognize my voice?"

"Of course, sir."

"Come and fetch us now!" Valerik ordered. "Hurry!"

"I'm on my—"

Valerik cut him off and pocketed the telephone. Five seconds wasted might well mean the difference between survival and extinction. In five seconds, he could rattle off three magazines from his machine pistol, enough rounds to kill sixty men. A single gunman with an AK-47 could—

Valerik stopped himself before his own imagination did him in. Clutching the Skorpion tightly enough to blanch his knuckles white, he tried to look calm and collected as he faced his aide, concerned that Bogdashka knew him too damned well to be deceived. A show of weakness now might prove as fatal in the long run as a bullet to the brain.

"He's coming."

"Then, all we have to do is wait."

"Not here," Valerik said. "It's too far from the yard. We might not hear the helicopter landing. Even if we did, it should be touch and go. The longer he waits for us on the ground, the more likely it is that none of us will get away.''

It was Bogdashka's turn to nod. ''He will be landing on the east lawn,'' he said. ''Our choices are to wait for him outside, or watch from somewhere close at hand, then make a run for it as he begins to land.''

They both knew that the closest door would be the exit from the kitchen, leaving thirty yards of open ground, at least, between the house and helicopter when they made their break. How many unseen snipers would be covering that exit from the house? How many times could they be shot, while running thirty yards?

''It's too far,'' Valerik said.

''Not from the library.''

''There is no exit from the library.''

''The room has windows,'' Bogdashka said. ''They open, yes? You still remember going in and out through windows, eh, Tolya? We watch and wait. The helicopter lands—''

''And we're no more than ten yards away.''

''Precisely.''

Smiling for the first time that he could remember in the past week, Valerik slapped his old friend on the shoulder. ''Let's be going, then,'' he said. ''No time to waste.''

''Be careful in the hallways,'' Bogdashka said. ''I don't believe they've reached the house yet, but we take no chances.''

Valerik checked his Rolex watch. A minute had already passed since he had spoken to his helicopter pilot. They were that much closer to salvation, to escape.

Bogdashka led the way, a ducking movement as he cleared the door, holding his AKSU with its stubby muzzle pointed toward the ceiling, so that he could swing it to the left or right with equal ease if there was any hint of danger. Valerik followed, his index finger resting lightly on the Skorpion's hair trigger. Extra magazines were heavy in his pockets, ruining the cut of his expensive jacket, but he knew that any ambush in the hallway would be over in a heartbeat. He would have a chance to fire, most likely, but reloading was a fantasy.

The library, he thought. A few more steps, and they'd be there.

WHEN HE WAS close enough to see Valerik's house with minimal obstruction from the trees, Bolan returned fire against the straggling defenders. He alternated 40 mm rounds with short bursts from his carbine, walking smoky thunderclaps across the open lawn, the blasts distracting shooters who might otherwise have focused on his muzzle-flashes, marking his location for return fire.

Bolan kept no count of those who fell. The only numbers game that held his interest was a rough assessment of the troops remaining who were still in any shape to bar intruders from the house. He also kept a sharp eye on his watch and tried to calculate how long the first police response would take, but it was futile guesswork. When he heard the first approaching sirens, he would know. Until then, he could only forge ahead and try to scan each target's face before he put the next man down, hoping to frame Tolya Valerik in his sights.

That was unlikely, Bolan knew, unless he made his way inside the house itself. And even then...

An engine revving, off to Bolan's right, brought him around in that direction, tracking as a sleek Mercedes limousine rolled into view, angling away from Bolan, following the driveway that would ultimately lead it to the highway.

If it was allowed to get that far.

He pegged the gap at sixty yards and lengthening, approximately half the M-203 grenade launcher's effective range for point targets. Bolan braced the carbine's stock against his shoulder and fired off a round, watching as a fireball billowed from the Benz's trunk, the rear wheels spinning off in opposite directions as the axle snapped in two. He guessed there wouldn't be much time before the gas tank blew, consuming anyone inside the limo, but he had to know if he had bagged his man, if this part of the game was finished.

Sprinting over open lawn, he was within a dozen paces of the crippled limo when the driver's door sprang open and a man lurched clear, reeling across the grass. Bolan knew instantly that it wasn't Valerik. Firing from the hip, he put him down.

And it was now or never. Take the risk and know for sure, or live in doubt. A few more seconds...

Bolan rushed the limousine and hooked the rear door open with his left hand, triggering a short burst from his carbine through the smoke that rushed to meet him. Leaning in, eyes narrowed into slits against the smoke and heat, he could see no one else at all inside the stretch.

Goddammit!

Raging silently against the driver who had tried to save himself and thereby wasted more of Bolan's precious, fleeting time, he turned and sprinted back toward the house. The secondary detonation of the limo's gas tank shoved him from behind and almost took him down, a little payback for the fatal boot he had delivered to the Benz.

Tolya Valerik wasn't in the car, which meant that he was probably still hiding in the house. No other vehicles had pulled out since the shooting started, but he saw two more sedans—a Lincoln and a Cadillac—parked near the southwest corner of the house.

No point in taking chances.

Bolan fed another HE round into his launcher, swiftly aimed and fired. The Lincoln shuddered, took it on the nose, its hood airborne before the engine blew back through the firewall, landing in the driver's seat. Reloading, Bolan aimed again and sent the Caddy to that high-priced junkyard in the sky. The two heaps settled side by side, tires melting in a lake of flaming gasoline.

The snap of bullets flying past his head brought Bolan back to his immediate surroundings, dropping prone beneath the hostile line of fire. Two gunners had him spotted from a range of forty yards and closing, firing from the hip as they advanced. If either had paused to aim, he might have done the job, but they were so caught up in laying down a screen of automatic fire that neither of them stopped to think the problem through.

Their loss, Bolan's gain.

There was no time to feed the smoking launcher, but he didn't need it. Sighting on the gunner to his left, Bolan squeezed off a 5-round burst that punched his target through a jerky little dance before he went down on his face. The other Russian may have noticed, but he gave no sign of it, advancing steadily, unloading short bursts from his AK-47, which were coming closer all the time.

His last rounds spattered dirt in Bolan's face, before the M-4 carbine rattled off an answer, stitching tidy holes across the Russian's chest on a diagonal. The Russian staggered, then appeared to suck it up and find his balance, making Bolan wonder if he had a Kevlar vest beneath his shirt and jacket, but the answer came a heartbeat later, crimson pumping from the blowholes in his chest, his eyes glazing over as he fell.

Bolan was on his feet and moving when he heard a new, familiar sound intruding on the ragged din of battle. Even from a distance, he immediately recognized it: helicopter rotors. He didn't know whose helicopter, whether it belonged to Valerik or the police, but it meant trouble either way.

Time was swiftly running out.

And where was Johnny?

"IT'S COMING!" Valerik blurted out. "I hear it!"

Craning out the open window, risking sniper fire, Bogdashka listened. There! He heard it, too! A helicopter was approaching from the west, and he told himself that it had to be their bird. If it was the police—or, even worse, pathetic vultures from the media, responding to a riot call—he and Valerik might be doomed.

Bogdashka didn't wish to think what would ensue if they were taken into custody. The arsenal of automatic weapons was enough to hold them overnight, at least, while federal agents and New York police debated other charges. There were corpses to account for, in Manhattan and now on the Long Island property. There was a good chance bond would be denied indefinitely. Even with a battery of high-priced lawyers on the case, it meant disaster. Prison time, or worse.

If they were taken by the law, locked up for any length of time, what would the others—Krestyanov and Pruett—do? Would they discuss the problem over drinks and wag their heads, deciding it would be much simpler if Valerik and his chief lieutenant simply ceased to be?

"Come on!" he urged Valerik, scrambling through the window first to cover Valerik's exit. Bogdashka heard his slacks rip, scraped his left shin painfully against the windowsill and nearly lost his balance on the other side. Cursing and windmilling his arms like a demented tightrope walker, he was able to prevent himself from falling, covering the east lawn with his AKSU, while Valerik tumbled to the grass behind him.

"Shit!"

"It doesn't matter! Hurry!"

He reached back for Valerik blindly, found one of his arms and yanked him to his feet. Overhead, the Bell JetRanger helicopter blotted out the moon, a prehistoric dragonfly that hovered momentarily before descending to the lawn. Its rotor wash whipped Bogdashka's hair around in spiky tufts and made him squint against the rush of wind, his open jacket flapping behind him like a superhero's cape. Valerik followed close behind him, letting Bogdashka take the worst of it, watching their rear with his Skorpion in case they were pursued.

The shooting started when the two of them had covered half the distance to the helicopter. Glancing backward, Bogdashka thought he saw a muzzle-flash, but couldn't tell if it was one of the attackers firing after them, or maybe one of their own soldiers, thinking he had found a target. Either way, the slugs were coming too close. Bogdashka braced the AKSU against his hip and fired off the magazine, some fifteen rounds, without believing he would score a hit.

It didn't matter now, as long as he could keep the bastard's head down, spoil his aim until they got aboard the helicopter and were gone. Valerik was firing, too, although the target was beyond effective range for his machine pistol. Sometimes, Bogdashka knew, it was enough to simply make some noise. It made you feel more like a man.

"Come on!"

Shoving Valerik toward the bird, Bogdashka followed closely, laying down a screen of cover fire until his magazine was empty. Seconds later, he was scrambling up into his seat, fumbling with safety belts.

"Get us out of here!" he ordered the young man at the controls.

The helicopter wobbled, lifting off so slowly that Bogdashka had a sudden urge to smash the pilot's face, but that would only send them plunging back to earth. Instead, he bit his lip and watched the muzzle-flashes below them, waiting for the bullet that would crack the canopy and drill a hole between his eyes.

It never came, although he thought—imagined?—that he heard the helicopter taking hits somewhere beneath his feet. The pilot seemed to hear it, too. He wrenched on the controls and swung the bird away in a long, looping arc, toward the darkness of Long Island Sound, leaving the battlefield behind them in a dizzy rush.

When they didn't explode in flames or plummet to the ground, Bogdashka swiveled in his seat, the safety harness biting at his groin and shoulders. Valerik, seated in the back, was staring back at him with vacant, shadowed eyes.

"Where shall we go?" Bogdashka asked his master.

Valerik thought about it for a moment, then leaned forward and addressed their pilot. "Where's the nearest airport? Not the one you've come from. Somewhere else, close by."

"There is Brookhaven," the pilot said. "It's not far. Or Suffolk County airport, roughly the same distance."

"Brookhaven," Valerik said. "We'll make arrangements for a flight out of the country. Not the major New York airports, though. They may be watching for us there. We'll fly from somewhere in New Jersey, or perhaps from Philadelphia."

"Fly where?" Bogdashka asked.

"What does it matter? As long as we get out of the United States." Valerik was silent for a moment, then he asked, "Do we have any soldiers left to meet us at the airport where we're going?"

"They would have to drive out from the city."

"No use, then," Valerik said. "We'd only call attention to ourselves. We'll keep the guns, instead, as long as possible."

Bogdashka settled back, the AKSU in his lap, and closed his eyes. He didn't know where they were going, but at least they were alive. They would concoct some explanation for Krestyanov while they waited for their flight out of the country. And tomorrow... Well, tomorrow would take care of itself.

EVEN WITH THE STUTTER of the M-4 carbine in his ears, he recognized the voice. "They're gone, Mack."

That was the pathetic truth, all right. The helicopter was beyond effective range, about to disappear behind the treetops, making for Long Island Sound. It could go anywhere.

"Yeah." He turned to face his brother, suddenly exhausted and disgusted with himself. "They're gone."

"Valerik?"

"Had to be. Two guys got on and the bird took off. I wasn't quick enough."

"Next time," Johnny said.

"If there is a next time."

"We should probably get out of here," Johnny suggested, and tipped his head in the direction of the highway, sirens warbling as the first squad cars approached.

"Sounds right. You want to use the boat?"

"Suits me."

Ironically, there was no one to challenge them as they retreated through the woods, back toward the Sound and Johnny's waiting motor launch. Any surviving members of the home team were apparently distracted by police arriving on the scene, drawn off to man the gates. Or maybe they all knew the boss had fled, and there was simply no point dying for an empty house that was about to be besieged by uniforms and television cameras.

"We'll find him," Johnny said, when they were roughly halfway to the beach.

"It's not that simple," Bolan told him.

"You mean without Hal's help?"

And that was part of it, no question. In the "old days"—like last week—he could have simply made a phone call to Brognola, telling him Valerik had slipped through the net. The big Fed would have sent the cavalry to cover every airport in the tristate area and shut them down, if necessary, until their man was in the bag. He couldn't do that now, because Brognola had already washed his hands of all involvement with the mission.

But that wasn't all.

"It's not just Hal," he said. "It isn't just Valerik."

"I know."

They had proceeded this far under the assumption that the Russian Mafia was operating, somehow, in conjunction with the CIA or certain elements thereof. They had sufficient proof, in Bolan's mind, to make the case, though it would never stand in any court. His problem, now, went well beyond the fact that he had failed to bag one Russian mobster at a given place and time.

Whatever the Valerik Family had going with the CIA, he had to assume the deal was still intact and moving forward. The Company itself had lost only one man, so far—well, two, if anybody counted Williams—and Bolan had no reason to believe the Langley team would back off from their goals because the weather got a little stormy.

Most of all, though, Bolan was unhappy for the simple reason that he still had no idea of what the larger game involved. Everything was smoke and mirrors with Langley, Chinese boxes, all means to a well-concealed end.

For all the blood and suffering, Bolan was confident that they had barely scratched the surface of the puzzle, and that was enough to depress him.

"Over here," his brother called, and Bolan moved to join him, smooth stones clicking underneath his boots. The boat was still intact, no sign that anyone had seen or tampered with it after Johnny came ashore.

Behind them, even through the trees, they could make out the throbbing pulse of emergency flashers, fire trucks and meat wagons joining the squad cars lined up on the highway. There was a brief, distant crackle of gunfire, and the lights began to move, like a forest fire spread by the wind.

"We make it to the Cherokee, we're home," Johnny said. "I've got extra clothes. The fit's not that far off. Some cold cream."

Bolan touched his cheek, remembering the warpaint for the first time since he put it on. He'd never make it past a roadblock with his death face on.

"Should be no problem." Johnny was already ankle-deep in the water, dragging the boat out to sea. "Head back to the motel, make sure Suzanne's all right and we can figure out what happens next."

What happens next?

That was the question. And for the first time in a long time, Bolan wasn't sure about the answer. They would need intelligence about Valerik's movements, something—anything—about his ties to Langley, and smart money said they would get little aid, if any, from Brognola or the team at Stony Man Farm.

Which meant that they would have to do it all the hard way, by themselves.

Just like old times.

* * * * *

*The heartstopping action
continues in The Executioner 269,*
SHIFTING SHADOWS,
Book II of
THE CONSPIRACY TRILOGY,
available April 2001.

**A journey through the dangerous frontier
known as the future...**

JAMES AXLER

DEATHLANDS

THE
SKYDARK
CHRONICLES
Book I

Savage Armada

Beneath the beauty of the Marshall Islands lies a
battleground for looting pirates and sec men in still-
functional navy PT boats. Ryan Cawdor and his warrior
band emerge in this perilous water world, caught in a
grim fight to unlock the secrets of the past.

On sale March 2001 at your favorite retail outlet.

Or order your copy now by sending your name, address, zip or postal code, along with
a check or money order (please do not send cash) for $5.99 for each book ordered
($6.99 in Canada), plus 75¢ postage and handling ($1.00 in Canada), payable to
Gold Eagle Books, to:

In the U.S.	In Canada
Gold Eagle Books	Gold Eagle Books
3010 Walden Ave.	P.O. Box 636
P.O. Box 9077	Fort Erie, Ontario
Buffalo, NY 14269-9077	L2A 5X3

Please specify book title with order.
Canadian residents add applicable federal and provincial taxes.

GOLD
EAGLE

GDL53

Take
2 explosive books
plus a
mystery bonus
FREE

Mail to: Gold Eagle Reader Service

IN U.S.A.:
3010 Walden Ave.
P.O. Box 1867
Buffalo, NY 14240-1867

IN CANADA:
P.O. Box 609
Fort Erie, Ontario
L2A 5X3

YEAH! Rush me 2 FREE Gold Eagle novels and my FREE mystery bonus. Then send me 6 brand-new novels every other month as they come off the presses. Bill me at the low price of just $26.70* for each shipment. There is NO extra charge for postage and handling! There is no minimum number of books I must buy. I can always cancel at any time simply by returning a shipment at your cost or by returning any shipping statement marked "cancel." Even if I never buy another book from Gold Eagle, the 2 free books and mystery bonus are mine to keep forever.

166 AEN C23F
366 AEN C23G

Name _____ (PLEASE PRINT) _____

Address _____ Apt. No. _____

City _____ State/Prov. _____ Zip/Postal Code _____

Signature (if under 18, parent or guardian must sign)

* Terms and prices subject to change without notice. Sales tax applicable in N.Y. Canadian residents will be charged applicable provincial taxes and GST. This offer is limited to one order per household and not valid to present subscribers.

GE2-00

James Axler

OUTLANDERS®

PURGATORY ROAD

The fate of humanity remains ever uncertain, dictated by the obscure forces that have commandeered mankind's destiny for thousands of years. The plenipotentiaries of these ancient oppressors—the nine barons who have controlled America in the two hundred years since the nukecaust—are now falling prey to their own rabid desire for power.

Book #3 of *The Imperator Wars* saga, a trilogy chronicling the introduction of a new child imperator—launching the baronies into war!

On sale May 2001 at your favorite retail outlet. Or order your copy now by sending your name, address, zip or postal code, along with a check or money order (please do not send cash) for $5.99 for each book ordered ($6.99 in Canada), plus 75¢ postage and handling ($1.00 in Canada), payable to Gold Eagle Books, to:

In the U.S.	In Canada
Gold Eagle Books	Gold Eagle Books
3010 Walden Ave.	P.O. Box 636
P.O. Box 9077	Fort Erie, Ontario
Buffalo, NY 14269-9077	L2A 5X3

Please specify book title with order.
Canadian residents add applicable federal and provincial taxes.

GOUT17

Gold Eagle brings you high-tech action and mystic adventure!

#123 DISLOYAL OPPOSITION

Created by
MURPHY
and SAPIR

THE RUSTED CURTAIN BOOK I

A secret Russian particle-beam weapon has long been suspected as responsible for the space shuttle Challenger explosion. Many scoffed...until the old Soviet Union dissolves and the weapon is sold on the Russian black market to the ruling council of Barkley, California—the most famous enclave of unrepentant socialists in the Western World. They direct it at American skies, making no planes, satellites or space shuttles safe until their very heavy price is paid.

Available in April 2001 at your favorite retail outlet.

Or order your copy now by sending your name, address, zip or postal code, along with a check or money order (please do not send cash) for $5.99 for each book ordered ($6.99 in Canada), plus 75¢ postage and handling ($1.00 in Canada), payable to Gold Eagle Books, to:

In the U.S.	**In Canada**
Gold Eagle Books	Gold Eagle Books
3010 Walden Ave.	P.O. Box 636
P.O. Box 9077	Fort Erie, Ontario
Buffalo, NY 14269-9077	L2A 5X3

Please specify book title with your order.
Canadian residents add applicable federal and provincial taxes.

GDEST123

Don't miss the high-tech, fast-paced adventure
of title #52 of Stony Man....
Be sure to get in on the action!

DON PENDLETON'S

STONY

AMERICA'S ULTRA-COVERT INTELLIGENCE AGENCY

MAN®

TACTICAL
RESPONSE

Three suspicious incidents occur that give the cyber
experts at Stony Man Farm pause: a nuclear incident
in Siberia, a hit on an FBI team protecting a Russian
mobster and the slaughter of an Israeli-American
archaeology team in the Bekaa Valley. It is up to Stony
Man® to determine if the incidents are connected in
any way...while averting a potential disaster!

Available in April 2001 at your favorite retail outlet.

Or order your copy now by sending your name, address, zip or postal code, along with
a check or money order (please do not send cash) for $5.99 for each book ordered
($6.99 in Canada), plus 75¢ postage and handling ($1.00 in Canada), payable to Gold
Eagle Books, to:

In the U.S.	In Canada
Gold Eagle Books	Gold Eagle Books
3010 Walden Avenue	P.O. Box 636
P.O. Box 9077	Fort Erie, Ontario
Buffalo, NY 14269-9077	L2A 5X3

Please specify book title with your order.
Canadian residents add applicable federal and provincial taxes.

GOLD
EAGLE®

GSM52